Far Below Human Eyes

Far Below
Human
Eyes

ANNABELLE HEALY

NEW YORK

LONDON • NASHVILLE • MELBOURNE • VANCOUVER

Far Below Human Eyes

Published in New York, New York, by Morgan James Publishing. Morgan James is a trademark of Morgan James, LLC. www.MorganJamesPublishing.com

ISBN 9781631952401 paperback
ISBN 9781631952418 eBook
Library of Congress Control Number: 2020939161

Cover and Interior Design by:
Chris Treccani
www.3dogcreative.net

Illustrations by:
Annabelle Healy

Morgan James is a proud partner of Habitat for Humanity Peninsula and Greater Williamsburg. Partners in building since 2006.

Get involved today! Visit
MorganJamesPublishing.com/giving-back

For all the children who wish they could fly.

TABLE OF CONTENTS

ACKNOWLEDGMENTS

I used to think getting published was like baking a pie; you make it, and it's done. But becoming an author is more like building an instrument—the tuning never ends, and you can't do it alone.

I'd like to thank my wonderful editor, Angie Keisling, who gave me terrific advice and encouraged me throughout the editing process. My gratitude also goes out to David Hancock, who not only believed in me but also gave me an amazing opportunity to pursue my dream.

I will forever appreciate all the people who read my rough drafts, celebrated with me, and asked me how my book was going even though it was completely irrelevant in their lives. Being friends with a writer is weird, and you guys are awesome (you know who you are).

I'd also like to thank my mentors: Mrs. Hollenbeck, who pushed me, encouraged me, gave me honest feedback, and fed me donuts, and Mr. Hollenbeck, who let me edit in his art class—without your class I would have gotten no sleep for six months.

Thanks to all my teachers, who demonstrated hard work, honesty, and diligence—except for one, who is my mortal enemy and demonstrates the true characteristics of an antagonist—thank you, sir. You are the best.

The biggest thanks of all goes to my crazy, wild, amazing family. Dad, thanks for reading stories to me from day one. Mom, thanks for keeping my head above water in high school and having long talks with me about boys. And to Owen, Patrick, Elyse, Ivan, and Lily—thanks for making sure I will never grow up.

And lastly, thanks to Jesus for pulling me through, being my best friend, and constantly reminding me that I will *always* be a child of God—no matter how old I am.

INTRODUCTION

My publisher suggested I address my qualifications when writing my introduction, and I did some hard thinking on it. Truthfully, I sat on my front porch after soccer practice and thought for quite a while. I won some awards, yes. . .

But what else? At first, I felt myself slipping into self-pity; *good grief,* I thought, *that's all?* And then I had the terrifying realization that I'm seventeen.

I started writing ten years ago, but the first thing I wrote sounded a lot like Doctor Seuss riddled with spelling mistakes, scribbled on a piece of bright pink paper. The first stories I told were in the third person to myself when I was potty training. The first books I wrote were bound together with ungodly amounts of scotch tape and cereal box cardboard. In fact, I didn't start typing up my stories until about four years ago.

So, I'm not a bestseller—yet. This is my debut novel. But my qualifications for writing this story are of a different kind.

We moved to my current house seven years ago. It was a transition that changed my life. One moment, I was surrounded with neighborhood friends. The next, I was marooned in a neighborhood just miles away, strange and unfriendly. I was convinced everyone who lived there was at least fifty years old. It was as if children had been banished from the community.

But despite the awful isolation, there was a pond behind my house, just across a small field. It was hardly a pond—more like a puddle with a few dragonflies. But I spent hours floating boats down the stream, trying to catch frogs, and weaving through the cattails. I was just a kid.

The setting gripped me. Two years later, I wrote *Far Below Human Eyes* by hand on notebook paper, storing each new chapter in a half-inch binder. I wrote it because I was lonely, and now that I think about it, that's a rather depressing motivation. But *Far Below Human Eyes* became my escape from the world. I wanted so desperately to fly, fly away on the back of a dragonfly, zip through the trees, and become so small nobody would pay attention to me.

But as I continued writing, I began to realize the true reason I wrote *Far Below Human Eyes.* Even Harold, two inches tall and orphaned, was so important to his story and had changed my life forever. Even *he* was important. *Harold.*

And what I learned is this: What is often *most* important is far below human eyes.

Harold's story demonstrates fundamental human struggles and emotions—loss, loneliness, revenge and grace, duty, inadequacy, betrayal, loyalty, and love. From his humble beginning as an orphan, to his struggle to catch a dragonfly, Harold's entire story revolves around a humble pond setting. A setting I, as a ten-year-old, explored and thrived in, discovering a kinship with God's beautiful creation.

So I might not be very qualified to write a book. I might not have the experience I'd like or the status I wish I had. I'm just a human—a high school girl who likes to tell stories.

But as a human talking to a human, I hope when you read Harold's story you feel the wind on your face, hear the sound of a babbling brook, and see the cattails swaying above your head. I hope you know how magical it is, how wonderful and beautiful it is, to live in a world far below human eyes.

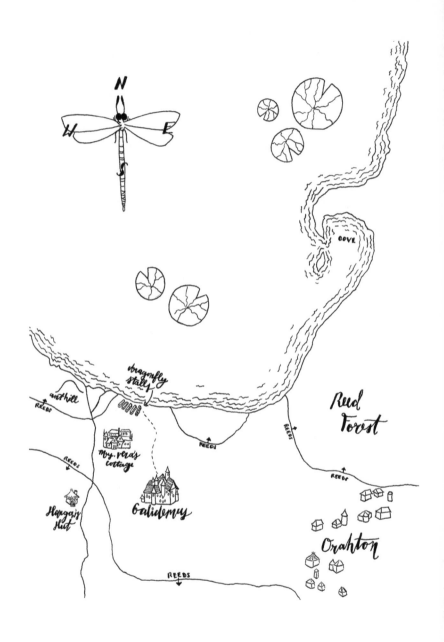

CHAPTER ONE

Harold

F ar below human eyes, there lies a town. It was built by men only inches tall, who build dwellings comparable to their size, on the shore of a minuscule pond. One might go as far as to call it an oversized puddle. But it was an entire world to the denizens of this land.

Harold was perhaps the only hope the little town, Orahton, had left. In the darkest night, beneath cattail forests casting long, dripping shadows and beside water black and cold, he was born. He could fit in the mouth of an acorn as an infant, sleep in a snail's shell.

But one night, everything changed. It was a night Harold's life twisted into something unexpected—the night when a seed of hope was planted in Orahton's coarse, dark soil. And one day, that hope would sprout, grow—blossom—into a tale that would be told for ages.

Mist shrouded the moon, blanketing the world in a cold, thick sheath on that dreadful night. It was late fall, the time when all things are dying, and winter was approaching fast. Decay seemed to cover the pond, blanketing the water in a thin sheet of filmy death. The ground was covered in the rot of late autumn, crunching beneath the feet of anyone who wandered by. Frost slithered like a snake between the yellow grasses, and the air was thick with chill.

The night found Harold wrapped in a blanket, clutched to the breast of his mother, who was running in the dark. Harold's mother was a beautiful woman; long brown hair swept in waves nearly to her waist. This was unusual, as these people commonly had green hair, the color of Harold's head. She stood just above two inches tall and had glossy green eyes that were almost always wide open and happy. Tonight was a solemn exception. Tonight, her eyes looked fearful, aware, and bloodshot. Each nerve in her body was taut with tension. She hadn't slept in days, but she refused to tire as she ran.

Behind her, the fog itself seemed to be chasing after her. A figure sat astride a thick, dark monster. The figure was black, even in the night, and it was pushing the lifeless creature onward. He flew on that ghostly shroud as one might soar on wings of death: he pursued without effort, thought, or remorse.

"You can only run so far."

Harold's mother knew of the dangers behind her. Her last hope was to run, with all her strength, to save her only son. Tears streaked her cheeks as desperation sank in. A painful stitch crept up her side. Her breath came in ragged gasps. If only she made it to the nearest building…

Almost there.

Finally, she could feel the stones of a pathway beneath her fleeting feet. A massive castle loomed before her, its cold stone face glaring down at her in the dark. She was just outside of the town; there weren't any other buildings surrounding the castle. But she didn't stop running; the figure riding the fog was still after her, engulfing cattails and reeds in a black cloud as he descended. The farther she ran, the closer the figure got.

As the woman stumbled up the steps of the castle, the man slid off his lifeless mount and stood behind Harold's desperate mother. She rapped as hard as she could on the huge castle door, to no avail.

"Help!" she screamed.

The man, who appeared long since deceased, chuckled at her effort.

"You can't save your child, even if you had all of Orahton on your side," he uttered. He seemed no longer man, deformed like the decay of early winter.

"He's yours, too!" she said, laying her baby upon the top of the steps.

"He belongs to nobody but you," the man said, a chill clipping his words. "No one will come."

"Flint, please, don't do this! Kill me, but please spare him. Please!"

"You both will die." The figure slowly progressed up the steps.

Harold's mother planted her feet between him and her son. The fear in her eyes was enough to kill a man, but a living one. This man was far from that.

The woman looked into his grey, shallow eyes. Even his hair was grey and as tufty as Harold's against his pale skin.

Flint raised his hand, all sympathy gone.

"Flint, no! Your son!" Harold's mother screamed.

"Silence!" he said. "He is no son of mine."

"Have mercy, please!"

"You know I have won, Marigold," Flint shouted. "It's all over. You refuse, you pay the consequences."

"Flint, this isn't you—" Marigold's face contorted in fear as the man stood right in front of her, face to face.

"Finally, after all this sickening time, I'll be rid of you and your child," he growled.

Marigold, powered by a newfound source of strength, whispered back, "You will not kill my son or win this game of yours. I will stand in your way if it is the last thing I do."

"Have it your way," Flint spat. With a flick of his wrist, the black, ethereal creature engulfed Marigold, a hound ripping at her existence with its iron jaws. With a scream, she disappeared into the night. Her voice evaporated into thin air. She was gone. Harold cried in his thin bundle of cloth.

Flint, both satisfied and hungry, peered into the child's feeble protection. He chuckled at the innocence of the child. How helpless it was.

"Meek child. You don't even deserve an exciting death."

Flint raised his hand and looked into the baby's tearful eyes. They were blue and bright. For a moment, a short one, he looked into the face of innocence. A slight hesitancy struck him, surprising him. Should he kill it, his heir? He could, of course, raise him as an ally.

"Enough!" he shrieked aloud, voice crackling like thunder in the night. He realized he had been breathing heavily and his pulse had quickened. He hated himself for it. "No hesitation."

Again, he raised his arms, death at his fingertips…

But nothing came. How could he end the child's innocence, the glow of his eyes? What was he thinking? He was feared among all. He had no weaknesses. He had done the impossible before. This was an easy task. He raised his hand a third time, triumph making him smile. He could get rid of it . . . now.

But again, he paused, thinking. Why would he kill the thing if he could leave it with the torture of being an orphan? He could let it live with the feeling of being the least loved. Why not wait and have the sweet taste of triumph in a decade or so?

Flint retreated from the bundle, never taking his eyes off the baby. He reached out a withered hand to the door and knocked, then bent down to examine his son. "I will be back, Harold, you will see. Just give it some time, and it will be all the sweeter."

He rose, a thin, dead smile on his lips, and disappeared into the dark, slipping away into the soupy air like a deep-sea creature. His black cape whipped behind him in one flick, and he was gone, leaving Harold alone in the cold, dead night.

She had heard the knock at half past two. First, she tried to ignore it. But it came again, the wretched sound, persistent and loud. She begrudgingly put on her spectacles and slipped off the bed onto the floor. The stone floor was freezing. Caution flared her nostrils, for a knock at this hour was not normal. The cold of the floor shocked her bare heels, telling her to turn back, to climb back in bed and sleep. But a nagging came in the back of her mind, a nagging like the catch of a fingernail on bedsheets, and she could not resist it.

Her eyes were still heavy from sleep, but as a teacher for the past two decades, early mornings did not bother her. And while her instincts still blared a warning, she was almost curious as to who was beyond the door. There had to be a reason for the visitor's impatience. It never crossed her mind that a villain could be standing right at the doorstep of her home, Orahton's fabled school—Galidemus.

She lit a candle to drive away the darkness and meandered down the frigid staircase. The feeble glow of the candle emitted barely enough light to guide her through the halls she thought she had memorized. She found the front door of the castle nearly frozen at the hinges, and with a pull she regretted, being well past middle age, the door swung ajar, revealing the small bundle on the doorstep. Leaving the candle on the floor, she rushed to the bundle to find a baby inside, crying in a terrible fit.

She pulled the baby indoors, retreating from the cold and dark. Her maternal instincts kicked in, but her heart was racing, and her hands shook from fear. After the child had warmed and stopped crying, she inspected him, finding him healthy, though premature. His eyes were the brightest blue she had ever seen.

She wished she knew what to do. Should she keep it or send it off to an orphanage? She would have to care for it until she found the right place for it. But what did she know about caring for a child? She had never married and certainly hadn't had children.

The poor child squirmed and fussed in her arms, his voice piercing the quiet within the castle. He was only a little older than a year. Without thinking, she began to rock the boy to sleep. After some effort, he was slumbering, his plush cheeks relaxed and calmed.

She wished she knew his name. The tiny creature seemed too young to send off, but she couldn't be a mother.

The floor was getting colder, and the candle she had dropped was losing light. The last thing she wanted was to grope around in the dark, holding a baby. Her back protested her position on the floor, and the chill that radiated from the open door sent a shiver up her aching spine.

As she stood up, a note tumbled from the baby's wrappings onto the floor. Scared of the message inside, she unfolded the tear-splotched paper.

To you I leave this child, you, whoever you may be, in full possession. His name is Harold and his parents are Flint and Marigold. Wherever he may be, give him the love I, as a parent, would have given him. Give him a good home, and please take care of him. He is more important than the stars.

Deepest regards,
Marigold

Thirteen years later. . .

CHAPTER TWO

The School

The morning sun streamed through the dormitory window of the castle, tickling Harold's nose. On typical days he tried to ignore the brightness of the morning. But today was different. Today was a big day.

Crawling out of his bed, doing his best not to wake up the other boys, Harold slipped into his woven boots, work pants, and plain cotton shirt. He stuck a knife into his boot and ruffled his tufty green hair. His warm breath made fog on the rusty mirror all the boys shared. His image was dusty, but he looked dressed for the occasion. His bright blue eyes sparkled in the morning light.

Breathing in the cool castle air, Harold looked out the dormitory's only window. It overlooked his home, the pond, and the little town of Orahton in which he lived. The school sat like a compass in the valley, front doors facing north, Orahton to the southeast, and the pond to the north. Outside, he could see morning frost clinging to the field grasses beyond the pond, slightly to the distant east. The pond was bubbling, fed by a small waterfall on the far northern side, and the cattails, which had not yet recovered from the harsh winter, swayed in the breeze. They rustled in the wind like sheets on a clothesline. The window Harold peered out of was cold and emitted a chill. He stepped away and exhaled.

Galidemus was the only secondary school in Orahton. It towered above other buildings and sat, distant from the town, in a valley in front of the pond.

Made from ancient gray stone, Galidemus was one of the oldest buildings in Orahton. It was notoriously cold everywhere inside. The halls and classrooms within wove around each other like a maze, and even Harold, who had lived there his entire life, still hadn't discovered every hidden space. Tall pinnacles rose into the sky like a castle, and the front door was massive and cumbersome, made from solid wood.

The school looked almost haphazardly designed; it was neither square nor rectangular, but portrayed strange angles and edges, as if shifted from a tilting of the earth. Harold liked to believe all the organized chaos gave Galidemus its character.

Harold could smell breakfast cooking. Huge corn kernels steamed while porridge was ladled into bowls the size of acorn caps. He could hear the slicing of fresh fruit and the sizzle of grease downstairs in Galidemus's massive kitchen—not to mention the groans of the many cooks as they squeezed a giant orange and tried to catch the juice into buckets. He rarely had orange juice because of the effort it took to make, but this was a special day.

Harold was almost excited enough to walk down alone, but he knew he'd better wait. He would be lonely and cold in the meal room if he went down early. He waited a couple more minutes to see if his best friend, Carnis, would awaken. As usual, Carnis didn't wake up on his own, so Harold thumped him on the head with his knuckles.

"Alright, then," Carnis mumbled.

"Wake up already. Don't you know what day it is?" Harold asked.

No response came other than a few spasmodic snores. Harold groaned and thumped him on the head again.

"Alright! Good grief!" Carnis said, climbing out of his bed.

"Don't you know what day it is?" Harold asked again.

"Who doesn't?" Carnis mumbled, pulling on his boots and clothes as Harold had.

"I can't wait to catch a dragonfly today!" Harold exclaimed.

Ever since he could remember, Mrs. Kernester, the school headmistress and Harold's official guardian, had encouraged him to be excited about the day he could catch his own dragonfly. Of course, he had lived in Galidemus his whole life, but since this was his first year of secondary education out of the four at Galidemus, he could finally catch a dragonfly as he had seen all the students before him do.

Dragonflies came out to mate only one day of the year. They flocked to the pond in swarms for only twenty-four hours. Harold's heart pounded with excitement.

"Did you see where I left my knife?" Carnis asked, not minding Harold's enthusiasm.

"Under your bed. Right there under your other boot." Harold pointed. "Aren't you excited?"

"About finding my knife? Absolutely!" Carnis teased, then, signaled by Harold's expression, said, "of course. You know how eager I am to wake up early, get dressed, shovel breakfast down my throat, and go out into this God-forsaken freezing morning to catch an insect twice my length."

Harold punched him in the arm.

"Ow! What was that for?" Carnis hissed.

"Don't be so sarcastic," Harold retorted. "I know you're excited."

Carnis sighed. "Alright, I'm excited as you want me to be. I'm just nervous I'll get a flunk. What if I don't catch one at all?"

"I wouldn't worry about it," Harold said.

Carnis had been Harold's best friend since the first day of school. Harold had lived in the castle as long as he could remember, homeschooled through his primary years by Mrs. Kernester herself, but when Carnis entered at the beginning of Harold's first official year at Galidemus half a year before, they stuck. Even though they were so vastly different, Harold was drawn to the relaxed ways of his friend.

Other boys in the room began to stir. Several had already headed down to breakfast.

"Should we go down for breakfast?" Harold asked. If there was one thing that got Carnis excited, it was food.

"You bet!" he exclaimed. He leapt out of bed, combed his light green hair in a flash, and bounded down the stairs, not bothering to wait for his friend.

As Harold caught up to Carnis, he thought about what having a dragonfly would do to his life. Of course, he wouldn't be so lonely during summers. Every one of his previous summers had been void of excitement, as there wasn't much to do in the empty castle. Galidemus was the only secondary school in the entire town, and it was a hot, lonesome place in summer. Each day he would explore some other preposterous way of entertaining himself. He remembered one time Mrs. Kernester had found him, as a toddler, in one of the bathrooms drawing watercolor on the bathroom wall with toilet water.

He wished for a taste of family, instead of the false feeling of kin Mrs. Kernester gave. She was a kind woman, but she wasn't real family, and she didn't have much time for Harold. He loved having Carnis around, who almost had more time than was good for him. He also loved being a fulltime student.

But unfortunately, summer was quickly approaching, and soon the loneliness would return. Harold's first year would end in almost three months. He didn't want classes to end, and he intended to cherish every moment he had left while he still had the chance.

The meal room bustled with students sitting at tables eating. Four long tables stretched out across the room. Flags had been draped around the immense room with the colors of each class to honor the occasion. Torchlight danced off of the walls, and paper dragonflies dangled from the ceiling to further the festivities. Food was stacked upon all the tables, delicious mounds that made Carnis's eyes gleam. The boys took their seats at the Algae table, to which they belonged. Usually jobs were inherited, and since Mrs. Kernester had been an Algae, Harold was now one as well.

There were four workmanships, or groups of people, in Orahton. The Reeds, who harvested boats from the area to serve as transportation, were always close to the Algaes, who were the hunters and fishers of the village, needing boats on a daily basis.

Then there were the Farmers, who farmed food for the whole town and distributed it for sale. They were the lowest class of all, but they were also the most pivotal in Orahton's economy.

And lastly there were the Royals, who ruled everything. They were the kings and queens of the land, only instead of one king and queen, there were hundreds. What was most ironic was that they didn't control anything. They were a responsibility to the rest of Orahton, so they had underlying power, but none in written law. With a reputation for being unfriendly, they had a dislike for almost all other classes.

"Good morning," said a girl named Petunia, sitting next to the boys' usual seats. Her twin brother, Snip, nodded beside her. Petunia and Snip, also Algaes, had been Harold's friends ever since the first day of secondary school at Galidemus as well. Petunia was confident and clever, but acted more like a mother than a student. She had freckles and green hair, though her shade wasn't as bright as Harold's hair was. Snip, on the other hand, was wiry and scared. He had the appearance of a worm, hair like a spider's web, and thin insect legs that sprouted from his thin frame. He stuttered when he was nervous and was grey all over. Even his hair was grey, which was an unusual phenomenon Harold couldn't recall elsewhere. Both were friendly and always ate with Harold and Carnis. Petunia even sometimes helped the boys with their schoolwork.

"Good morning," Harold replied, sitting down to enjoy the magnificent breakfast. Carnis had already started inhaling his. "Royals aren't too happy, I take it?"

"I doubt it," Petunia replied, munching on a strawberry seed.

Royals, unfortunately, were not expected to own dragonflies. They weren't really expected to *do anything*, so they were quite an unhappy lot on days like these.

"I heard it might rain today," Petunia said, "but I'll be happy, rain or shine. We're catching our dragonflies today! I hope I'll get a blue one. I heard those are the best."

"Lightning Backs, that's what they're called," Carnis said through stuffed cheeks. He was an expert on dragonflies and always watched professional races during the summer. "Them and the yellow ones."

"I don't know," Snip squeaked, finishing up his piece of toast. "I hope to get a Sapling. They're much safer."

"A Sapling?" Carnis laughed, as if it were a joke. Saplings were the slowest dragonflies and were colored an unattractive brown.

"*I* want a fast one, whatever it is," Harold said.

"At least one that flies," Petunia added.

"Attention!" boomed a voice from the front of the room. Harold turned his head to see Mrs. Kernester standing on the platform at the front, demanding the attention of all the students. Her pale red hair was tied into a loose bun. Her eyes squinted beneath her square spectacles, and a wrinkled smile beamed on her face. A dull green dress that looked like a robe was pulled around her simple, overweight frame. Harold smiled at her.

"Is it time already?" Carnis moaned. "I'm not even finished yet—"

"Shhh," Petunia hissed.

"Good morning students!" Mrs. Kernester said as she waited for the room to settle. "I'd like to speak a few words to our first-years before they embark on their dragonfly-catching quest this morning." Her voice was charged with excitement. "Once you are dismissed, you will exit the East wing and wait for further instructions. I suggest you exercise caution. More injuries happen on this day than any other at Galidemus. Please be careful. And as a precaution, be observant of the skies. It could rain soon, and you all know very well how dangerous that can be. Please return if there is any such inconvenience. You will all have an opportunity to catch a dragonfly, mark my word.

"Remember students: life in Galidemus, Orahton, and the entire pond evolves around dragonflies and us riding them. Once you learn to fly, your dragonfly will become your transportation, your comrade, your freedom, and your lifesaver. You will treat your dragonfly like he is a good friend, and the day it dies is the day you will part. Take this task seriously. Your survival depends on the dragonflies. Catch one, and your life will begin."

Harold felt adrenaline rush through him as he thought of the task before him.

"Best of luck to you all!" Mrs. Kernester smiled. "Remember your training. It was meant for today and these last three months. Off you go!"

The meal room exploded with noise and movement. After wolfing down a last quick bite of breakfast, the four stood up to leave. Harold felt his heart beat faster and faster as he and his friends filed outside.

As the crowd spilled through the front doors, Puella, one of the worst Royals, stepped on Harold's foot before she shrank back into the meal room. She always picked on him because he was different than most other students, having lived in Galidemus his entire life.

"Hope you break a leg, schoolboy!" she snarled.

"Just ignore her," groaned Petunia, who was walking behind him.

Harold sighed.

Outside was chilly and wet. Behind them, Galidemus loomed, stones dark and cold, spires frowning down at their audience. The ground was soft and squishy from the melted frost. The eager students grouped into a clump and waited nervously for the race to begin.

All around them dragonflies were buzzing, in all shapes and sizes, colors and patterns. Most flew over the pond and around the waterfall, some in the forest of reeds upon the bank, some high in the morning sky. Harold's jaw dropped at the sheer magnitude of the horde. He had not seen the swarm so close before. It looked like a chaotic ballet, displayed in every color of the rainbow. There had to be hundreds of them!

Petunia nudged his elbow and gestured toward the sky. "Looks like rain," she said.

The sky was grey and heavy, like someone had colored the clouds with wet paint and it had started dripping. Harold could tell the rest of the first-years had noticed, and they looked concerned. He glanced over at Snip, who was still finishing his toast with a scared look in his eyes. He was probably more frightened of the rain than anything.

Suddenly, Ms. Dywood, the dragonfly riding instructor, shouted from the front of the crowd. "I expect utter silence!"

Everything quieted immediately. One would be a fool to ignore Ms. Dywood. She had a nasty temper. Ms. Dywood was lanky and cranky, as Harold had heard the other boys say, and he knew it to be true. Her hair was tied into a tight ponytail, as it always was. Possibly the most startling thing about her was her hair, which changed color depending on her mood. Right now, it was a pale coral color, indicating irritation and annoyance.

"Today, as you all know, is dragonfly hunting day," she barked.

The way she said *hunting* made Harold shiver.

"Welcome to the Day of Gathering! As you probably already know, today is the day all the dragonflies come out from hibernation to feed and mate. The way you catch your dragonfly is entirely up to you. However, no one has ever successfully caught a dragonfly without the technique I am about to teach you. So pay attention."

She strode over to the pond shore, not too far from where they were standing, and everyone trickled behind her. Floating gently in the water lay a small boat made from a dead leaf that curled up at the edges to keep the water out. They were the kind of boats the Reeds usually harvested and were easy to find in the fall, when leaves died. Though they weren't too sturdy, they rarely sank. She stepped inside it without much effort to gain her balance and continued.

"You will all be using these to catch your dragonflies," she said. "There will be a whole fleet of them at the base of that hill."

Ms. Dywood gestured to the highest elevation point near the pond. It was an old abandoned ant hill that lay not far from the water, just northeast of Galidemus.

"From there, you will drag your boats up the hill and balance them on the top. Today appears gusty enough, so you should be able to catch a good wind. When you do, you'll fly over the water into the thick of the dragonflies. I'll give you a net to catch one with. If you catch one, land in the water and paddle back to shore. If you don't catch one, try again. If you fail to catch a dragonfly today, you'll have to wait until next year to try again. Am I clear?"

Harold swallowed in fear and nodded. Climbing up the abandoned ant hill was tough without carrying a boat and net as well.

"Your nets are already in your boats. And please don't fight over who gets what. I promise you, they are all exactly the same. Get to work!"

The group jumped to life. Students fought over which boat was the best and argued about which dragonfly they would catch. Harold, Petunia, Snip, and Carnis hung back to regroup.

"Should we set up as a team?" Petunia asked.

"I think we should stick together," Snip said, biting his nails. "That way, if any of us gets in trouble, we won't be alone."

"Hold on," Harold said, gesturing to Ms. Dywood, who was glaring at their backs. "Are you sure this is alright?"

As if in answer to the question, Ms. Dywood strode over, arms crossed.

"This is an individual activity," she snapped, "no teams allowed. Now hurry up! If you wait any longer, you'll be the last in line."

Harold left his friends, a sense of fear in his eyes. He hated doing things alone. What would Snip do? He was afraid of leaving the group just to use the restroom. Suppose he couldn't catch a dragonfly at all? Suppose none of them would be able to catch anything since they were so dependent on one another?

He hoped the rain would hold up. Glaring at Ms. Dywood's back, he steeled himself and set off toward the hill. So much for teamwork.

Squinting over at the hill he must climb, he never dreamed he would soon face much more than a wild dragonfly alone.

CHAPTER THREE

Catching A Dragonfly

H arold plucked a boat from the few that were left at the base of the hill. His small leaf boat was brittle and brown, like the crust of some stale bread, and heavier than he would like. The net inside his boat was about an inch long and seemed insufficient to catch a four-inch long dragonfly. He doubted whether he could catch anything bigger than a gnat in it.

The climb up the hill was treacherous. The slope was wet, and mud clung to Harold's clothes, making him shiver. A rank film covered him, and he stank of cold soil. His boat was heavy and awkward, and his net relentlessly grabbed at his legs and tangled in his boots. Without his friends to talk to, he began doubting if he could catch a dragonfly at all.

But Harold felt determined. At least it hadn't started raining . . . yet.

As he approached the top of the ant hill, he noticed other students taking the leap off the crest in their leaf boats. The wind swept some into the air, some into the freezing cold water.

After joining a line that was slowly advancing to the top, he glanced around for his friends. He could spot Carnis several boats ahead, but Petunia and Snip were nowhere to be seen. They were probably behind him down the hill.

Everyone else in line looked nervous and shaky, either from the cold or the fear of failure that so firmly gripped them. They refused to make eye contact with one another, quiet as worms. In fact, they even looked like worms, cold and slicked in a thin layer of mud. The top of the hill remained silent, except for the quiet trickle of water from the pond and the whistle of the wind. The stillness and anticipation made it seem like a funeral.

Soon enough, it was Harold's turn. He positioned his boat on the precipice, hoping it wouldn't be swept away. Once it had steadied, he climbed in, holding his net ready. He didn't have to wait long for the wind. Suddenly, his little boat lurched. He tightened his grasp on the edges of the leaf, and all of a sudden he was flying over the pond.

The feeling was exhilarating. The sky itself seemed to brush Harold's face, and the adrenaline made him forget the cold. He was flying!

He could see the pond streaking below him in a blur of blue. He could see other boats flying, their occupants waving their nets in wild arcs.

Dragonflies buzzed everywhere. Hundreds of them, in all shapes, sizes and colors, flitted like fairies around him. Harold glimpsed a Lightning Back darting above him. Hundreds of Saplings darted about. Other types Harold had never seen before flew with ease above and below him. Some were even orange or green, and some were so big they could carry three people on their backs.

He was so absorbed in the wonderful feeling he almost forgot about catching the dragonflies themselves. Whipping back into focus, Harold waved his net wildly at the dragonflies buzzing around him. He hadn't really thought of a strategy, so he just waved his net around like a madman instead. The insects seemed so close, but right before one would snag in his net, it darted out of the way. The net was frustratingly short.

All in a matter of seconds, the boat landed in the water, and Harold laid down his empty net as he drifted back to shore. Clenching his fists, he tried not to fling his useless tool overboard. He most certainly wouldn't get a replacement.

"This whole thing is useless," he grumbled to himself. "This net is useless and this boat is way too heavy. Why don't they make them longer?"

As if in response, the wind fluttered around him, spinning his boat in wild circles. Harold gripped the leaf boat's stem for balance, nearly tumbling in the water. As if his circumstances weren't hopeless enough. . .

Suddenly, he realized he was holding onto a stem, which was long and sturdy, perfect for a new net handle.

Harold gripped the stem and pulled with all his strength, snapping it off the leaf. He pondered attaching it to his net to make it longer, and, glancing down at his boots, promptly removed their laces. Fastening it together, he grinned at his new, longer net. *Now* he had a better chance of catching a dragonfly.

Powered by a new strength, Harold looked toward the shore, which wasn't far off. Soon, the boat scraped the ground, and he clambered ashore, newly fashioned net in one hand and boat in the other. After a short walk, he had almost reached the base of the old ant hill. But before he could begin his second climb, Ms. Dywood's slithery voice called out behind him. Harold felt the hairs on his neck raise.

"Harold!" she scolded, yanking his improved net from his grasp. "Playing games, are we? Getting yourself an advantage so you'll win? I never handed out nets like this."

Harold swallowed, watching as Ms. Dywood pocketed his shoelaces. "I tried the first time, and it seemed ridiculous to have a net so short—"

"Excuse me?" she barked.

"I figured I'd just make it a little longer with what I had already," Harold confessed. "I didn't know it was against the rules or anything, I swear."

"Harold, do you not know that I've taught here at Galidemus for twenty-one years?" her voice was pulled so tight Harold feared it would snap.

"Yes, ma'am," he nodded.

"And do you know, in those twenty-one years, every single student I have ever taught has used the same exact nets?"

"Yes, ma'am."

"So why do you think I should make a special case for you?" she snarled. Her pale orange hair flared to a deep crimson.

"Alright, here." Harold handed his net to her and turned his back to walk away. He could go without Ms. Dywood's wrath today. But before he could do as much as take a step, Ms. Dywood gripped him by the shoulder and spun him around. Her face contorted in fury.

"Dare to cheat again, and I'll have you expelled," she seethed, as if it were a real threat to a boy whose home was the school. "And you'll never get a dragonfly if I don't let you. I'd be careful about what you say, Harold. I run this operation, and I can take your dragonfly away anytime I want. Hear me?"

Harold nodded. He didn't care that spittle was flying into his face. He just wanted to get away from this madwoman.

"Here's your new net," she spat, handing him a normal, smaller net. "Now get to work!"

Harold *did* get to work. Dragging his net and boat behind him, he scrambled up the hill, not daring to look back. He forgot entirely about his shoelaces, at least until mud started seeping into his shoes, making his socks wet and cold. It had all happened so fast he could barely recall why Ms. Dywood had been so furious. Regardless, he would have to stay out of her way. Nothing could stop him from getting his dragonfly.

Up at the top of the hill again, Harold gazed into the sun. It had to be at least noon by now. Fewer and fewer students remained, and the dragonflies were slowly returning to their homes. He had to hurry or he might be the last student to catch a dragonfly. Or worse, the only student to not catch one at all.

Down he flew again, waving his net wildly. Again, he swooped to a stop on the pond surface empty handed. Anger flushed his cheeks. How long would it take for him to catch a single bug? If only Ms. Dywood had let him use a better net . . . it had been his idea, anyway. All his friends had probably already caught their dragonflies by now, even Snip.

His enthusiasm dwindled even more as he floated back to shore. By now it was well past noon and the morning light had bloomed into the warm glare of the afternoon. He would only have one more chance to catch a dragonfly before the sun sank. He was so exhausted. Could he do it? He was arguably the last person left in the hunt. Soon they would call for dinner and Harold would be forced to quit. He wouldn't have another chance until next year!

"Snap out of it!" Harold demanded aloud, using his net to paddle to shore. He could not lose hope. He would catch the biggest, fastest dragonfly there was on his next run. He just knew it!

Onto the shore he ran again, then up the old hill. His feet slipped in the mud and sand. Fatigue climbed up his limbs and into his body. He noticed how hungry he was. But the possible reward of a dragonfly powered him forward.

He was gasping for breath by the time he reached the top. Balancing his craft carefully upon the precipice, Harold waited for the wind, his dripping net poised for flight. He *would* catch a dragonfly this time—he could feel it.

Finally, a gust of wind picked up. Harold went soaring for the third time, swishing his net back and forth, trying desperately to snag just one insect. The dragonflies darted back and forth, evading his maneuvers, flying just out of Harold's reach. He slashed, closed his eyes, knowing he would hit water at any moment.

A voice in his head whispered frantically, awakening him from his despair.

"Open your eyes! Quickly! Choose your dragonfly!"

Harold's eyes whipped open. His senses seemed acute, his stress alleviated.

"Choose wisely."

Harold swung his net with all the force he could muster, reaching out with all his strength, and snagged a young Sapling by the tail. A surge of excitement flew through his nerves as he pulled in his desperate catch. The dragonfly thrashed violently, nearly tearing the net from Harold's grasp, but he held firm. He almost had him, he was almost there. . .

The boat crashed into the water and jolted from impact. The dragonfly flung itself into the water, tearing free of Harold's grasp. In one last desperate attempt at catching his dragonfly, Harold dove in after the Sapling.

The water was freezing and stunned his nerves as he dove. It took all his self-control not to inhale from the shock. But his dragonfly was nowhere to be seen in the murky water. Harold resurfaced, caught his breath, and dove again. But it was no use. The insect swam away. Harold had failed to catch his dragonfly.

Limp as a cooked noodle, Harold pulled himself into his boat. He stood up and gazed around the pond. The dinner bell rang faintly in the distance. The small Sapling lay wet and weak on the shore of a distant island, petrified in the setting sun. It would probably freeze in the night. Would it die in the cold temperatures? Harold hoped not.

He lay in the bottom of his boat for a while, listening to the water. The sun had set and the stars were now appearing, little glowing gnats flocking to the sky, devouring the day that had just ended. He was so tired. But now he had to go back to shore, empty handed, and deal with his miserable failure.

When he finally felt strong enough, he sat up and started home, eyes downcast in frustration.

On the mossy shore stood a cross Ms. Dywood, her arms folded and her hair flaming again. Her thin shadow wavered in the little light there was left. As displeased as she was, Harold didn't fear her in his pity. He climbed ashore, telling himself he would ignore the onslaught of words she was about to hurl at him.

"I have only one thing to say to you, Harold," she said when he stood before her, lips pressed together into a firm scowl. "You are the first student I ever taught that failed to catch a dragonfly on your first day. I am incredibly disappointed in you."

Harold didn't dare look into her eyes.

"Now go get some dinner and go straight to bed. You must be terribly ashamed."

Harold complied, walking silently back toward the school. Ms. Dywood stayed behind, collecting discarded nets. Harold hoped she would freeze out in the cold.

The cold night air cut through Harold's thin, wet clothes. He felt helpless. His failure had been all his fault. It wasn't the net's fault. All the other students had used them. It wasn't the wind or the boat's fault; they had worked just fine. It wasn't even Ms. Dywood's fault. It was all *his* fault. He just wasn't good enough to catch a dragonfly.

As he approached the tall front doors, Harold noticed a slender figure leaning up against the erect stone wall. He recognized the features of a young girl, hair green and primped. He didn't have to study the figure to know who it was; he knew by a quick glance it was Puella.

He debated traveling around her and through the back of Galidemus, but it was a hike and Harold was already exhausted. His stomach growled, and he hated making Mrs. Murphey keep his food warm for too long. Annoyed as he was, it was not a sacrifice he could make. He approached the spoiled Royal.

"Shove off, Puella," Harold groaned, ready for her verbal assault.

"I only wanted to congratulate you," she snickered back, eyelashes fluttering. "Don't be so rude."

"I just want to get some dinner," Harold said.

In defense, Puella stood in front of him, to keep him from getting inside Galidemus.

"What do you want?" Harold demanded.

"Only a little fun," she replied. "How was your swim? Just look at you! You look like a drowned rat!"

"Done yet?" Harold asked, trying to sidestep her.

"Not at all. I was just getting started," she snickered. "Why did you go for a stupid Sapling anyway?"

"It was the only choice I had left!" Harold retorted.

"It wouldn't be your only choice if you had done a better job in your first two flights."

"How did you know I had been on two previous flights?" Harold asked. "You must have wasted a lot of time watching me."

"I only knew because Ms. Dywood told me," she spat back.

"I doubt that."

"Well, the point is, I'm glad you failed, Harold," Puella said. "I'm glad you have no dragonfly and that you are now the embarrassment of the whole school. You deserve worse. In fact, you'd be a great Slug Spotter. What do you think of that?"

That did it.

Slug Spotting was a dirty, boring, and terrible job only the poorest took on. It consisted of sitting around and watching out for massive slugs. The pests were troublesome to villages because they destroyed crops and slimed up boats. The Slug Spotter's job was to spot the slug, then to lug the boneless mound of jelly into the water to drown.

Harold thought he deserved *much* more than that.

"You think you're such a princess just because you're a Royal," Harold seethed. "You're the one who deserves to be a Slug Spotter! In fact, you're such an *idiot* you deserve to be a *Ferral*!"

The words tumbled out and Harold clamped his mouth shut. They certainly weren't going back in. Puella gasped and ran away, skirt trailing behind her. Harold stood motionless. Had anyone else heard? No, that didn't matter. Puella would tell the entire school by morning. He was doomed.

Calling someone a Ferral was just about the worst thing anyone could say. It was worse than profanity. Profanity was just words. Ferrals were actual things. People, really. Ferrals were the outcasts of the town: evil, dark, and feared everywhere for their terror. They claimed allegiance to a chief, who directed their vengeful attacks. They were sometimes barbaric, sometimes cannibals, sometimes murderers—and they terrorized pondside developments. But the worst part was that Orahton had often been assaulted by the rogue tribe of outcasts, and many an innocent man had fallen under their sword. It was *horrible* to call someone a Ferral.

Harold squatted on the ground and held his head crowned with green tuft in his shaking hands. He just sat there, stunned for several minutes as the sun sank and the moon appeared. Stars began to pepper the sky.

He had been idiotic to call Puella such a thing. Even if she deserved the title, he would be in tons of trouble in the morning. That is, *if* he survived the night.

Eventually, Harold decided he should go inside, before people thought he went missing. As he stood, his gaze shifted to the far side of Galidemus, where he could barely see his three friends meandering in his direction, just walking up the hill. He waited for them to see him, then walked over to meet them. He tried to forget his misfortune, knowing his friends had probably done much better. If anything, he hoped their day had been better than his.

Petunia was the first to speak. "Harold, I—" she faltered, unsure of what to say. "I wish you could've caught one."

"It's alright. Don't feel sorry for me," Harold mumbled.

"No, don't act like that. It was just bad luck," she said, attempting to console him.

"Petunia, I had three tries!" Harold fumed, "I had plenty of luck, chances, and resources. I have no one to blame but myself!"

"I heard you nabbed one," Carnis said, looking down at his nails. He seemed almost as unhappy as Harold.

"Sure I did, but it doesn't matter. I still lost it. And plus, it was a Sapling."

"You'll get another chance next year," Petunia encouraged, "and I promise I will let you borrow Bortle if you want."

"You named your dragonfly Bortle?" Harold asked, changing the subject.

"Yes, and Snip and Carnis caught one, too," she said. "Want to see?"

"I guess," Harold lied. Even Snip—scared, weak Snip—had caught a dragonfly. It didn't make sense.

With Petunia in the lead, the four students set off toward the back of the school where the dragonfly stables stood. Harold had never been to this area of the property before, and it proved to be quite a distance from Galidemus's main castle. Over the hill were rows and rows of stalls, all made out of wood, all just big enough to hold one dragonfly each. There had to be hundreds of them. The shacks were spaced evenly, like small barracks, some quivering as their occupants slammed into the sides of the walls. Dragonflies did not appreciate being confined.

As Petunia led them to her stall first, Harold noticed both Snip and Carnis seemed to be sulking, as if they were unhappy they had caught anything at all. They should've been happy, Harold thought. At least they caught *something*.

Petunia's stall was silent inside as she slid her small key into the latch. The door swung open to reveal a medium-sized dragonfly that was peppered with shimmering blue spots. The small insect cowered in a corner of the stall, spherical eyes flashing. It was beautiful.

"She's a girl," Petunia said enthusiastically. "Isn't she pretty?"

"Very," Harold agreed. "What kind would you say she is?"

Carnis, being an expert on such things, spoke first. "Some sort of mix, I'd say," he murmured. "Most likely the offspring of a Sapling and a Lightning Back."

"Is she fast?" Harold asked.

"Fast enough," Petunia said. "I can't believe I actually caught one!"

Harold nodded. His mind was distant, in another place. "Should we go to see Snip's now?"

"Oh, well, I—" Snip mumbled.

"Snip, just because you aren't happy with your dragonfly doesn't mean you won't show us," Petunia scolded. "Let's go."

Snip's stall was one row over from Petunia's and rattling violently. Harold was startled at the effect.

"It's a bit hyper," Snip squeaked, shivering as they walked. He insisted his sister open the door for him. And when she did, it was only a crack.

Harold peered inside. What he saw startled him.

The biggest, brightest Lightning Back Harold had ever seen lay crouched inside, as if ready to pounce. The insect was massive, insane. It throttled the walls by slamming into them and shrieked when it couldn't escape. Its wings spanned the entire shed.

"Snip, how in the world did you catch a thing like that? It's crazy!"

"That's what *I* asked him," Carnis moaned. Harold could now tell why he had been so sulky. Carnis, the dragonfly connoisseur, was jealous.

"Well, I—I don't really know for certain," Snip stuttered. "It just sort of plopped in my net and here we are."

"The thing's got to be the best catch of the day!" Harold gasped. "Not to mention the fastest!"

"*Too* fast," Snip frowned, "I had been hoping for a simple Sapling or something like that.

"Snip, this dragonfly is awesome," Harold said. "I wouldn't replace him for the world. What did you name him?"

"Bott," he replied.

"Bott?"

"Bott."

"That's it?" Harold clarified. "A dragonfly like this ought to be named something much cooler than just Bott. Nothing cool like Speedwing or Windracer?"

"Just Bott."

"Alright, then. Bott," Harold said, a bit disappointed. "He's a slick dragonfly."

"Thank you," Snip sighed, though he didn't sound very grateful. "Let's go see Carnis's now."

Carnis grumbled.

"Why so glum?" Harold asked as they walked down the row to Carnis's shed.

Carnis unlocked his door and swung it wide open. Harold was afraid the dragonfly might escape, but when he saw what was inside, he didn't worry any longer. The dragonfly Carnis caught lay in a blob in the corner, pale in color and very small. It didn't even look like a dragonfly. Its wings were short and limp, and its body was lethargic and mushy. "Is it—is it alive?" Harold asked.

"Oh, you bet it is," Carnis growled, grinding his teeth.

"How did you catch it?" Harold asked, stifling laughter.

"You'd *better* not laugh," Carnis growled. "It was an accident. I was going to dump it, but Ms. Dywood saw me first. Now I'm stuck with it forever."

"At least you *caught* a dragonfly," Petunia suggested.

Carnis frowned. "I'd rather catch nothing at all!"

"Why don't you and Snip trade?" asked Harold.

"Impossible," Carnis replied, "I already asked Mrs. Kernester. She said I should learn to cope with my stupid dragonfly no matter how miserable she is."

"Well, you must've given her a name, right?" Snip asked.

"Her name's Sickworm."

"Well, it certainly fits her, doesn't it?" Harold joked. Nobody laughed.

"How about we all go to supper?" Petunia suggested. "I know it's late, but I'm sure there's something left to eat."

The others consented. Carnis closed his stall, perhaps harder than necessary, and the four friends marched back toward Galidemus, a tall, prickled shadow in the darkness. Harold watched the stars flicker into being and knew his day was not yet over. He was not yet done with the Sapling he had injured. He would not give up that easily.

CHAPTER FOUR

Swiftless

The meal room was vacant, and Harold could see four lonely bowls sitting on the Algae table. As usual, their soup was still piping hot; Mrs. Murphy, the school cook, always made sure even late students got a warm meal when they arrived.

Harold took his seat at the empty Algae table, as did his friends. He wolfed down the warm soup in minutes. Skipping lunch had made him starving, and the calming effects of the soup made him sleepy. He yawned as he listened to his friends' detailed accounts of the day, though he listened attentively. Were there secrets to obtaining a dragonfly? Or was it all just good luck? If there was a method, he wanted to learn it.

"At least the weather cooperated," Petunia said, the soup cheering her soul.

"I'm glad only one of us had to get wet," snickered Harold.

Petunia shot him a look. "Cheer up, Harold. This soup is amazing!"

"It tastes great," Carnis agreed, bits of noodle and vegetable dangling from his mouth. If there was one thing that could cheer Carnis up, it was food.

"How did all of you catch your dragonflies?" Harold asked. He wanted to know what he had done wrong and hoped he could glean some advice. "I want every detail."

Petunia was the only one not chewing, so she spoke first. "It was pretty easy for me," she said. "Nothing but a bit of stretching before."

"I didn't even *intend* to catch mine," Carnis admitted. "It was floating upside down in the water, so I went to see if it was alright. It was still alive, but just barely. I figured if I left it there, it would drown. So I put it in my boat to take it to shore, but Ms. Dywood was watching me, and she made me keep it! *Honestly*, if she'd only let me have a chance . . . it was really early in the day, you know."

"How'd Snip catch his?" Harold asked. He was most curious about how his frail friend had caught such an enormous dragonfly.

Snip looked like a scrawny rat. His grey hair was sweaty and matted, and his thin limbs were rattling. His knees were knocking against each other, but even Snip seemed to be feeling some of the calming effects of the warm soup.

"Oh, well, it sort of ran into me," Snip said.

"What?" Harold exclaimed, snorting soup up his nose. He dried his face with a napkin and cleared his throat. "How?"

"Well, I was just finishing up a piece of toast, and it . . . it came after me."

"So I suppose Lightning Backs love toast, then?" Carnis inquired, his voice tinged with an undertone of jealousy.

"I suppose," Snip said. "With jelly."

"Well, even though *I* didn't catch one," Harold said, making sure to lower his voice, "I think I might still be able to. I mean, before next year."

"What? How?" Petunia asked. "You aren't planning on breaking any rules, are you?"

"I'm sort of already in hot water," Harold explained. He then told them all about his day, how he had fashioned his net and how angry Ms. Dywood had been. He told them about how he called Puella a Ferral and about the small, wet Sapling across the pond.

"And so," he continued, "I think I just might be able to ferry across the pond tonight and *catch it*."

"No. Absolutely not," Petunia stated. "You can't. You might get more detention, or worse, get expelled!"

"Petunia, I *live* here. They can't expel me," Harold explained.

Petunia rolled her eyes. "Rules are rules. And just think of if we failed! What if we crashed the boat? Or what if the dragonfly wasn't even there? What if *we* got in trouble instead of you?" This latter proposition she stated with such repulsion Harold could only clench his fists gently upon the table to contain his frustration.

"I didn't say you have to come," Harold stated.

"Well, if you're set on going, I can't just let you go alone. I *have* to go with you," Petunia said, exhaling with moral confliction.

"You don't *have* to," Harold said, mimicking her voice. "We can go alone."

"You guys are idiots," she said. "Of course I have to go!"

"You really don't," Harold insisted.

"But if I don't, I'll be worried, and then if something happens to you, I won't be there!"

"Whatever," Carnis laughed, "I think it's a great idea!"

Carnis had broken more rules in his life than he had eaten meals. "I'll come, of course, but we'll have to work out some wrinkles first. If we get caught, will you take full blame?"

"I guess so," Harold nodded.

"How will you catch it?" Snip asked. He had known from the beginning this was a bad idea. However, Petunia had an answer for that one.

"I know where Mrs. Kernester's office is. The keys to the net box and dragonfly sheds are in there. But that would be breaking rules." She twisted a lock of her hair with anxiety.

Harold was a bit uneasy about it too, but a dragonfly's fate depended on this endeavor. He convinced himself it was a good idea, pushing thoughts of possible mishaps out of his head.

"Petunia, if we don't go out there, that dragonfly will die in the cold, and I won't have a dragonfly for the entire year."

"What if they don't let you keep it?" she asked.

"That doesn't matter," Harold replied. "We'll have saved a dragonfly by then."

"Alright, so what's the plan?" Carnis asked, rubbing his hands together.

They huddled together, and Harold explained the plan he had formulated in his mind. They all agreed that Harold and Carnis would retrieve the keys and meet Petunia outside afterwards. Snip, who had been too scared to do anything else, insisted he keep watch on the dormitory for them in case any suspicion mounted. They would be leaving late, and other students might notice their absence.

Once Harold, Petunia, and Carnis got outside, they would borrow a couple of boats from the shore and paddle to the island. If they couldn't find the dragonfly there, they'd go home. But if they did, they would capture it and head home, returning the boats in the process. Then they'd lock the sapling up, return the keys, and go back to sleep like nothing had happened. It was foolproof—or so they thought.

Just as they were finishing their plan, Mrs. Murphy came bursting through the kitchen doors, several bowls of steaming soup balanced on her arms, hands, and head. She smiled, gaping at their presence. Mrs. Murphy always treated the students like children of her own— or, rather, babies of her own. She was constantly fretting about Snip's weight. She was quite round and carried a bloated behind, and her hair was always put up in a fancy bun, pale green in color. Her aging face was always smiling.

"Oh, I'm so glad you returned!" she passed out more bowls of soup.

"Mrs. Murphy, we already had our soup," Harold explained. "It's very good, though."

"Oh, nonsense," she chided. "I mean, just look at the lot of you! You all need your nutrition, and Snip is terribly thin. Eat up! Go along, don't be afraid."

Carnis didn't complain, but the others picked at the extra food. Seeing their reluctance, she began spoon-feeding Snip.

"Not—hungry!" Snip said, trying to shove her away. But it was no use. Mrs. Murphy was too heavy to budge. Her arms were fit from lugging pots around all day, and she was nothing to mess with. Taking the cue, the others began slurping their soup and smiling. Mrs. Murphy seemed pleased.

"So, I heard all this whispering out here," she said, as if she were a gossiping girl at a slumber party. "What's it all about?"

"Oh, nothing," Harold insisted, thinking he was hiding his nervousness better than he actually was.

"Oh, come on. Spit it out. I won't tattle," she insisted. While Mrs. Murphy was technically an authority figure, she rarely seemed like one and would do anything for a juicy bit of gossip.

"Fine," Harold nodded halfheartedly. "We were just whispering about how... er... how strange the weather's been, and how filthy Ms. Dywood looked this morning. Quite an eyesore, isn't she?"

Carnis stifled a giggle, but Mrs. Murphy didn't seem to notice.

"Oh, I know. She's been so wretched these days," she nodded, "I am almost sure she's interested in *somebody*."

Harold smiled perhaps a little too broadly, regained his composure, and nodded, "most certainly."

"Have you noticed how fast her hair turns?" she continued. "It's almost certain!"

"Quite certain, if you ask me," Harold played along, trying not to laugh.

"Well, I'd best get going, then," Mrs. Murphy said, picking her large body up. "Ta ta, and stay out of that Dywood's way. She's obviously insane."

And off she went back to her kitchen, leaving the four to laugh in hysterics. It was no surprise Mrs. Murphy didn't make it as a teacher. She would never punish any of her students even if she was ordered to. Finally, when the laughter subsided, they finished their extra soup because it really did taste good.

The rest of the evening was uneventful, but Harold could barely contain his excitement as he waited. He resolved to lay in bed while he waited, but staring up at the dark ceiling was painfully boring. It was hours before the other students began falling asleep, some trickling into the dormitory early and some so late, Harold wondered how they could function the next day. At midnight, Carnis meandered into the room and quickly fell asleep, but Harold dared not move until he heard everyone in the room snoring.

Finally, he decided it was late enough, and he crawled out of bed. He hadn't slept a wink, but he hardly felt tired. Careful not to wake the other boys, Harold tip-toed over to Carnis's cluttered bedside and poked him on the cheek. Carnis snored on, unaware and unbearably loud.

"Carnis, wake up!" Harold whispered. No response. He shook him harder.

"What? Oh, uh, Harold," he mumbled, smacking his lips, "remind me why we are waking up so early?"

"Carnis!" Harold whispered, "the PLAN. Remember?"

"Oh, bother. *That*. Right. Okay, I'm up."

"Let's go."

The boys slipped out of the dorm as quietly as they could, passing Snip as they went, who sat leaning against the door frame, barely keeping awake.

"Good luck," he whispered up as they passed.

"Thanks," Harold whispered. "And thanks for keeping watch for us. Good luck staying awake."

"Hey," Snip chuckled nervously. "I've got this."

They left the commons and crept through deserted halls and down some unused staircases as Petunia had instructed them. Finally, they came to Mrs. Kernester's empty office, but what they found was shocking.

Harold gasped when he looked inside the chamber. The desks and chairs were overturned, and the pictures on the walls hung askew. A decorative rug on the floor was half folded over, slumped up against a bookshelf that had all the books taken out. The chair that once held Mrs. Kernester as she dealt with private matters was turned over on the floor, its legs broken. The trashcan was smashed and its contents lay scattered all over. Drawers on the desk lay open and emptied, and papers were everywhere. But most unusual about the whole mess were several mud splotches positioned like footsteps on the floor. They shimmered in the moonlight coming from the open window, not having been mopped up at all.

Harold walked over to the desk where a name plaque had fallen to the floor, just to confirm this truly was Mrs. Kernester's office. It was.

"This place is a wreck," Carnis stated quietly.

"I know," Harold agreed, "and this is the place where we're supposed to be. How strange. Something must have happened."

Carnis looked at the mud splotches, tapping his foot in the grime. They were just the size of footprints. "Weird."

"I hope Mrs. Kernester is okay," Harold whispered.

"Oh, I'm sure she's fine," Carnis whispered back. "No alarms have been sounded, and she's not here. I'm guessing it was a break-in and we're the first ones to notice."

"Huh," Harold wondered. He couldn't think of anything in her office anyone wanted to steal.

"Let's get out of here before anyone notices," Harold urged, "find the keys."

It didn't take long to spot them. They hung in plain sight on a hook on one wall, and Carnis snatched them. They jingled in his grasp. Harold put his finger to his lips and they tip-toed out of the wrecked room. After briefly using the keys to gather three nets and open Galidemus's main oak doors, Harold and Carnis slipped out into the night to find Petunia waiting on the steps.

"How'd you get out here?" Harold asked, handing out the nets. She hadn't had a key to escape.

"Window," she replied, "it was surprisingly easy. Now, let's get going. The dock's not far."

The rest of the trip was spent in silence until they reached the docks. The moon was not quite full, a tantalizing misshapen circle in the sky. The clouds had cleared, stars multiplied from horizon to horizon, and the night teemed with the noises of nature—the soft breath of the wind, the rustle of leaves, and the prattle of trickling water. The water itself seemed fairly calm, and many boats were left abandoned. No one fished at night, save maybe the night-fishers, who caught nocturnal fish. This was one of the things that concerned Harold, being spotted by one of these midnight trawlers.

The group picked two moderately sized boats to borrow, and Harold shoved off in one while Carnis and Petunia sat in the other. The current flowed swiftly in the direction Harold had been hoping for.

They spent the rest of the cruise in silence, even though they knew they couldn't possibly be heard by anyone on shore if they rustled. All the same, it was only a matter of time before a booming voice reached their ears from shore, nearly giving them all a heart attack.

It was a loud voice, a man's voice, but it was oily and slick like a crawdad's.

"Juniper, did you misplace my boats? We need them tonight."

Harold gulped.

"No, father," said an equally sulky voice, though younger sounding. His voice was doleful, morose. Like his future had been stripped from him. "I don't know where they could be. Something smells fishy."

"Well, of course if smells fishy," Juniper's father replied harshly. "We're on a dock."

"I haven't failed to notice that, Father."

Harold glanced over at Carnis and Petunia. They both looked rather pale, and Harold knew he would get no answers from either of them. What could he do? His brain seemed to be in a constant state of panic ever since they had started this whole mission.

"Hey, do you see that?" called the younger one, Juniper, again. Harold's heart skipped a beat.

"Out there on the water?" his father clarified.

"Yes, it looks like two boats."

Harold ducked in the boat, trying not to be seen. Carnis and Petunia did, too, and everything held still. Harold gulped.

"They couldn't have drifted, could they?" asked Juniper. There was no noise, so Harold assumed the father had nodded.

"Let's go check them out," he said.

Harold froze, thinking with all his might. They were about to be caught by a couple of night-fishers. He couldn't let that happen. Finally, he willed his body to respond and began paddling furiously to the opposite shore. They could make it if they paddled quickly. He whispered to Carnis and Petunia to do the same, but they didn't need to be told. They paddled as hard and quietly as they dared, trying their best to not be seen in the drifting boats. But Juniper and his father recognized the sudden change in pace. "The boats are moving faster!" Juniper called out. "Someone is stealing them!"

Harold moaned and paddled harder.

"They are!" Juniper's father exclaimed. "Quick, into a boat!"

A great scuffling ensued onshore as the two night-trawlers scrambled into boats. Harold prayed they were slow, which was a lousy prayer, since these people were night-*fishers*. Still, anything was possible.

Finally, the island came into sight. It wasn't far off, and the fog made it seem farther than it really was. They could make it. They could make it...

"Hey, you!" called the father over the rush of the water. "Stop this instant and return our boats!"

Finally, they bumped into shore. Harold scrambled to shore, soaking his boots in freezing water. Then he pushed his boat off far away, toward their pursuers. As Carnis and Petunia jumped out of their boat, Harold readied to push that boat off as well, but Petunia gripped his arm.

"How are we going to get back?" she whispered.

"Trust me," Harold said. There was a moment as she looked into his eyes, searching for something to trust. Finally, Petunia nodded and they let the boat go.

They scrambled to hide on the island, running as fast as they could. They flung themselves into the thick vegetation, not caring about the brambles and thorns. After they were hidden and had caught their breath, they waited for the night-fishers to find their boats and leave. It took a while. Finally, a shout sounded over the water.

"Here they are, father!" exclaimed Juniper. Faintly, Harold could see them taking a new direction on the water and he breathed a sigh of relief. They had escaped.

After a couple more minutes, the three students stood up, stretched, and regrouped.

Petunia glared at Harold as he ruffled some water out of his hair. "How are we to get back?" she asked, hands on her hips.

"We'll figure out something," Harold said. "There're plenty of resources on this island. We'll be fine."

"So much for a foolproof plan," she muttered under her breath.

Carnis sighed, eyes drooping from exhaustion. "Let's go find the Sapling, all right? You guys look and I'll build some reed boats for us. Got it?"

Petunia nodded.

"You won't just make mud castles, will you?" Harold clarified.

"Good grief, I can be helpful once in a while, can't I?" Carnis retorted.

Harold snickered and ran off with Petunia to catch his dragonfly.

It didn't take too long to circle the island. The first time they circled it, they couldn't find a trace of anything, but after their second run, they looked more carefully and finally discovered a small Sapling cowering in some tall grasses toward one side of the island. The dragonfly was plain and tan, with faint dark speckles beading its short tail. The insect was small, even for a Sapling. But it had some defenses. The hook at the end of its tail was still intact, despite all the rough pulling Harold had done to it. Its eyes gleamed in the moonlight and its small antennas stood up at the noise Harold made while approaching it. However, regardless of its alertness, the dragonfly didn't move at all as they got closer.

"Hey, look," Petunia pointed to the insect's wings. "They're frozen to the ground."

As Harold looked closer, he noticed they were. The wetness of the crash earlier in the day had soaked the dragonfly's wings through and through, and they had frozen in the icy March temperatures. Harold felt sorry for it. This was all his fault. He stroked its frozen wing gently, hoping to calm the poor creature, but it only shriveled in pain. And that was when Harold noticed it.

A deep gouge had been ripped on the dragonfly's left wing, leaving a painful scar. The tear seemed fatal, or at least lessened it chance of ever flying again. Harold gingerly touched the rip, noticing a sort of pattern in the injury, as if carved by hand. But the image made no sense to him. He showed Petunia the scar.

"Oh, no! The poor thing!" she cried. "It looks like it will never fly again."

"I doubt it will," Harold sighed, "this is all my fault. I managed to fail on the most important day of my life *and* maim a dragonfly in the process! I'm useless—"

"Stop it now," Petunia scolded, "this didn't happen without reason. How about you give it a name?"

Harold scowled at the bug. It would be lucky to live. "It's just going to die anyway. At best, it'll survive, but won't be able to fly. Why do I have to name it?"

"It deserves better than this. Name it," she replied.

Harold sighed. The dragonfly deserved *something*. But he would only miss it more when it died if he gave it a name. Oh well.

"Swiftless." Harold stated, "that's what I'll call it. Only because it can't fly."

"I like it," Petunia smirked slightly, then covered it with a warm smile. "Let's go see how Carnis is getting on now."

After carefully lifting his frozen wings, they managed to move Swiftless into their two nets in a position where they could easily carry him. Swiftless shivered in the midnight breeze, so Harold reached for his cloak to drape around his dragonfly, but found nothing there.

"Uh, Petunia, did you take my cloak?" he asked, adrenaline pumping into his body. His heartbeat quickened, pounding like a warning beacon in his chest.

"No, why?"

"Uh-oh."

Harold and Petunia stared at each other for a moment. Then Petunia gasped.

"Please don't tell me you left it in one of the boats," she pleaded.

"I think I did," Harold replied softly, "and I think it had my name written on the tag."

Petunia moaned. "Look what you've done now!"

"Shoot! I know, I'm sorry," Harold apologized, but he knew if the night-fishers took any notice of the tag, he would be in serious trouble. There weren't many Harolds in the village.

"Well, there's nothing that can be done now," Petunia sighed, "and you're the one whose name is Harold, not me."

"Think of how *I* feel," Harold groaned.

After a short walk and a lot more lifting, the duo reached Carnis and the shore. Carnis was very focused, but the one boat he was working on was mangy and small. Harold sighed when he saw the sad raft. At least Carnis had been eager to help. The boat was made from three fat reed rods, all different lengths and clumsily cut. There were no sides to the boat, nor anything to catch a breeze or paddle with. And smudged in wet mud on the floor of the craft read *Absolute Failure*.

"Carnis, please don't tell me you spent more time on the name than actually building this thing." Petunia moaned.

"Accurate, isn't it?" Carnis asked as he laughed. "Did you catch it?"

Harold nodded, gesturing to Swiftless.

"Ouch, almost looks as bad as Sickworm," he sighed. "What took you so long?"

"Its wings were frozen and two are broken," replied Petunia, "and it's getting colder out here by the minute."

"His name?"

"Swiftless," Harold said, rubbing his hands together to keep them warm. "And we discovered I might have left my cloak in the bottom of the boat we stole."

"Ah—wait, what?" Carnis shuddered. "You did what?"

"I left my cloak in the bottom of the boat."

"The one with your name on it?"

Harold rolled his eyes. "Yes, the one with my name on it. It wasn't my greatest moment, alright?"

"Good grief, Harold," Carnis laughed. "You're a walking disaster."

"We'd best get going," Petunia shivered, cutting off Harold before he could defend himself. "It's cold out here."

It was difficult work getting three people, a dragonfly, and three nets on an unsteady raft in the dark. Their first attempt failed, and Carnis soaked his whole torso in cold water. On their second attempt, Harold and Petunia got soaked while they tried not to get Swiftless wet. But finally, on their third try, they managed to get everyone safely aboard without tipping.

After some quick high-fives and a small, feeble celebration, they began paddling back to shore using their hands. Harold's fingers became numb within seconds. At least at this pace, they would be home soon.

Before they could get far, however, an uneasy noise came from the thicket of the island. The snapping of a twig, the sound of feet stepping lightly between the brush. Harold and his friends paused to hear the commotion behind them, holding as still as possible. Harold could see the faint outlines of some figures in the bush, a pair standing opposite one another. The first was a woman, slender and slouched, her short hair tied up into a tight ponytail—a familiar hairstyle. The second was a man, though he was unlike anything Harold had ever seen before. From what he could see from his low vantage point, horns protruded from the man's skull and gills were carved into his neck. Fins spiked down his spine, and his hands and feet were webbed. Most unusual of his features was a tail, long and scaled, which swished back and forth in the undergrowth as he stood. He spoke in a strange voice, like the sound of water in a rushing river.

"Good evening," the man grunted. His greeting was void of kindness of warmth.

The woman stuck out her chin. "Stark, your choice of destruction was extremely foolish."

Harold gasped, then looked at his two friends, who were equally shocked. They knew this voice. They had heard it today, no more than a few hours ago. It was Ms. Dywood.

"You shouldn't be so daft," Stark growled, "you know perfectly well my reasons."

"Yes, I understand," Ms. Dywood grumbled, "but you haven't the faintest idea of the valuables in there and the time it will take to clean up. It'll create pandemonium. I'm only playing along with this—"

Stark stuck out a slimy finger and brushed Ms. Dywood's chin. She shrank back in disgust.

"Oh, Merryl, naive, naive. You just don't see it yet. Mrs. Kernster's office was the perfect place. Open your eyes. Who will win this war?"

Ms. Dywood kept silent, and Carnis and Harold shared knowing looks. They were talking about Mrs. Kernester's destroyed office, undeniably. Petunia looked terribly confused.

"Were the students frightened?" asked Stark.

"Not yet," Ms. Dywood replied, "we are announcing it tomorrow morning."

"Not a minute later," Stark growled, "He doesn't like to wait for the job to get done, Merryl."

"I am loyal only to Mrs. Kernester," Ms. Dywood snarled.

Stark chuckled. "We will see. We will see."

"It's late," Ms. Dywood observed, "We should go."

"Remember, Merryl," Stark nodded, "no later than the morning. Do not delay."

Stark suddenly plunged into the water quite near to Harold's boat, but he didn't seem to notice their embarrassing craft. In fact, he didn't even resurface. After the ripples had disappeared, Ms. Dywood moved. For a moment, Harold was afraid she'd come right their way, but instead she turned her heel and disappeared into the thicket of the island. Harold breathed a sigh of relief.

"That was Ms. Dywood!" Carnis exclaimed.

"And what about Mrs. Kernester's office?" Petunia whispered. "Did I miss something?"

"Me and Carnis found it on the way here," Harold explained. "The place was battered up. Tables overturned, chair legs snapped, bookcases tipped over. And mud splotches on the floor..."

"It looked like a break-in," Carnis added. "And what in the world was Ms. Dywood doing out here, at this time of the night?"

"I don't know. To be fair, she might ask the same thing about us," Harold chuckled. "But who was that guy, Stark?"

"I suppose the question is, *what* is Stark?" Petunia wondered aloud.

"I don't know that either," Harold sighed, "I've never seen such a thing."

"He had horns and a tail and just dove into the water like some kind of fish," Carnis gawked.

"You don't suppose either Ms. Dywood or Mrs. Kernester are working for him, do you?" Petunia asked, worried.

"I don't know," Harold said a third time. "Mrs. Kernester would never do such a thing." He then noticed faint rays of sunlight on the horizon. "We need to go, it's almost morning."

Away the group paddled, silent and thinking. The only noise that could be heard was the lapping of water upon their sad raft and the chirps of early morning birds that were nesting in the reeds. The sounds were so soothing Carnis fell asleep and Harold had to paddle double. He snorted awake when they bumped ashore, a bit confused, but otherwise conscious. They all climbed off the raft and set *Absolute Failure* into the current again, to cover their tracks. Harold was glad to see it go.

After a brief stop at the stables to lock Swiftless up snug and sound under a warm blanket, they headed back to the school, dawn creeping in. Petunia returned the nets and the keys and headed to her dorm as the boys returned to theirs. They found Snip asleep on the floor, all tuckered out with red lines on his cheeks from lying against the door frame. But Harold was hardly disappointed. He had a dragonfly—finally.

Harold had far too many questions to sleep. He had come to terms with this exhausting reality long before. So, lying in bed after undressing from his wet clothes, he waited patiently for morning.

CHAPTER FIVE

The Boating Lesson

Harold had hardly slept when the others started rising from their beds. He found himself in a state that was not quite asleep, but just nearly enough to make rising a chore. It had only been an hour or so since he returned from catching Swiftless, so he hadn't been able to get much rest.

Listening to the other boys' snickering while he got dressed informed him that he was now the talk of the school, and not in a good way. Everyone seemed to have discovered overnight that he called Puella a Ferral. It wasn't a good feeling to be pointed at several times in a morning. And as if the snickering wasn't enough, Puella had told the teachers about the whole incident as well. They were sure to take her word for it; she was, after all, a Royal.

Harold had awakened to a note pinned to his dormitory door saying he would serve detention. But his punishment was quite different than he expected. Reading the note that rested on his bedside table, he realized he had been ordered to clean Mrs. Kernester's destroyed office that night.

Harold was shocked they were allowing *anyone* in the room, but he preferred it to sitting and doing nothing. The thought of another late night seemed exhausting, but he was eager to investigate the office.

The curious splotches of mud on the floor had to be from *something*, and Harold had his theories.

The fact that Mrs. Kernester's office had been broken into also spread like wildfire throughout the school. Students were talking about it in fearful voices, and teachers were warning them to be careful during every class period. They even made an announcement during breakfast about it, claiming there had been a break-in, though nothing had been stolen. Nobody was to enter the room unless they got permission, and apparently Harold had been one of the select few to get it. He wished it was on better terms, but he was glad to go so he could investigate. The thought of it almost helped him to forget his exhaustion. Almost.

In the meal room, Harold and Carnis sat down at their regular seats, next to Snip and Petunia. Snip was in his usual frightful mood but was at least rested. Petunia, on the other hand, looked disheveled and half asleep, her hair sticking out in all directions.

"Good morning," she moaned.

"Good morning," Harold said, forcing a smile. He looked down at his breakfast—a big steamed corn kernel and a bowl of thick cream. Both were just cool enough to eat. He munched slowly—it tasted delicious, but he wasn't very hungry. He was too eager to tell Mrs. Kernester about Swiftless to eat. From the beginning, telling her about his adventure had been part of his plan. He hoped he wouldn't get in too much trouble. It would have to be told tactfully, but with enough luck, he might be able to keep Swiftless. That is, *if* the insect had survived the night.

"Petunia said everything went well?" Snip asked, still nervous about the night before.

"Oh, certainly not everything," Harold sighed, sipping his cream, "but we got the job done."

Just then a great splash erupted next to Harold, soaking his pants with cream. Harold glared at Carnis, who was sputtering and gasping next to him. Apparently, he had nodded off in his breakfast.

"Petunia filled me in," Snip said, ignoring Carnis. "Did you really leave your cloak in the boat you borrowed?"

"Yes," Harold replied numbly.

"That's terrible."

"I know."

A moment of silence followed.

"Does anyone want to come with me to ask Mrs. Kernester about Swiftless?" Harold asked. He knew their little expedition would not be kept a secret for long, and he knew he would have to tell Mrs. Kernester some time or another. He could trust her.

But Carnis just snored.

Petunia shook her head, staring into her breakfast.

Snip averted his eyes.

"Alright," Harold nodded, "I'll just go by myself then."

As soon as Harold finished his breakfast and changed out of his cream-soaked pants, he grabbed his school bag and set out to find Mrs. Kernester. He typically didn't see her very often during meal times, so he wandered the school in search of her, hoping to find her by chance. He checked her office briefly, which was still vacant, muddy, and destroyed. The mess seemed a lot worse in the morning light. He was not looking forward to cleaning it that night.

He then checked outside, in the remedies class she taught, and in the west tower, where she usually spent her free hours, but she was nowhere to be found. Finally, Harold gave up and walked down the hall to his next class when he spotted her not far off. He scurried up to her.

"Good morning, Harold," she said, smiling beneath her spectacles. She didn't appear busy, walking down the hall by herself. "Is there anything I can help you with?"

"Actually, yes," he replied. "I need to speak with you in private for a moment."

"Of course, dear," she replied. "I suppose I can spare a few minutes."

They walked to the library and sat down in two plush chairs, apart from the other few students that studied there. Harold took a deep breath, choosing his words carefully.

"Mrs. Kernester, you know how I couldn't catch a dragonfly yesterday?"

She frowned. "I do. That is unfortunate. I know you were looking forward to having one."

"Well," Harold continued, "I need to tell you about a certain dragonfly."

He explained everything, telling her as carefully as he could about the events of the night before. He tried his best to leave out most of the rule-breaking parts, but Mrs. Kernester could sniff a lie a mile away, which was saying something for someone two inches tall, and she hastily pointed them out.

Soon Harold found himself telling the entire story, save perhaps the encounter with Ms. Dywood. At the end, he knew he was in trouble. Mrs. Kernester's usually happy face had creased into a frown and her vibrant hair seemed to grow darker.

"Harold, you know by doing what you did, you and your friends have broken at least ten rules in the span of a little over three hours," she said once he had finished.

"Swiftless would've died had I not saved him," Harold insisted.

"I understand your intentions, but you were in serious danger last night. A regular student would get expelled for this behavior."

Harold sighed, then remembered his friends were considered regular students.

"Mrs. Kernester, I am really sorry," Harold said, "and I am not trying to run away from anything I deserve, but I have to ask that you go easy on my friends. Petunia would be furious at me if she got in trouble. It was my idea, and I doubt she would ever speak to me again if you expelled her."

Mrs. Kernester chuckled and her irritation disappeared from her face for a moment. "I understand, but you will have to take full blame for all you and your friends did."

"I will," Harold gulped, "and may I keep the dragonfly?"

"Under normal circumstances, I would set the insect free," she replied, "but considering you are in a tight spot already, I will let you keep it. And I doubt the insect would be able to survive on its own. But you must be ready to be responsible with such an injured dragonfly. It might not recover in your care."

Harold could barely contain his relief. He hadn't noticed how much he had hoped for keeping Swiftless until now. Before, he had just been a wet dragonfly that needed help. Now it was Harold's dragonfly, and no matter how injured or hop it was, Harold would look after it. "Thank you, Mrs. Kernester," he sighed.

"Now for your punishment," she said, pausing for thought. She couldn't expel him, but she was not eager to let him go unscathed, either.

"What do you most hate at Galidemus?"

Unable to resist, Harold said sarcastically, "Well, being with Mrs. Murphy for too long is pretty terrible."

Apparently, Mrs. Kernester was not in the mood for jokes. "Well, Mrs. Murphy for the day, then, if that's what you decide. Yes, that should work."

Harold's stomach plummeted. He suddenly regretted the joke.

"What? No!" he shrieked. "I mean, of course there are worse things, aren't there?"

"You tell me," she replied.

"Perhaps cleaning the bathrooms?" Harold shrugged, hoping that anything would help him escape from this predicament. But what had he expected? Breaking this many rules required justice, and he had been prepared to take it. He couldn't shrink out of it this time. He hesitated. "Actually, never mind," he sighed, "I deserve it. Send me to the kitchen. What day should I go?"

Mrs. Kernester smiled beneath her spectacles. "Two days' time. Does that sound reasonable?"

"Sure," he gulped. "Thank you for letting my friends off. And if you don't mind not telling Ms. Dywood, that would be fantastic."

Mrs. Kernester laughed. "I understand. Now get going! Classes have already started!"

She shooed him out of the room, and they parted in the hall. Harold then headed in high spirits to his first class of the day, boating class. He was never particularly excited about boating class, but today, after the news he had just acquired, he could take anything with a smile.

Mr. Porthand, the boating teacher at Galidemus, rarely engaged in conversation with the other teachers, probably because most of the teachers didn't know how to operate a boat. But even if he had someone to talk to, Harold didn't see him much outside of his classroom environment.

Tall and slim, Mr. Porthand had unusual brown hair that was matted and out of place. He liked to wear casual layered clothes and he didn't make much effort to disguise the actual age he was. Overall, he was a kind man, and Harold didn't mind him in the least. He was probably one of his better teachers, but he was far from perfect.

One thing that constantly nagged Harold about boating class was that it was never engaging. They seemed to read about boating plenty, and Harold had seen Mr. Porthand sail a handful of times, but they never seemed to go boating themselves. Little did he know, that was about to change this morning.

Harold walked into the classroom with a smile on his face, even though he was several minutes late. He expected not much had happened in his absence, but he couldn't have been more wrong. When he arrived, it seemed as though a cyclone had swept the room.

The place was completely empty. Not a single desk, chair, or book was left. The entire class was sitting on the floor.

Shocked, Harold took a seat on the floor next to Carnis near the back. Carnis had fallen asleep again—this time slumped on the floor, head hanging. Harold felt sorry for him. Snip was sitting towards the front of the crowd and Petunia was standing at the front of the classroom with Mr. Porthand.

"And I suppose Harold is here as well," Mr. Porthand smiled, ignoring the whispers from the rest of the class at his arrival. "It is well past time to begin," he continued, "and I would like to make an announcement before we start."

He gestured Petunia closer and cleared his throat.

"Today we are going to do things a bit differently," he said. The class murmured. "As Miss Parker and Mrs. Kernester have been so keen to point out, my teaching methods have been slightly flawed."

An air of anticipation penetrated the room. Harold scrunched his nose at the thought of Petunia pointing out a teacher's flaws.

"I would like to apologize. It is an easy mistake to make, not being quite as interactive as a teacher of my stature should be," he nodded. "As one says, *I listen and I forget, I see and I remember, I do and I learn.* I think something different for a change would be beneficial to us all."

The class consented with more enthusiasm than Harold expected. Maybe he wasn't the only one tired of not doing anything.

"Therefore," Mr. Porthand continued, "today we will have class outside. The weather is fair enough. How does that sound? To further the change, Mrs. Kernester herself thought it would be best if we moved the classroom *itself* outside permanently, or at least for the rest of the semester. We will now be taking classes under a porch of sorts out on the east side of Galidemus, not far from here. All the chairs and equipment have already been placed outside. So, if you will be gracious enough to change rooms with me, it is not far off."

Everyone was shocked. This arrangement was long overdue, but it was far from expected.

As students filed out of the retired classroom, Harold tried his best to wake up Carnis. He was completely unconscious. He tried the gentlest approach he could think of, but eventually he gave up and shook him hard instead. Carnis opened his eyes a crack.

"Harold? Don't tell me I've been dreaming this whole awful day and that we have to go catch Swiftless again," he moaned.

Harold laughed. "We're done with that. And keep quiet; we don't need to advertise our adventure. It's boating class now, and we're changing rooms. You should come along."

Carnis just stared blankly at him.

"You look really tired," Harold noted.

"Growing boys need sleep," he sighed, "lots of sleep."

He shook his head slightly, as if to shake off the sleepiness like the dew on a dog's coat, then stood up and walked out of the room into the torrent of students heading to the new classroom. Harold ran after him and followed at his friend's side.

"You sure you're okay?" he asked.

"I'm fine," Carnis replied, "just tired."

"*I'd* say!" Harold laughed.

The new open-air classroom was not much different from the old one. Other than being outside and looking like a square gazebo, the desks were arranged the same way they had been before. But even though not much was different, the place was peaceful. The pond trickled in the distance, and the trees swayed in a gentle breeze. Even though the classroom wasn't close to the pond, a path led from the patio to the shore across the valley for easy access to boats. The wooden platform that served as a porch for the classroom was wet and a bit squishy, like the wood had been rotted from the inside out, and the destruction couldn't be seen yet. Harold liked the new place already. All the students took their seats, but Mr. Porthand had them quickly stand again.

"We'll be out on the water today," he winked.

Snip, who had decided to cower next to Harold, moaned.

"I hate this place," he grumbled, "what if it gets cold out here? And an assignment out on the water? This is ridiculous!"

"We have quite a few boats to spare," Mr. Porthand said, gesturing to the path that led to the pond, "and today we are going to give them a test run. I would like each of you to pick a partner."

Harold snapped a glance toward Carnis, who was sleeping again.

"Both of you will grab a boat. One of you will operate the rudder, or the stem on your leaf boats, and the other should operate the oars. Then, after you are all situated, you will guide your boat a few inches out where I will be waiting, perform a left and right turn, two spin movements, and then return to this dock under my supervision.

"Now, don't worry too terribly about this assignment. As you haven't done much boating yourselves, I don't expect much. But I will tell you, after this school year is over, you should be able to perform these exercises effortlessly. Does anyone have any questions?"

No one raised a hand.

"Very well then," Mr. Porthand nodded, "off we go."

Harold quickly grabbed Carnis, who was following at a slow waddle, and led him down the path with the rest of the class. He felt like he was leading an elderly person into a wheelchair. Carnis was barely able to move, let alone pick up a rudder and steer a boat. Harold hoped they wouldn't flunk the entire thing.

On the other side of the group of migrating students, Petunia seemed to finally be letting go of Snip for once in her life. Instead of grabbing his arm, as she always did for nearly every occasion, she carefully walked over to a boy named Owen and asked if he wanted to be her partner. When he agreed, she blushed furiously.

This arrangement, however, was anything but sweet to Snip. Being left by himself made him quiver under pressure. Soon there was no one left to pair with except for the rejects of the class, himself and a girl named Martha Hamm. Martha was overweight and had an upturned nose. She was probably two times Snip's size. Around Galidemus, other students called her piggy.

The class followed the path to the water's edge, where several leaf boats sat waiting. It was a decent walk, but it only took a few minutes. Soon everyone had selected a boat, and Mr. Porthand was sorting out who would go in what order. Harold and Carnis were chosen first, while Snip and Piggy were fifth and Petunia and Owen third.

Harold gulped as Mr. Porthand ushered them out on the water, guiding them with his own boat. Everyone would be able to see them from the shore. Immediately, he felt like he was carrying dead weight. Already Carnis had fallen asleep in the bottom of the boat. How would he be able to make all those sharp turns without a person at the rudder? Slowly they edged forward to where Mr. Porthand was waiting, making a little trail in the water. Mr. Porthand smiled at Harold, then looked down at Carnis.

"Sleeping?" he asked.

Harold chuckled. "Tired, I guess."

"Will you be okay on your own?" Mr. Porthand asked.

Harold nodded, waiting for his first instruction.

"You're doing well so far. Make a right turn, please."

Harold tried his best, but steering with a rudder and paddling at the same time was just not working. Mr. Porthand scribbled something in his clipboard, then looked up again and ordered Harold to now make a left turn.

Harold tried, very slowly. It took nearly ten minutes before the demonstration was over. Mr. Porthand frowned at Carnis as Harold finished his desperate spin.

"It is unfortunate," he sighed. "Carnis picked a terrible time to take a nap."

Harold rubbed the back of his neck. "He's a fine sailor, but he had a late night. I did, too. We're all a bit tired."

"Well," his teacher continued, "whether Carnis is a good trawler or not, I'm afraid he has gotten a bad score on this assignment. You did well for carrying so much dead weight. You are free to go back to shore."

Harold nodded and paddled slowly to shore. He then watched as the other students took their turns. They all did noticeably better. Before long, it was Petunia and Owen's turn. Owen was fit and Petunia always studied before class, so of course they aced the test. From what Harold could see in his boat near the shore, he was impressed. Soon they sailed back, both in deep conversation. Harold envied their comradery.

After the first few runs, the process became boring and monotonous. Each student's performance was just the same as the one before, and Harold could feel his head bobbing gently as if upon waves. He was losing his focus, but willed himself to stay awake until at least Snip's turn. And by the time the fifth round arrived, Harold had no trouble focusing.

Out they went, Piggy paddling and Snip steering. Piggy was so heavy she weighed down the front of the boat, almost sinking it. Snip was so nervous, his hands could barely grip the rudder. It took ages for them to reach the intended spot, even longer than it had taken Harold. At one point, Mr. Porthand grew impatient and told Piggy to pick up the pace.

"Put your back into it, Martha!" he shouted from his boat out on the water. Piggy started paddling even harder, flinging water into the air in all directions. They suddenly sped forward, landing right in front of Mr. Porthand's boat.

From a distance, Harold could see Mr. Porthand nodding his approval, then ordering them to proceed with a right turn. Everything appeared normal.

Until, of course, Mr. Porthand ordered them to stop turning. If anything, they spun faster.

"Alright then," Mr. Porthand frowned, "that's good, but you can stop spinning now."

Snip nodded, and pulled harder on the rudder, making the craft turn faster. Piggy, focused on making her teacher proud, continued to row with fierce concentration, making the boat spin even faster. Mr. Porthand extended his hand, shouting at Piggy and trying to show Snip how to stop the boat. But out of panic, Snip pulled on the rudder harder. Harold could no longer make out the differences between Snip and Piggy anymore; he only saw a spinning blur on the water.

The students on shore noticed the mishap as well. Some pointed, while others laughed and shouted names toward them. Harold could see Owen out of the corner of his eye asking if Snip was Petunia's brother. "Oh, of course not," she chuckled.

Out on the water, Snip pulled harder and harder on the rudder and Piggy kept rowing, jabbing the water so fast, Harold couldn't tell if she still intended to go faster or to slow down. Mr. Porthand shouted for them to stop, but they just went faster, splashing water everywhere.

By now, the whole class was doubled over laughing at the sight. Harold couldn't keep from chuckling, but he knew it was only a matter of time before they would capsize. Hopefully Piggy could swim.

Then suddenly, a horrible noise penetrated through all the laughter. Piggy had leaned over the side of the boat and tossed her cookies, and whatever else she had eaten for breakfast, to the horrible sounds of laughter and disgust from the shore. Finally, she dropped her paddle in the water, and the boat came to a stop, rocking in the ripples it created.

All was dead calm as the boat drifted to a stop. Mr. Porthand paled at the sight of Piggy, who was still leaning over the side of the boat, but

Snip was even paler. He finally released the rudder from his panicked grip.

"Get to shore," Mr. Porthand breathed. "See the nurse immediately. Both of you. Go. Now."

At last, Snip obeyed a simple command and paddled slowly to shore. The crowd began to chuckle, and then to whisper and gossip as Snip and Piggy scrambled to shore. Harold cringed as Snip ran down the path towards the classroom again, followed closely by Piggy, who was bright red with embarrassment.

The lesson continued. The only trace of the incident was Mr. Porthand's dirtied boat and the slightly colored water out in the shallows.

The rest of the class ended normally, and they were dismissed on time. Carnis had to be woken up to have a talk with Mr. Porthand after class, but other than that, nothing more unusual happened for the rest of the morning, which Harold was perfectly content with.

Unfortunately, it was short lived.

CHAPTER SIX

The Monster
Beneath the Door

"So, you are the only one in trouble?" Petunia asked.

"I took full blame. I promise," Harold assured her.

"Thanks for keeping us out of hot water," Petunia said beneath ringed eyes.

Harold nodded, glad the issue about Swiftless had been resolved. Since Snip's boating class failure was a sensitive topic, Harold avoided talking about it, updating his friends instead.

In turn, Petunia told them how great Owen was at boating, while Carnis snored on the table and Snip played with his food. He had just returned from the hospital wing and didn't have an appetite. He tried to apologize, but it had been no use. Piggy was stubborn and angry, and refused to talk to him, despite the incident being her fault, too.

Snip had been teased all morning, and as if things could get no worse, Petunia returned to her old motherly state, worrying about Snip like he was some small child. Of course, Snip never protested. He preferred to keep quiet and stare at his food instead.

Harold was annoyed with him. Now they were the laughingstock of the school.

But even if he was irritated, he couldn't ignore his excitement. After lunch, they would be flying their dragonflies for the first time. And even though Harold knew Swiftless couldn't fly yet, he was eager to make sure he had survived the night.

He also couldn't wait to see Ms. Dywood's face when she saw Swiftless. The thought of it made him chuckle with triumph.

It seemed ages until lunch was finally over. Harold was so impatient he nearly shot to the ceiling at the ring of the morning bell. As they piled out of Galidemus and toward the dragonfly sheds, Harold dragged Carnis along. He was a little more awake after eating some food, but he was still groggy. He was like a candlestick, slowly melting the longer he burned.

Harold was getting pretty tired, too, but nothing could crush his excitement, not even exhaustion. Ms. Dywood was waiting, a big ring of keys dangling in her fingers. She seemed smug, and when she spotted Harold in the crowd, she scowled. But she didn't say a word, spatting out a few quick instructions for the other students to find their dragonfly's shed and wait. She would make her rounds.

"Be careful," she warned, "some might be a bit anxious still. Eh, Snip?"

All eyes trained on Snip. He wilted like an embarrassed flower.

The students dispersed, and Harold took his place at Switless's new stall, which wasn't too far from Carnis, Petunia, and Snip's. Then he waited, peeking hopefully through the little cracks in the wooden walls. It was too dark to see anything inside.

It seemed ages until Ms. Dywood reached his stall. Finally, she started down his row, first helping Carnis with Sickworm, which required no effort at all, then Petunia and Snip, which required all of her strength. Finally, she came to Harold at the end of the row. She glared at him as she approached. Her hair deepened into a dark red.

"And why are you here, you little worm?" she snarled.

Harold nearly started laughing, but forced a serious expression. "I'm supposed to be here, aren't I?"

"Are you an idiot?" she growled. "*You* did not catch a dragonfly, am I *correct*?"

"Yes, I did," Harold smiled.

"Do you think this is some kind of game?"

"Not at all."

Ms. Dywood focused her sharp eyes directly into Harold's. Harold dared not blink.

Finally, Ms. Dywood jammed the key into its lock and swung the door open with such force, Harold was afraid it would come right off its hinges. She stared inside. And there, silent and still, lay Swiftless.

Ms. Dywood gasped. "How did you—?"

"I caught him yesterday, remember?" Harold said, biting his lip.

"No," she frowned, scratching her head. She scrutinized him. "This is all a joke isn't it?" she growled. "This is just a ridiculous prank you and Carnis pulled off."

Harold shook his head, trying to portray honesty as best he could. Ms. Dywood studied him like a book, but she couldn't detect any dishonesty in his expression. She clenched her teeth and walked into the stall with Harold at her tail.

"This dragonfly is seriously injured," she noted, fingering Swiftless's wing. Her manner suddenly changed between species; with humans she was rarely kind, but dragonflies spoke her language. Her eyes rested on the rip in his wing. "Looks pretty bad."

"When he fell in the water, it ripped his wing pretty bad," Harold lied. He didn't actually know how Swiftless had been injured. Plunging into the water couldn't have injured him that badly, but he was just glad to see Swiftless was still breathing.

"He fell in the water?" she asked with surprise.

Harold gasped, cursed to himself, and then retold his story. In the end, the story morphed into him finding Swiftless just after the dinner bell, injured and abandoned on the shore. Ms. Dywood didn't seem convinced, but she was too irritated to press him further. Once he was finished, she examined Swiftless more carefully. He seemed to be in good health, except for his wing.

After circling him twice, she moved in closer to look at the rip in Swiftless's two wings. She squinted, as if finding something tangible within each papery wing.

All of a sudden, she screamed. She cowered in the far corner of the stall, a shaking finger pointing at the rip.

Startled, Harold stood up. "What's the matter?"

"The sign!" she muttered under her breath.

"What sign? What's the matter with his wing?" Harold demanded, his heart racing.

"On his wing . . . how did he hurt his wing?" she asked frantically.

Harold looked at the rip in Swiftless's wing closer. He saw no 'sign'.

"How did he hurt his wing?" she demanded again.

"I don't know," Harold confessed, "he had it when I found him. It could have happened in the water."

"Stark," she muttered.

"Excuse me?" Harold asked, his attention acute.

"Never mind. This is a bad sign," she said. "Go see Mrs. Vera. She might be able to fix his wing. But if she can't, nobody can. He might never fly again."

Harold gulped. "Mrs. Vera?"

"Yes. You know where her cottage is."

"Yeah."

"Then go now," she demanded. "Hurry."

Harold picked up a rope leash from the floor, attached to Swiftless's neck, and dragged him out of the shed. Thankfully, Swiftless was glad to leave the claustrophobic shed.

A bit shaken, they trekked toward Mrs. Vera's—the school's vet and animal studies teacher—who lived in a cottage that also housed a menagerie of creatures. While most of the teachers lived in Galidemus itself, Mrs. Vera always claimed she preferred an off-the-grid lifestyle. But everyone knew the real reason she stayed out of the main building was that her animals made a terrible ruckus, and Mrs. Kernester wouldn't permit it. With so many creatures in such a contained space, Harold had always wondered how she could sleep at all.

From what Harold remembered, Mrs. Vera's cottage was small and rickety. He had only been there a couple of times, all on account of various things Carnis had done to the local flora and fauna. However, as he rounded the bend on the well-trodden trail that led to Mrs. Vera's house, he realized it seemed to have grown at least twice in size since then.

One main structure stood in the center of the whole complex, painted a sky blue. Dozens of smaller buildings branched off from this one, each painted a different color. In the windowsills where one might plant flowers or shrubs grew short grasses she used for animal feed. All the windows were open, and if Harold was lucky, he just might glimpse a strange creature peeking out of a window to nab a taste of the grass. A tall chimney made of hard sand and clay poked out of the top of the main building, puffing merrily. A design was painted on the chimney, a little mural of dragonflies racing among colorful flowers. Harold walked up the dirt pathway toward the comfy door centered in the middle of all the structural confusion. A crisp red cross was painted on it.

Harold knocked cautiously. Before he could even rap twice, the door swung open to reveal a slightly overweight woman with bright yellow eyes; she looked like a tomcat. Her hair was a burnished bronze color and her hands were large and dirty. She smiled a gritty smile, one that was missing one too many teeth, and brushed her muddy hands on her rosy apron. "And what brings you here, Harold?" she asked, leading him and Swiftless inside.

"Something with my new dragonfly, Swiftless," he replied, adrenaline pulsing through his veins.

"Say no more!" she exclaimed. "I know exactly how to treat it!"

They stepped inside, and Harold was bombarded with a zoo of creatures, all large and colorful and loud. He tried to take in all that was crammed into the front room. Groups of various creatures sat in clumps around the chamber, each corralled into tight boundaries. Most of the creatures Harold had never seen before. Of the ones he could distinguish, he spotted slugs, worms, maggots, snails, tadpoles, and some fish in a big container of water. The room was crowded and stuffy, smelling like old musty straw. Dusty air filled the room, a stench evaporated from the floorboards, and dust motes formed as the sun cast in through the window.

Mrs. Vera led them to the back of the main room where several halls branched off into different sections of the cottage. A hearth glowed on the back wall, and a friendly pot of soup was bubbling over the fire.

From there she turned down one of the hallways and into another room of equal size as the first.

The room housed strange creatures. Water striders clumped in a shallow puddle, outdated styles of water travel. A mouse sat sleeping in the corner, its body rising and falling steadily with each breath. Woodlice crawled in circles around a corral, strong as oxen. An enormous frog sat belching in the center of the room. They passed through quickly and walked up to another door on the far side. Mrs. Vera carefully turned the knob and slipped inside, guiding Harold and Swiftless in after her. She quickly shut the door behind her, to keep whatever was inside contained. Harold gazed around the room and discovered the reason for Mrs. Vera's caution—the room was full of dragonflies.

Dragonflies were everywhere. Fast ones, slow ones, fat ones, skinny ones, bright ones, dull ones. Harold couldn't keep from thinking how Carnis would react to such a sight. Most seemed to be injured, from simple scratches to being nearly torn in two. Most were flying, hovering just below the ceiling, making an eerie throb of wings beating above their heads. They chirped and made noise at the newcomers.

"Quiet!" Mrs. Vera yelled. All fell silent, and the dragonflies scurried to where they were apparently supposed to be—on the floor and out of the way. "And stay that way until this little squirt is taken care of."

She took Swiftless's leash from Harold and set him on a small bed in the corner of the room. He had been laid right between two of the brightest dragonflies Harold had ever seen, both Lightning Backs, one blue and one yellow. The blue one was hovering a tad above ground and thumping its head into the wall like it was drunk. Mrs. Vera glared at the Lightning Back, her eyes almost commanding his stillness. Finally, the Lightning Back ceased, and she proceeded to take a look at Swiftless.

"You said something about his wing," she noted, not taking her eyes off her patient.

"Yes," Harold nodded, pointing to the patterned rip on Swiftless's two left wings. "Ms. Dywood said you'd be the only one who could fix it."

"She's most certainly right," she mumbled, holding a roll of tape in her mouth. "Nobody appreciates me these days. I mean, at least a bit of acknowledgement would suffice…"

She bent over the torn wings to look at them closer. But before she could even start bandaging, she shrieked in terror.

"AAAAAAAHHHHHH!"

"Oh, not this again," Harold groaned, his heart jump-starting once more.

"The sign!" Mrs. Vera gasped.

"What sign?" Harold yelled. "Everyone keeps talking about a sign, but I don't see anything! Will somebody please tell me what the 'sign' is?"

But Harold would get no such answer. Mrs. Vera had promptly passed out on the floor, knocking her head into the hardwood floor. All the dragonflies stared in her direction as if an explosion had just ignited in the room. Everything fell silent. The blue Lightning Back began thumping into the wall again.

Harold rushed over to Mrs. Vera, kneeling beside her head, which had rolled to the side.

"Mrs. Vera?" he asked, lifting her head to feel a knot forming under her auburn hair. But she wouldn't respond. She was out cold.

"Well, great," Harold sighed, "now what?"

Swiftless peered in his direction with wide eyes.

Harold stepped over to his dragonfly, again looking at the rip in his wing, but found no image or sign at all. It only looked like a few vague scratches. He stood up and took hold of Swiftless's leash.

"I guess we leave," he decided. "How do we get back?"

Harold glanced out a small open window. It was nearly the middle of the afternoon. His first riding lesson would soon be over. He should hurry back. But the matter of Swiftless's wing was still unresolved. He couldn't participate in riding lessons if he had nothing to ride. It seemed everyone he met was terrified of the injury. Mrs. Vera had fainted! Even Ms. Dywood seemed afraid of the 'sign', and Ms. Dywood was afraid of *nothing*.

But nobody would tell Harold why. Who could he ask? Surely Mrs. Kernester was too busy. She wouldn't know, and he had already bothered her today. Possibly Mr. Porthand? He was usually cool and collected. That would be his next best option. Dragging Swiftless behind him, they exited the way they came from and wandered into another room.

The place seemed a lot more sinister without Mrs. Vera around. The thick air stifled Harold's breath, making him pant. Every sound, every rustle, was magnified, and Harold's ears twitched. Even the shuffling of his own feet became a monotonous pattern that made him uneasy.

Through the two rooms they traveled, then through a third, but no exit came in sight. If anything, the rooms seemed to be hosting stranger, more dangerous creatures. He passed rooms of slugs, then rooms of rats, and then rooms of snakes. A huge wolf spider crouched in the corner of one room. Poisonous insects buzzed in another. Harold began to doubt his sense of direction as they traveled deeper and deeper into the cottage.

Suddenly, they came upon a dead end—a small room with a small door, shorter than Harold's shoulders. The hairs on the back of his neck raised, evidence of something sinister, something only the sixth sense could pick up, a reek of death and danger. Swiftless cowered in the corner of the hallway, away from the door. A note was hanging on the knob, written in fancy handwriting:

DO NOT ENTER!
Those who enter will face a slow and gruesome death. Nobody, under any circumstance, is to enter or disturb this room. That includes Mrs. Grundy Vera, Veterinarian and fellow teacher of the school of Galidemus. This is private school property.
DO NOT ENTER!

Harold recognized the handwriting as Mrs. Kernester's. He could recognize her scrawls anywhere. But she had never cared about dangerous animals. She had never been a big fan of any creature at all.

Something was fishy.

It even *smelled* fishy.

No, wait, that was the smell leaking from the crack in the bottom of the doorway. He glanced around, making sure he was alone. Unable to contain his curiosity, he bent down, sinking to his knees to look beneath the door. It was dark inside, too dark to see anything. The smell was pungent near the bottom of the door, the smell of decaying flesh and rotten fish. Harold couldn't stand it much longer.

Suddenly, a movement in the dark. A flash so quick he would have missed it had he blinked. A pair of blood red eyes flickered open. They fixated on the crack and bored into Harold's mind, and Harold began to sweat in panic.

"*Death*," the creature rasped.

"*Death . . . kill . . . bloooood.*"

Harold leapt to his feet, heart pounding in his chest. The voice stung his ears. He tugged on Swiftless's leash, trying to escape this horrible place. But Swiftless wouldn't budge. He was rooted to the ground, like a stone statue.

"*Blood . . . human bloooood—*"

"Come!" Harold panted, feeling his mouth go dry. "Swiftless!"

But Swiftless wouldn't move.

"*Kill—*"

Harold could feel his hands shaking, his face dripping in sweat. He felt dizzy and pulled as hard as he could on Swiftless's leash. The slippery leash fell out of his hands, making him tumble to the ground. His head slammed to the floor. He covered his ears, trying to block out the noise, but the voice somehow spoke into his mind, penetrating his soul. His eyes swam into focus on the leash in front of him, and he reached for it again, gripping it like it was a lifeline.

"*Smell Blood.*"

Finally, as if broken by some spell, Swiftless ran out of the room, dragging Harold to his feet. They raced through the building, flying through halls and past creatures, the voice still ringing in his ears. It was searing his body. Slowly, as they progressed, the creatures became more harmless, and more familiar.

They stumbled into the main room and rushed through the front door, collapsing on the dirt path. Both of them were exhausted and out of breath. They lay there, staring at the sky. Harold never thought he could have loved and loathed doors so much in the same minute. He could faintly sense the feeling returning to his fingers and the dampness on his face drying. He was still panting after several minutes. Oh, the sky was so beautiful! Harold had never noticed it before. Everything was so nice. So nice…

Harold woke to a brushing on his face. His eyes snapped open to find Swiftless staring with round, crystal eyes into his face.

Harold sat up and gazed around. Everything came flooding back, all that had happened. How long had he been asleep? He didn't recall being tired at all. The sun was low in the sky, and it seemed to be mid-afternoon now. Harold moaned as he rubbed the back of his head where he had fallen. He could feel a knot already there.

He stood up, stretched, and looked around again. He thought about the creature he had seen beneath the doorway. The thought sent chills up his spine.

Swiftless was in a good mood as he led Harold back to the school. Everything seemed a bit foggy, but the more he walked, the more he remembered, like how he needed to ask Mr. Porthand about Swiftless's wing. This time, he would, hopefully, tell Harold why all this was happening.

The duo walked farther along, Swiftless at the front, until they reached the stalls. It was as if Swiftless were locking himself up. He nudged open the door and went inside, waiting for Harold to close the door.

Harold smiled. "I'll be back before the day is up," he promised.

Now alone, Harold headed back to the familiar walls of Galidemus. As he walked, thoughts raced through his mind. So many questions had arisen in one day, he felt his mind had been slogging in a wet marsh and was beginning to sink, bogged down with questions.

What was the sign? Why was it so threatening? Would Swiftless ever be able to fly again?

And what about that terrible creature, the monster beneath the doorway? How had it been able to talk to him, and why was it such a secret? Even Mrs. Vera hadn't been permitted to see it, and she was the *vet*. So why was it so special? And what did Mrs. Kernester have to do with it?

As he walked into school, he tried to remember what class was next on his schedule. He was almost sure it was Mrs. Kernester's Home Remedies class. But that would have to wait. He had to show Mr. Porthand Swiftless's broken wing.

He arrived at Mr. Porthand's new classroom with haste, only to find another class in session, a class that was probably two or three years ahead of him. The period wouldn't end for a while. It looked like they were taking the same boating test as Harold had, only executing it with much higher precision.

Harold sighed, and plopped himself down with his back to the corner post supporting the roof of the open room. He watched the older students for a while, as time passed like molasses. Eventually, he dozed, unable to keep his eyes open any longer. He was startled awake when the older students began to return from the water, and Harold leapt to his feet and waited at the front desk until all the students had left, even though Mr. Porthand still hadn't returned from the water. If he didn't hurry, Harold would miss his next class, too.

Just when he was getting ready to leave, Mr. Porthand came to shore, clothes wet and muddy. He seemed surprised to see Harold.

"Harold! What brings you here?" he asked, taking a seat at the front desk.

Harold sighed. "Will you come with me for a moment down at the stalls? I have something urgent you need to see."

"Of course," Mr. Porthand nodded.

As they walked back to the stalls, Harold tried as best he could to retell for the third time how he had captured Swiftless. Mr. Porthand was a great listener and didn't interrupt once; he in fact seemed curious and impressed at Harold's feats. After he told everything he could recall, Harold voiced his concerns about the rip in Swiftless's wing, and how Ms. Dywood and Mrs. Vera had been terrified of it.

"She literally passed out," Harold said.

"She what?" Mr. Porthand asked, taken aback.

"She freaked out," Harold continued, "both of them did."

"Let's have a look at this wing," Mr. Porthand nodded.

They reached the stalls in silence, and Mr. Porthand unlocked the door.

They both walked inside, and Mr. Porthand knelt down to examine Swiftless's wing. He frowned, immediately recognizing the sign, whatever it was, but wasn't terrified like the two before. He just knelt there, staring.

He finally broke the silence. "This is bad."

"I'm just glad you didn't explode like the others did," Harold teased.

"This is no time for jokes," Mr. Porthand countered, "this is a dangerous sign. I had no idea they would strike so soon."

"What?" Harold asked.

"Come outside with me for a moment," Mr. Porthand insisted, "there is much we need to discuss."

They walked outside, taking seats on the dirt path between the stalls, their backs to the wall of the next row. Mr. Porthand sighed, folding his hands.

"I had hoped I could tell you this later, but the inevitable has arisen," he said. "I also don't know how to put this lightly. Harold, have you ever wondered how your parents died?"

Harold was taken aback at the question. Of course he had wondered this, but had never known for certain. He didn't have the nerve to ask Mrs. Kernester. He had been told they just left him there, a long time ago. The sting, the hatred that had arisen in him, was venomous. He remembered yelling at them, begging for answers, even though they were dead. But why did they leave him here? Why did they get rid of him?

But there was something—always, something—a thought. The thought that it wasn't their fault, that it was all a story untold. He had always wondered. It was unfair he had no parents and no last name. All the other kids had at least one parent. He had none. He missed them every day. So instead of confessing he had never thought of them before, he admitted the truth.

"Yes," he sighed, "I didn't even know them. But I miss them."

"I do, too," Mr. Porthand nodded, sadness creasing his face.

"You knew my parents?" Harold asked.

"Did I know them!" he laughed bitterly. "Did I know them? I knew them; they were closer to me than many others. I know how your parents died. I can tell you, if you'd like."

Harold nodded slowly, afraid of what he might hear.

"Very well, then. Before I tell you this, you must understand, Harold, it is not what a man is but what a man can be. A man's potential is his worth, not his past, not his heritage. Do you understand?"

Harold nodded. His mind was racing.

"Your parents were great people," Mr. Porthand nodded. "They were—" He paused. "Harold, while your mother is truly dead, your father is actually still alive."

Harold felt his breath stop, his eyes dilate in confusion.

"But at the same time, he is, in a way, dead." Mr. Porthand continued, "He is lost. The life in him has long since faded. Harold, your father is the chief of the Ferrals."

Harold was stunned. He couldn't speak. His mind was screaming, spinning like driftwood at sea.

"But that makes me—"

"The heir to the Ferral tribe," Mr. Porthand nodded. "Remember, Harold, it is the potential of a man that is his worth, not his heritage."

"How did my mother die?" Harold asked in a voice so strained he could barely recognize it as his own. "How does this explain Swiftless's wing?"

"One question at a time," Mr. Porthand nodded. "Your mother was killed by your father, in an attempt to save you. She married your father when he was a kind man. But something changed. Something snapped. When he joined the Ferrals, your mother refused to join him. And so, your father killed her. How you were spared, I do not know."

Each of Mr. Porthand's words cut Harold deeply; they were nives to his conscience. He found that he couldn't speak.

"You wish to know their names," Mr. Porthand nodded, reading Harold's mind. "Marigold and Flint. Your father goes by Golgothar these days, though. A twisted word for skull. But he was always Flint Porthand."

"What?" Harold asked, standing up. Mr. Porthand stood as well. "Flint *Porthand*?"

"Your father is... *was* my brother," he nodded.

"You're my uncle," Harold said. "You're my uncle!"

"Yes."

"My last name is Porthand!" he gasped, "I have a last name!"

"Yes."

"Why didn't you tell me sooner?" Harold demanded. "I've always wondered . . . you knew all this time and . . . how come you never told me?"

"Harold, I am so sorry," Mr. Porthand sighed, "it was extremely dangerous to tell you. Your father, I believe, has been secretly after you for years. The innocence of not knowing has kept you safe. Imagine if it got out that this school was housing the current heir to the Ferrals! People would go after you, even if you weren't guilty of anything. The main reason I teach at Galidemus is to keep an eye on you. You are essentially an outcast prince, Harold. Think about that for a moment."

Harold's head was spinning. His father was alive! He was the heir to the Ferrals... Mr. Porthand was his uncle, and he had a last name. All at once. . .

"I have a family," Harold sighed in relief, tears filling his eyes. "I have a name—I *am* something—"

Mr. Porthand smiled at him. "Harold, you always *were* something. Do you realize that?"

Harold said nothing.

Mr. Porthand squinted into the sunset. "I miss your father, Harold," he said. "He was my only sibling. I don't know what happened to him."

Harold looked into the sky. He knew he missed them, too. He thought about them every day. He wished none of this had happened, that he could be normal like the other kids, instead of being the principal's adopted son. He wondered what it was like, being normal that way. He thought of Mr. Porthand, how his own brother had done the things he did. He thought of all the pain he must be burdened with.

"You're probably wondering how this all ties into Swiftless's wing," Mr. Porthand finally said after a long silence. "The 'sign' on Swiftless's wing was scratched there by someone. It is the sign of the

Ferral tribe. That is why the other teachers were so terrified of it. Do not be mistaken; I am terrified as well. I don't know who put it there, or how, but it was obviously used as a warning. I knew they would strike soon, but I had no idea how soon. Now I know. Harold, you must be wary. This sign means someone was watching you when you failed to catch Swiftless, and knew you well enough to know you would go after him."

Harold glanced at the rip on Swiftless's wing. It seemed to be a pattern of sorts, like a crude number eight turned on its side, but hardly recognizable. Would he have to see the sign of the Ferrals on his dragonfly's wing forever? Would he forever see the mark of his blood on Swiftless?

"I can fix his wing," Mr. Porthand said, "it shouldn't take long. I have a certain method for such ailments. Leave me in his care for a few days, and all should be well. Will you be alright?"

"I think so," Harold nodded, "it is just so much all at once."

"I understand," Mr. Porthand nodded, "shall we head back for supper?"

"Is it supper already?" Harold said.

Mr. Porthand looked at his watch. "Well, it's after seven. Are you hungry?"

"Sure," Harold lied. How he could be hungry after receiving such news, he didn't know.

They walked the whole way back in silence, both deep in thought. Twice, Harold considered telling Mr. Porthand about the monster beneath the door, but reconsidered. Harold had discovered enough for one night—any more would make his head explode. The matter would have to wait. He was bruised and tired, and he still had detention that night, cleaning Mrs. Kernester's office. He knew he needed to rest; it would be a long time before he would fall asleep again.

CHAPTER SEVEN

Mrs. Kernester's Office

Harold could hear his own footsteps on the cold, stone floor as he walked to Mrs. Kernester's office for detention. The room was deep in Galidemus, nearly the center of the labyrinth of halls and classrooms.

Harold had just finished an eventful dinner, even though he hadn't eaten a bite. During the meal, he explained everything to his friends, telling them about the monster beneath the door, Mr. Porthand, and the sign. He told them about Mrs. Vera, his last name, and why he had skipped two classes. Carnis couldn't stop laughing when Harold told them about how Mrs. Vera passed out, receiving a concussion. Of course, they had their doubts, but Harold didn't care. He was still stunned at the news and hadn't been in the mood to talk much, so he quickly retold his story and left to Mrs. Kernester's room, eager to investigate.

After a while of meandering through cramped halls, Harold finally spotted her office. This time, the door wasn't askew as it had been before. Instead, it was closed, with a neat little plaque hanging on the doorknob. A message was inscribed on its face:

Harold (no middle name, no last name) will receive detention by cleaning Mrs. Kernester's office until it

is spotless, on account of harassing a young Royal lady, tonight from 8 pm until it is clean, however long that will take.

Signed,
Ms. Dywood

Harold chuckled at the note. "No last name."

He opened the door silently. Nobody was inside. The room was cold and dark, so Harold lit a lantern that had been strewn on the floor. The light it cast made the place seem eerie; shadows leapt from the skeletons of furniture; the flicker of the flame seemed to whisper caution.

Harold looked around, noticing the wreck hadn't changed from when he first saw it. Furniture was still broken and overturned, pictures still hung crooked on the walls, the rug was still clumped. Everything was dusty, as if a great length of time had passed since the break-in, even though it had only happened a day before. The trash bin was still empty, its contents spilled on the floor. The large bookcase on one wall had books missing, now set in uncomfortable positions on the floor, their bindings broken and spines protesting. The place was creepy, and Harold would be glad to finish this job as quickly as he could.

But he couldn't help noticing something was missing. What was it? No one had touched the room, every splinter lay at peace, beyond hope of mending. Not even the floor betrayed footprints.

But something was missing from that night Harold had first stumbled upon this room...

It was the mud splotches. The strange puddles were gone, the dirt swept, yet nothing else in the room had been touched.

Harold wondered who had mopped them up and why they would want to remove that one piece of evidence. After a quick look around the room, Harold's fears were confirmed. Any evidence of Stark, the horned, amphibious man that Ms. Dywood had spoken with, was gone, and nothing unusual was apparent. Dismayed, Harold grabbed a mop and started to clean.

The work proved a lot harder than it looked. Heavy furniture had been overturned, and it required all his exhausted strength to move them. The giant rug that covered nearly the whole floor had to be put back, but in doing so, he had to move all the furniture out of the way first. Many of the knickknacks and accessories of the room had been destroyed, and Harold had no way of fixing them. He was sweating and tired, having to take breaks every so often, wishing he was asleep. It did not matter where; to him, he just wanted to rest.

While he cleaned the room, he searched carefully through every scrap, every splinter, in search of any small fragment of evidence that might have been left behind. But the rubble betrayed nothing. He wished he was able to dust for fingerprints, but he knew he couldn't.

Hours passed. Harold slowed down at the passing of each minute, his eyes lowering to half mast, then flicking open again with a sudden jerk, his will to stay awake overtaking his physical needs. It was well into the night by the time he straightened the last plush pillow and tucked in the last damaged book. The room looked quite clean, but Harold was too tired to fire up his pride. He groggily blew out the lantern, leaving the room nearly pitch-black, and left, not bothering to close the door behind him.

His feet felt heavy, like they had been weighed down by muddy boots. He could barely keep his eyes open. Only a little farther to the dormitory . . . only a little farther to bed . . . he could make it.

Up one more staircase, through one more hallway. . .

A large flight of stairs spanned before him, stretching into eternity. He was too tired to climb them all. Harold yawned and stretched, lying down on the wooden staircase. It felt surprisingly comfortable. The moment his eyes closed, he fell into a fitful sleep.

He was falling—falling forever it seemed. Where was he falling? He was falling in the dark, he couldn't see a thing. Suddenly, the darkness around him burst into color, bringing alive a small room with a tiny door on one side. A familiar stench permeated the air, like rotten fish and decaying flesh. There was Swiftless, cowering in the corner of the room. He looked scared. A note was tacked on the door. Harold recognized the handwriting. He felt sweaty, though he didn't know why. He somehow knew his skin was pale and the blood had drained from his face. But why? Why did this all seem so familiar?

Suddenly a raspy voice broke the silence.

"Death . . . Kill . . . Bloooood . . ."

Then he remembered. With a sudden jolt of panic, he commanded his limbs to act. He tried to run but his legs wouldn't move. He tried to pull on Swiftless's leash, but his muscles didn't respond. He was a lifeless wooden form with his terrified mind trapped inside.

"No!" he yelled, but the voice overpowered him.

"Human bloooood . . . Must kill—"

"Help!" Harold called, but his voice wouldn't work. He tried to scream, but his voice only collapsed into a dying whisper.

"Blooooooooood . . ."

"No!"

Suddenly, the small door burst open, and a sound like a thousand burning souls erupted around him. A light flashed, and everything he could see disappeared into nothingness. Darkness enveloped him, his breath was stifled, his sight smothered, his senses muffled. Then the light came back, flooding his vision with a new scene.

He was riding on a dragonfly above an island, a small island in the pond. He didn't recognize where he was. He looked down at the dragonfly, surprised because it was familiar. The dragonfly was Swiftless, and Swiftless was flying—but how? He didn't know where he was or how he got there. He focused into the water, which was churning and frothing like something was breathing underwater. A noise was coming from the murky depths, a chant. It was saying something, but what, Harold couldn't tell. It came from not one voice, but many, wordless underneath. What were they saying?

The chant became louder and louder, thundering until Harold had to cup his hands over his ears. And still it was penetrating his mind. He tried to block it out, but couldn't. He felt dizzy and nauseous, his consciousness was slipping.

Then the chant exploded around him and out of the water. Out emerged an enormous monster, black and scaly, like a dragon but worse. A demon. A killer. A monster. It reared its head at Harold, spoke in that raspy penetrating voice.

"*Kill . . . bloooood . . .*"

The screams under the water strengthened, evolving into words and language. They were humming a single word, over and over, lulling closer and closer like some deep-sea predator.

The scene began to dissolve, and the voices became clearer. More and more left as the scene blackened, until only two voices were left, speaking in clear tones. He could hear them, what they were saying. They were calling someone. They were calling *him*.

"Harold?" the higher one called.

Then a lower one. "Harold?"

Harold's eyes snapped open and a rush of light overcame him. He blinked, sat up, and looked around. His neck felt kinked, his back bruised from the uncomfortable staircase. Petunia was bent over him on his left side, Carnis on the right. Snip waited patiently at the bottom of the stairs.

"Harold," Petunia smiled, "you're awake. How did you fall asleep on the stairs?"

"Awake?" Harold asked. His dream hadn't felt like a dream at all. It felt so real. He could smell and feel in that dream. Nobody can smell and feel in dreams.

"Yes, awake," Carnis gasped, "and thank goodness. You were doing some creepy things in your sleep, mate. Talking about monsters and yelling and calling for help. That's how we found you down here. Thought you were possessed."

Petunia furrowed her brow at him. "It was just a bad dream."

"It couldn't have been," Harold said. "It was so real."

"Dreams can be like that," Petunia chuckled.

"You don't understand," Harold insisted, "didn't you hear the voices?" His mouth felt dry and his tongue was sticky.

"Other than ours, no," Carnis responded.

"You heard voices?" Petunia asked.

"More than that. Screams. Calls. Swiftless could fly and the monster beneath the doorway was there, and I don't know where I was, but it all seemed so familiar. The monster was talking again."

"You need better sleep," Petunia insisted, concern knitting her face. "You haven't gotten much lately. Classes won't start for a while. Get some rest."

"I'm fine," Harold said, not sounding convincing at all. "It was just a crazy dream."

"Get some sleep," Petunia repeated.

Harold was about to object, but he couldn't. Sleep still sounded so tempting. "Fine."

"We'll be down at breakfast," Petunia said. "Get some rest. We'll see you in class."

Harold nodded numbly and walked back up to his dormitory. He felt like a blind man trying to make his way to the bathroom. His skin seemed like it was going to crawl right off him.

Not bothering to take off his shoes or change his clothes, he slumped into bed, closing his eyes the second he hit the pillow. His head was throbbing. He knew he should sleep, and he wanted to, but so many questions swarmed his mind. He didn't want to fall asleep for fear of having that awful dream again, but he was so tired. He finally gave in to the questions in his mind; it was no use ignoring them.

His dream had been so vivid, so strange. How had it felt so real, yet so unrealistic? Swiftless can't fly. And the monster beneath the doorway was much too small to be the monster in the pond. Where had the mud puddles gone in Mrs. Kernester's office? Should he tell Mr. Porthand about the monster? He was pretty sure he had Animal Studies today. Would Mrs. Vera recognize him?

Then it clicked. He had to get answers about the monster. Who could he better ask than Mrs. Vera? She had no idea he had seen the beast. But she undoubtedly knew of its presence in her home. He would ask her during class.

Feeling refreshed, he gathered his things and headed out of the dormitory, thinking of Swiftless. He would see how he was doing later. The thought made him feel even less tired, and he walked with a new force in his stride to class.

It had only been a dream.

Harold rushed to breakfast, finding his friends already gone, and ate alone in the bustle of the meal room. Without anything to distract him from his thoughts, he stared out the small square windows that lined one wall of the meal room and pondered the bright morning. For the first time in his life, he longed for the way things had been, and wished he could spend a day out on the pond like he used to with Mrs. Kernester. The weather was perfect. A cool breeze chased the morning warmth away, bringing the temperature down to a crisp early spring chill. The pond seemed calm and fresh, and the sky was dappled in big, puffy clouds, white as snow. Eventually, he gave up eating and staring outside where he longed to be, and finally headed to Animal Studies.

Harold was one of the last students to arrive. Harold joined his friends quickly, noticing almost everyone had already taken their seats. He hoped they weren't too frightened of him. Petunia smiled warily in his direction as he sat down.

Mrs. Vera hardly noticed Harold and acted as if he were just another student. This made Harold feel a little better, and he sighed with relief as she started class.

"Good morning, class," Mrs. Vera said in a loud, commanding voice.

A few dull replies echoed around the room.

She smiled cheerily, then held up a bag of something Harold couldn't identify. He gulped as he noticed it was wriggling in her grasp.

"This morning we will be studying maggot larvae."

Harold felt his stomach sink. The rest of the class moaned.

"Now, now," she smiled, waving a hand in dismissal, "I know they can be a bit horrid, to be frank, but listen here. How might you get rid of them if they invaded your home? Surely you'd want to take care of such a mess. Why hesitate to learn such a vital skill?"

The class fell silent.

"That's right. Now, did you know maggots are the larvae of flies?"

The class did not share her enthusiasm of maggots, and Harold's face remained blank.

"Many maggots feed on rot, particularly meat and sometimes rotting wood, and they love darkness. Most hate sunlight, so that could be one way to rid them in your home. Shine light on them. Natural sunlight is best. You better be taking notes," she added as she looked around the room.

The class quickly retrieved their pencils and papers from their bags. Mrs. Vera continued. "Maggots will serve as our final study. You will all pick out maggots of your own and take care of them until they hatch into flies. When they morph, we will set them free. Today we will choose and defume our own maggots, or get rid of their awful stench; they don't smell terrific at first. I'll pass around the defuming solution."

Mrs. Vera promptly opened the sack she was holding and dumped its contents onto the floor. Girls screamed at the sight. Thirty or more white, fleshy maggots writhed across the floor towards the students' feet. They looked like a bunch of bulbous bananas, unpeeled from their skins, only much worse. Some students wretched, others cowered on their desks to get away from the repulsive larvae.

"I agree," Mrs. Vera nodded matter-of-factly. "They don't smell nice at all."

Around the room she went, handing each ill-spirited student their maggot, along with a spray bottle of defuming solution to rid them of their smell. Soon the room's smell of rotting flesh was replaced with the fresh, minty smell of the defuming solution. When Mrs. Vera came to Harold's desk, she plopped a particularly fat maggot onto his desk with a gloved hand, along with a small bottle of defuming solution. Thick white slime dripped from her gloves and onto Harold's notebooks and pencils. Harold cursed under his breath, yanking his things away, and the maggot writhed in protest. Harold wasn't too happy with his new partner either.

Just as Mrs. Vera was about to move on to the next student, she looked squarely into Harold's face. A sense of confusion overcame her expression.

"You do look so vaguely familiar," she sighed. "What is your name again, young man?"

Harold was shocked. Mrs. Vera had known him since he was little . . .why couldn't she remember his name now? Then Harold remembered how she had fallen, passed out, and smashed her head on the hardwood floor of her cottage. Could she still be suffering from a concussion?

"Peter Prickle, ma'am." He forced a fake smile. "Such a pleasure to be in this wonderful class!"

"It *can't* be!" she exclaimed, all the curiosity wiped from her face. "Not the one and only Peter Prickle who is so magnificent at growing pansies, is it?"

Harold hesitated. "I'm your man!" he smiled, puffing up his chest.

"Why, *I'll* be! I had no idea you were in my class! Forgive me. Didn't I last see you at the flower fair? You had grown those beautiful purple and yellow pansies in your garden, and I had walked by to admire them, and then you said—oh, Peter, dear, what did you say?"

"Er . . . I said, 'nice day,' didn't I?" Harold grinned, heart beating fast. "And then I said, 'aren't these flowers magnificent?'"

"That's right!" Mrs. Vera chuckled, "those pansies were absolute beauties. Well, it is such a pleasure to have you in my class. It's a wonder I haven't noticed you before. Too much work, I tell you. Please, whatever you need, just ask."

And just like that, she swept to the next student, and continued to pass out maggots and spray. As soon as she was distracted, Harold burst into giddy laughter, with Carnis beside him. They were nearly in tears.

"Peter Prickle, harnesser of flower power!" Carnis chuckled when they both got themselves nearly under control. "Some concussion *she* had!"

Harold laughed, feeling guilty for her memory loss but secretly grateful. From now on he was Peter Prickle, at least in Animal Studies.

"I like it way better than Harold Porthand, if you ask me," Carnis continued under his breath. "Suits you!"

"Shut up," Harold laughed. "I'd better not hear Peter Prickle anywhere outside of this classroom."

"Yeah, whatever," Carnis snickered. "Look, Harold, I just wanted to ask you if you were okay, from earlier. You seemed really freaked out back there."

"I'm fine, really," Harold sighed, "it was just a weird dream. It was so real—kind of freaky. Thank goodness I was sleeping."

"Yeah," Carnis agreed. "I'm glad you got sleep, though. Let's start defuming these flesh bags."

They sprayed and sprayed, probably overdosing, but when they were done, their maggots didn't smell quite as terrible. At least the rotting flesh smell was gone. By the time they finished, Petunia came over to their desks, with Snip at her side. They were both pinching their maggots at a distance.

"Harold and Carnis," Petunia scolded, "you should be ashamed of yourselves! Lying to Mrs. Vera?"

"I had to!" Harold protested.

"I know, but how many names is that now? Three? Let's see, Peter, Harold, and Mr. Porthand. In two days! What is *wrong* with you guys?"

"Just luck, I guess," Harold joked, snickering under his breath.

Petunia sighed, setting her maggot down on Harold's desk. Snip did likewise with Carnis's.

"It's not funny," she said, spraying her maggot again. "Good grief, Susan, you really do smell."

"Susan?" the boys chimed at the same time. "It has a *name*?"

"Oh, I know. It's pathetic, but it's required." Petunia sighed. "You know Mrs. Vera. She thinks we'll make a better, more personal connection with our pets if we name them. I'd rather eat slug slime, but for a good grade…"

"Required?" Harold grumbled.

"I don't *want* to make a better, more personal connection with a maggot!" Carnis added, standing up in fury.

"I know, I know," Petunia said. "Don't look at me like it's my fault. Rules are rules. Here, Harold what are you going to name yours?"

Harold sighed in exasperation. Did he really have to name a *maggot*? This was ridiculous. Mrs. Vera was a nutcase.

"Lard, I guess. Yes, that's fitting. He's the color of lard, anyway."

"Okay then," Petunia said, wrinkling her nose. "Frank and realistic. I like it."

There was a moment of silence as all four of the friends stared at Lard, as if willing him to die on the spot.

"Well, then," Carnis spat sarcastically, "I'll just call mine *Crap*. Suits him, doesn't it?" Carnis's maggot writhed like it had been salted.

"Snip named his Belchy," Petunia explained, nodding to Snip's maggot. Snip paled as his new pet secreted a gooey substance on Carnis's desk.

Carnis moaned. "Go take your Belchy somewhere else if it's going to crap all over my desk," he demanded. Snip timidly held Belchy a bit above Carnis's desk, but the worm was still dripping. Carnis groaned.

"And this is Susan," Petunia said, "I would name her Pig-Nosed Half-Dead Maggot for emphasis on how awful a creature she is, but it's a bit long and that's basically her definition."

More silence followed as they all sprayed their wretched larvae pets with more defuming solution.

"Harold, are you sure you're okay?" Petunia asked, after a while. "You were really shaken up by that dream. Do you think it's something serious?"

Harold felt like a small child, the way she was talking to him. But Petunia made everyone feel like that. "It's fine, it was only a dream."

Petunia raised an eyebrow. "A lot of weird things have been happening lately. This could be serious. Are you sure there's not more to this dream?"

Harold was surprised at her words. She had just voiced his inner concerns.

"Well, to be honest, it was . . . weird. Not normal," Harold confessed. "I felt horrible when I woke up, and it felt so real. I could smell, I could see clearly, I could hear, I could feel. It felt, I don't know, like it *was* real, if that makes sense?"

Petunia nodded. "What was in your dream?"

"Stuff… repeating itself. And new stuff, too," Harold said weakly. He retold the whole dream to them as best he could, trying to remember all the details. His skin began to crawl again just thinking about it. After he finished, Petunia sighed.

"I don't know, Harold. Or Peter, or whoever you are," she teased. "You're right, it is odd. It's unlikely any of it will come to pass. But then again, many strange things have been happening. You should probably tell Mrs. Kernester or somebody you can trust. But you always have us, even if we're an odd bunch." She smiled into his eyes. Harold chuckled and forced a smile.

Suddenly, Mrs. Vera rapped her stick on the desk, calling attention to the class. The comfort Petunia had provided melted away as she and Snip returned to their seats with their maggots and solutions.

"Has everyone named their maggots?" she asked. The class reluctantly nodded.

"Good," she smiled, "I know most of you were hesitant to name such lowlife, but it is required. I'll come around to clean up and gather your maggots and solutions, and then I'll pass around a sheet for you to write your Maggot's name next to your own. And please, no crude names."

Nearly everyone groaned, including Carnis. The sheet passed around, and when it came to Carnis, he hastily scribbled down Matt on the paper in sloppy handwriting. After the room had been cleaned up, Mrs. Vera spent the remaining time explaining to the class the useful properties of maggot slime, demanding a short essay on it by the following week.

Just before class was dismissed, Mrs. Vera asked a question no one usually paid attention to. Only this time Harold did.

"Does anyone have any questions?" she asked.

This was his chance. Harold took a deep breath and raised his hand.

"Yes, Peter dear?"

The class, a bit confused with his new name, turned his way.

"What is the most dangerous animal in your cottage?" he asked.

Silence filled the room. All movement ceased as the color drained from Mrs. Vera's face, leaving her blanched, expressionless. Her bright, glowing eyes darted around the room as she gathered her things.

"I—sorry?"

"What's the deadliest creature in your cottage? Currently speaking, of course."

Mrs. Vera stared at Harold for a moment, lips pinched into a thin line.

"I—well . . . I would say the . . . er . . . The Scarlet Speckled Rattler, I'd say," She smiled weakly, giving a false chuckle. "Nasty bite, that one has."

There was a moment of awkward silence.

"Is there anything else?" she asked politely.

"Yes," Harold paused for thought. "Do you have any creatures that can—I guess that can talk to you? Like through your mind?"

"Talk?" her voice faltered, "have you learned anything outside of botany, Peter? Of course not!"

"I only thought I'd ask," Harold nodded, taking a mental picture of her horrified expression. "I suppose we should head out, shouldn't we?"

"Yes, class is dismissed," Mrs. Vera said hurriedly. "Have a nice day!"

CHAPTER EIGHT

Mr. Porthand

"**D**id you hear her?"

"Oo bet I id!"

"Carnis, don't put so much in your mouth next time," Petunia scolded.

They were eating lunch together, several classes after Animal Studies. Carnis had stuffed his face with duckweed pie, cheeks bulging, speech slurred.

"I think she knows," Harold said.

"Me, too," Petunia said, stabbing her food. "I had no idea you would ask her, but it was a good idea. I guess acting as Peter Prickle was pretty lucky cover. She seemed shaken."

"It was so ob-ious!" Carnis said, food flying from his mouth.

"Carnis, spit that out right this instant!" Petunia ordered like a distressed mother, pointing a finger at his plate. Carnis spit a huge amount of food onto his plate, half-chewed and slimy. "Don't eat so much next time."

"But remember when I told you about the sign? Even Mrs. Vera wasn't allowed to mess with the monster. So why was she so freaked out?" Harold asked.

"I don't know. I've never seen her so scared before."

Harold sighed, stabbing a small bite of pie with his fork and resting it on his tongue. It tasted nutty and sweet, with a sugar dusting on top.

"Do you think she peeked?" he wondered out loud.

"Mrs. Vera is not one to ignore orders," Petunia said, shaking her head. "If anything, she might have stumbled upon it by accident."

"The door is all the way in the back of the building," Harold argued, "she wouldn't—couldn't go back there on accident if she already knew about it."

"What if she didn't know about it?" Petunia asked, almost to herself. "What if some Ferral or something smuggled it inside? What if she got spooked?"

"The sign on the door was written by Mrs. Kernester," Harold reminded. "She would have let Mrs. Vera know a new creature was in her home."

"It's all very strange," Carnis nodded, staring at a large bite on his fork. He looked at it for some time before setting it back down on his plate to cut it in two. Then he put the smaller bite in his mouth with a groan. "Eating small bites is ridiculous! How am I supposed to eat my meal when I have to go so slowly?"

"Carnis," Petunia sighed, "your regular bites would finish the whole pie in three swallows. Grow up."

Carnis shot her a sarcastic glare, then set to playing with his food like a child.

"Do you suppose she's taking orders against her will?" Harold continued. "Or perhaps she's keeping it on purpose, but she still doesn't like the monster. Maybe she's in trouble."

"That's a long shot," Petunia said. "What do you suppose she's controlled by? Mind control?"

"No, but . . . I don't know," Harold sighed exasperated. "It's all so weird, and I don't know why."

"We'll get more clues," Petunia insisted. "What do you think about all this, Snip?"

Snip shrugged across the table. He was nearly shivering, having a hard time cutting up his pie. His round, scared eyes looked across the table at the three friends.

"Can't you guys stay out of trouble? Ever since Harold flunked on catching day, everything's gone upside down. Why do you guys have to cause so many problems?"

Harold clenched his fists, frustration pumping through his veins. The mere thought of Snip accusing them of being too ambitious made him furious. Snip didn't even know what ambition was. He had always joined in their conversations, but he was never really a part of the group. He always followed along, but he never helped with anything. And deep inside, Harold knew he was a nuisance. Did he think they were doing all these things for some thrill? Harold certainly didn't want to do all he had been doing without good reason. And now Snip thought they were causing trouble? On purpose? He couldn't stand this anymore.

"Snip, listen," Petunia sighed. But Harold cut her off. His anger bubbled so hot it overflowed.

"You think this is some kind of thrill game we're playing?" he asked. "You think we're doing this for fun?"

"No, but—"

"You were never there, Snip! You didn't help us with anything! You were too scared to join us with catching Swiftless. You stay in the dorms all the time. You refused to talk to Mrs. Kernester with me, you refuse to appreciate your super awesome dragonfly. You just watch and listen, but you've never had to be brave. Never. You're not a baby anymore, Snip! Grow up!"

Snip's eyes widened at the onslaught of words. Harold stood up and planted his hands on the table in anger.

"You don't help! You don't even try. So stop telling us we're doing something wrong when you don't even know half of what we're doing this for. If you think it's a bad idea, walk out. You're not a help anyway! We're looking for advice, but all you can tell us is to quit! Unlike you, we can't just walk out of any situation because we are too small and insecure to face the real world. So if you have nothing positive or helpful to say, then leave."

Snip held completely still, staring Harold down. A single tear ran down his cheek.

"You just don't understand, do you?" he whispered, voice cracking.

He shook his head and stood up to leave. Then he ran out of the meal room, his friends looking after him. As soon as he was out of sight, Harold sighed and unclenched his fists, regretting his words. How could he have been so ruthless? He addressed the elephant in the room in the worst possible way.

"Harold!" Petunia scolded. Tears were streaming down her cheeks. She stood up to go after her twin but sat down again hopelessly. She sobbed even harder, covering her face with her hands.

"This is terrible," she cried, covering her face in her hands. "How could I let this happen?"

Carnis placed his hand on her shoulder. "It's not you, Petunia."

Harold sighed, rubbing his neck in stress.

"I'm so sorry, Petunia. I shouldn't have said anything," he apologized. "I feel terrible."

"No, no," Petunia said, catching her breath a little. "You're right. But I feel so bad leaving him to cope by himself. I can't leave him all alone."

She stood up, tearing away from Carnis's grasp, and ran out of the meal room. The table fell silent as Harold and Carnis stared at Snip and Petunia's unfinished food.

"She needs to let him go," Carnis sighed.

"I know, but—" Harold said, unsure of what to say.

"You were right to say what you said, mate," Carnis nodded, though Harold wasn't so sure. It almost made him feel worse. He began to pack his bags.

"See you at boating class," Harold said, standing up.

"You didn't even finish your food!" Carnis gasped.

"Not hungry," Harold said. "You can finish it."

"Suit yourself," Carnis said, devouring Harold's pie. "Try to stay out of trouble."

Harold squeezed his eyes shut as he walked out of the meal room. He wished he could crawl in a hole and hide.

Harold could see the hot afternoon sun shining through white, puffy clouds. The haze made the sun seem bright yellow, almost neon, and the clouds glimmered. Birds of all kinds swooped and dove over the water to catch bugs. He spotted kingfishers, swallows, robins on the banks, and finches in the trees. Deer grazed in the meadows beyond the pond, some with huge antlers covered in a brown mossy fuzz. Most of the deer were still losing their winter coats, thick fur in some places and thin fur in others. A breeze was still blowing steadily over the pond, making the tree sway. Spring was still a way off, but nature began to betray signs of life as the days got slightly warmer, temperatures finally rising above freezing.

Harold was sitting on the roof of Mr. Porthand's new classroom. The lofty place hadn't been too hard to reach. Some tall grass grew close to the wall on one side, and Harold only had to climb a blade and hoist himself onto the low roof. It had a terrific view, with only the western span of his surroundings shielded from sight.

Since Mr. Porthand had not yet returned from lunch, Harold decided to wait for class on the roof where he could think things over. Why had he been such an idiot? He knew, of course, what he said was true. But everyone already knew that. Only one person didn't.

Snip himself.

And Harold had just insulted him, in front of all his friends. How stupid he had been! Snip *was* useful, wasn't he? He *had* stayed guard for them when he had gone to save Swiftless. Well, for most of the time.

Maybe he just needed a little more time to grow up. But he was fourteen! He couldn't go on like this.

Harold sighed in frustration, and something shifted below him.

"Harold?" Mr. Porthand asked, peering up from below. Harold must not have noticed his arrival in his deep thoughts.

"Mr. Porthand?"

"What are you doing up there?" he called up. "You seem troubled. Come down."

Harold jumped off, landing right in front of Mr. Porthand, whose boots were muddy. He smiled.

"What's the matter?"

"What have you been doing?" Harold asked, surprised at his disheveled look.

"I just paid a visit to Swiftless," Mr. Porthand nodded. "He is doing well. But first, tell me what is troubling you."

Harold sighed. He didn't have much of a choice but to confide in him. "I said some things to Snip I shouldn't have said," he managed to say. "But when we ask him for advice, all he does is tell us to quit. He says what we're doing is dangerous."

"It was dangerous, what you did to save Swiftless," Mr. Porthand nodded, "but it was also the right thing. You shouldn't quit, and I'm glad you didn't."

Again, Harold considered telling Mr. Porthand about the monster beneath the door.

Again, he refrained.

"I don't know what to do," Harold sighed, "Petunia protects him like he's two years old. Whenever I try to tell them something, I just end up hurting them. Today at lunch, I told Snip he was useless. Now I feel terrible."

"Some things, Harold, cannot be fixed by only yourself," Mr. Porthand said. "I had to learn that myself a while ago with your father. I felt helpless, because I couldn't do anything to save him. I was frustrated and lashed out at him in anger. Do not make the same mistake I did. People can be frustrating, but sometimes our interference makes things worse. The best approach is to be gentle. Snip will respond much better to kindness than to criticism."

"I guess you're right," Harold sighed. "I regret what I said to him. I know I should've been gentler. But it is so hard when he isn't changing. I feel like I have to correct him. It's impossible to be kind to him when he's being . . . when he's . . . I don't know."

"It is difficult," Mr. Porthand agreed, "but all the same, we ourselves must try to get better. We must look at ourselves before attacking others. While it's easy setting someone straight with unkind words, it typically makes the whole situation much worse."

"I know," Harold frowned. If only Snip could change right this instant, he thought, things would be so much easier! He wished he could erase the whole noon hour and start fresh again. He wished he hadn't even spoken.

"I can tell you're still troubled," Mr. Porthand nodded, "but see how your father turned out. Sometimes I think it was all my fault, even though I know it wasn't. Don't make that same mistake."

Harold nodded.

"Your dragonfly is healing extremely well," he added.

"That's great," Harold said, glad to hear good news. Again, he thought about the monster beneath the door. Should he tell Mr. Porthand? Would he get in trouble? Or would he be mad at him for hiding the secret? If he hid it longer, it could become more dangerous. But if he told him now, he would be in hotter water than he had been in all year. He bit his lip in indecision.

"Something is still bothering you," Mr. Porthand prodded. "You've seemed overly worried about something these past few days, but I know it's not Swiftless or Snip. What is it?"

"Nothing."

"If you don't wish to tell me, that's fine," Mr. Porthand said, putting his hands up, "but please don't lie to me. I know you're bothered by something."

Harold sighed. He couldn't tell him yet. Not yet. "Later," he said.

"Very well then," Mr. Porthand sighed, "if you wish to wait, be my guest. That's your decision to make."

There was a long moment of silence.

"Why don't you come and visit me later today?" he offered. "You could see how Swiftless is getting along. You can even bring your friends. I think you will be surprised at Swiftless's *swift* recovery."

Harold smiled. "Sure," he nodded.

Just then, the classroom doors opened and students flooded the open deck. Mr. Porthand winked at Harold and returned to his front desk position. Harold sat in his desk, waiting for his friends to arrive, but also dreading their appearance. While Mr. Porthand's talk had helped him, he felt like he had to set things right now more than ever.

Several minutes passed, but they never came. Just before class began, Carnis burst through the doors, taking a vacant seat next to

Harold. He seemed happy enough, the same old Carnis. But still, after a good quarter into the class, Petunia and Snip were nowhere to be seen.

Mr. Porthand soon asked the class to write a short essay about the boating lesson they had the day before. He seemed to have returned to his old, academic ways of not doing anything interactive or hands-on. The whole Snip incident must have shocked him back into mind-numbing discipline. The breeze was cold as it swept through the classroom, cutting right through Harold's clothes.

As Harold tried to focus on the task at hand, he couldn't help but think about Petunia and Snip. By the time class finished, he barely had an opening sentence to his essay, and groaned as Mr. Porthand demanded they be finished by next class.

He gathered his things, thinking about his weekend. Tomorrow, he would be helping Mrs. Murphy in the kitchen *all day*. The thought made him sick, and he pushed it to the back of his mind. He longed for a normal weekend. Last weekend had been normal. But the time that had passed since then seemed like eons.

Later, Harold found himself alone with Carnis at dinner. Neither of them had seen Petunia or Snip all day. They ate solemnly, keeping quiet almost the entire time. Eventually, Carnis broke the silence.

"Don't forget about tonight," he said.

"Tonight?"

"Weren't you going to stop by to see Swiftless with Mr. Porthand?"

Harold scrunched up his nose. "Wait, how did you hear that? I thought we were alone."

"I only heard the end of it," Carnis said defensively. "I couldn't resist."

"Well, thanks," Harold groaned, "now I remember."

"Hey, don't be so grumpy," Carnis chuckled, "aren't you excited Swiftless is healing well?"

"I guess so."

"Oh, come on—*I guess so*?" Carnis chuckled. "Don't be such a drag. And to think you had to cheer *me* up just a few days ago…"

"Fine, I'm excited," Harold shrugged with a faint smile. "Would you like to come with me?"

"Absolutely," Carnis agreed, "and we should probably leave soon. But before we leave, could I finish your potato? It looks neglected."

"Knock yourself out," Harold smirked. "I'll be waiting in the dormitory. When you finish, we can meet there and head out. Sound like a plan?"

Carnis smiled through bulging cheeks. He tried to speak, but his voice was muffled by potatoes, so he settled for a thumbs-up.

Harold chuckled at his best friend. He definitely wouldn't be losing him anytime soon.

CHAPTER NINE

The Night Flight

Harold and Carnis waited until all the other Algae boys had fallen asleep. Once again, Snip was nowhere to be found among the beds of slumbering boys, and Harold was concerned. No one knew where the twins were, and they hadn't attended any classes since lunch.

Long after it was time to sleep, Harold crept out of bed. His light footfalls felt loud in the complete silence. He carefully slipped on his boots, yawning as he stretched. He realized he had fallen asleep and hoped he hadn't slept too late. He was still exhausted from sleeping only briefly on the stairs the night before.

As quietly as he could, Harold tip-toed over to Carnis's bunk. He was snoring loudly, uncovered from his sheets. Drool leaked from the corner of his mouth and onto his pillow.

Harold opted for a gentler approach of waking him first. This proved difficult. After shaking, jostling, and even slapping, Carnis was still snoring. Harold whispered in his ear, then spoke softly, but to no avail. He considered leaving Carnis to sleep and going on by himself. That way, he would be more rested for tomorrow. But he had seemed so eager to come with him. Harold shook him again, brushed his face, and even tickled his nose with his sleeve. Nothing seemed to work.

Finally, Harold attempted his last resort. He bent down close to Carnis's ear and whispered, "Dinner time!"

Carnis startled awake. "Dinner? Where?"

"There's no dinner," Harold said hastily.

"Then why'd you wake me up at such an ungodly hour?" he nearly yelled.

Harold cupped his hand over his mouth. "SHHH! It was the only way to wake you up!"

"What for?"

"Carnis, honestly! Remember? We were going to visit Mr. Porthand and Swiftless. Do you remember that?" Harold sighed.

"Oh, right," Carnis groaned, "alright. Fine. I'll get up. But next time, don't fool me. You know how excited I get when I hear anything about food."

Harold sighed. "I still don't how you maintain your normal weight."

After a bit of scuffling, both boys were ready. Carefully, they slinked through the dormitory door, down some stairs, and past the girl's dormitory. Again, Harold wondered about Petunia. Was she sleeping soundly in one of the beds? Or was she missing, just like Snip?

Keeping to the shadows, the boys walked quietly toward the teacher's wing, the section of Galidemus where most of the teachers slept and lived, all but Mrs. Kernester and Mrs. Vera.

Harold had always disliked that hall. It branched off the school on the second level, and it looked like a hallway in some stony hotel. It was even more eerie at night.

Down the hall they walked, being as quiet as they could. If they woke one of the sleeping teachers, they'd surely get detention. Unfortunately, Mr. Porthand's quarters were positioned at the very end of the hall, facing a different direction than all the other rooms. Instead of facing west, his room faced south and was the last door before the hall ended in some stairs.

Suddenly voices drifted up the stairs at the end of the hall, right next to Mr. Porthand's room. Harold's heart skipped a beat. The thought of detention moved him to open the closest unlocked door. The room was vacant, an empty teacher's quarters, and the two slipped inside, closing the door quietly behind them. Harold put his ear to the door to listen.

They could hear two voices, both muffled by the door, but distinct and defined. One was high, the other throaty and low. Both were strangely familiar.

"The boy has taken care of it," said a hushed voice. It sounded like Ms. Dywood.

"Not a smart move, Meryll," the low voice growled. Harold was startled at the sound of Stark's voice. Once again, the pair was talking during the dark hours of the night in secret, but this time they were lurking *inside* Galidemus.

"He is only a boy, Stark," Ms. Dywood sighed.

"Do not underestimate what he can do," Stark growled. Harold was shocked at how angry he sounded.

"Did you forget whose son he is?" Stark continued. "You know how powerful he can get. Think of how much power that can be transferred through to his offspring. It is only a matter of time, Merryl. Do not underestimate him. Have you noticed anything suspicious?"

"Not that any of us could tell," Ms. Dywood stated, "he seems oblivious."

"Once again, I am warning you," Stark growled, "do not look past him. He is smarter than he appears."

"She raised him herself," Ms. Dywood continued. "She always said he was just a stupid little boy."

A twinge of betrayal struck Harold. It was obvious they were talking about him. And Mrs. Kernester had raised him. She had said he was stupid? That was entirely out of her character. He couldn't believe it.

"It does not matter what she says he is like," Stark snapped. "How much time does she really spend with him these days? She's so busy."

Harold clenched his fists in frustration. He hadn't spent time with Mrs. Kernester in so long, he nearly forgot what it was like to eat dinner with her, go out on the pond together, work on homework together— mother and son.

He wished he wasn't so angry.

"I guess you're right," Ms. Dywood nodded. They passed the room the boys were hiding in and kept walking down the hall.

"Let's take a turn here," Stark offered once they reached the end of the hall. "I do not wish to wake the other teachers."

Just like that, they were gone, and Harold could no longer hear their voices. He turned around to face Carnis, who was sitting on a dusty, old rocking chair. He was barely keeping awake.

"Did you hear that?" Harold asked.

"The gist of it," Carnis responded, standing up. Dust billowed from the sudden disturbance, creating dust motes beneath the glow of the moon through the open window. Everything in the bedroom seemed old and dusty. "They were talking about *you*."

"They were," Harold nodded, "but I don't know why. It was those two again."

"They do seem to be getting together often." Carnis sighed, "What are the chances of us eavesdropping on them twice?"

"I don't know," Harold said, creaking the door open. "Let's go."

Harold's knuckles had barely touched the surface of Mr. Porthand's door before it was answered. Apparently, he had been waiting for them the whole time. His hair was combed, and he still wore his day clothes.

"Finally," he sighed, "I was beginning to think you forgot about me."

"Sorry," Harold apologized, "we got hung up on the way. We can tell you later."

"Here, come inside," Mr. Porthand smiled, "you can tell me about it now, if you wish."

He led them both inside, where Harold had never been before. The room was clean, but sparse. All that lay inside was a bed, a nightstand, a chair, a rug, and a large chest, shoved under the bed. A flickering lantern lay on the side table, and some books lay on the chair. Mr. Porthand cleared them off, allowing Carnis to sit on the chair, seeing how tired he was. Harold and Mr. Porthand sat on the bed. It felt springy and rough, with scant sheets to cover it.

"What is it?" asked Mr. Porthand.

Harold told him about spying on Ms. Dywood and Stark twice in a row, now, and all they overheard. Mr. Porthand was intrigued.

"I will have to keep an eye on her," he said when Harold had finished. "Thank you for sharing. I heard some muffled noises, but I wasn't paying attention. It concerns me—"

He paused, staring intently at the floor, thinking. "I suppose we'd best get going. It's getting late. Swiftless will be excited to see you two."

Outside, the air was warmer than Harold had felt in some time. Usually, in early spring, winter still dominated the nights. But tonight felt perfect, and even smelled a little like rain. The moon was half-full, creating a wedge of light in the sky. But despite the moon's ample light, Mr. Porthand carried his lantern with them, carving a path through the dusk.

It was much more pleasant sneaking out at night with Mr. Porthand to guide them. He carried an air of safety with him. He also carried the keys, and this helped when they needed to get through the massive oak front doors.

Down they trampled through the valley toward the stalls, the lantern casting fiery shadows against the matted ground and the tall blades of young grass, which appeared to be rising from the dead. The ground was neither muddy nor dry, and the pond surface in the distance shone with the light of the stars, as if the sky were looking in the mirror, posing its best. The stalls threw moon shadows in a westerly direction. Crickets chirped loudly, hiding in the foliage. A pair of ducks drifted gently on the surface of the pond, making ripples in the glass-like surface.

Harold gazed back at the school behind him, making sure they weren't being followed. They weren't, but his eyes found Mr. Porthand's new classroom squatting against the castle wall. It loomed there like a skeleton, exposed to the whims of the weather.

"Mr. Porthand?" he asked quietly.

"Yes?"

"Why did you *really* switch classrooms? I'm pretty sure you wouldn't have changed stations just because one student wanted you to."

There was some silence.

"You are correct," Mr. Porthand replied after some time. "I wouldn't have. You want to know the truth?"

Harold nodded.

"It was about a week ago that Petunia intruded my classroom, suggesting a more engaging lesson" he said. "I was mostly bothered, but I listened. I've always known I could do better, but it is—just part of my nature. Every time I try to improve, something disastrous happens. This time, it was Snip's accident."

Carnis chuckled.

Mr. Porthand continued, "However, before she could finish, Mrs. Kernester herself came through my doors. I offered to dismiss Petunia, but she said she could stay, so she stayed and waited. Mrs. Kernester delivered a message. I was to switch classrooms next week due to— what did she say—'private school issues.' No other reason. That was it. Then Petunia conveniently interjected with her thoughts, and Mrs. Kernester agreed my new outdoor position would offer many more opportunities for a hands-on experience. Then she left."

"That's it?" Harold asked.

"That was all," Mr. Porthand said. "No apology, no pay raise, not even a date I should make the move. Quite frankly, I'm not sure why I had to switch."

"Sounds like a lot of secrecy," Carnis said.

Harold twiddled his thumbs. He could tell what Mr. Porthand was thinking.

"You don't suspect Mrs. Kernester, do you?" he asked timidly.

Mr. Porthand sighed, "Now, don't take me wrong, Harold, but I do think she's up to something. Not to be said negatively, but she has been more secretive about her business now than she ever has before. Much more mischief has arisen. Of course, I'd like to believe it's for a good reason."

Harold sighed. Surely, Mrs. Kernester wasn't guilty of anything, was she? If she was, it could only be for the right reasons. She was the most kind-hearted person Harold had ever met. Her purposes had to be worthy.

They reached the stalls in a hush, and Mr. Porthand led them to Swiftless's cubicle, unlocking it with a single rusty key. He gave the key to Harold, admitting it may come in handy in the future for practicing. Harold accepted it with gratitude and tucked it in his pocket, and Mr. Porthand swung the door open. Inside was Swiftless, but not lying down as he had before.

Swiftless was hovering just above the ground in his tiny shed. Swiftless could fly?

Harold gasped and ran into the stall, wrapping his arms around his dragonfly. Never had he been so happy to see one of the most common insects on planet earth. Swiftless reared his head in joy, jostling Harold around and wrestling in excitement.

Carnis stood still at the entrance to the shed, mouth agape, arms limp. His eyes had grown twice their normal size.

Harold laughed and played, trying to hold back tears of relief. How he had so wanted Swiftless to fly! A couple of days ago, he couldn't have cared less about such a disappointing mount. But those words rang in his ears again as he hugged his dragonfly, the words that had filled his mind when he snagged Swiftless in the first place: *Choose your dragonfly wisely. Choose wisely.*

Now Harold *knew* he had chosen wisely. He had chosen the best dragonfly he could possibly imagine. Swiftless, no matter if he could fly or not, was Harold's dragonfly, and Harold loved him. After what seemed like eons of pure joy, Harold stood up, a smile creasing his face.

"How did you do it?" he gasped, "how did you save him? His wing was beyond repair. And it has only been a day since I gave him to you!"

"Yeah," Carnis nearly whispered. He still stood frozen at the mouth of the shed, jaw unhinged.

"Can you keep a secret?" Mr. Porthand smiled.

Harold nodded.

"Never," Carnis said honestly. "I don't think I ever have."

"Well, I'll tell you anyway, just because you were honest," Mr. Porthand said, laughing. "I used spider web, from a special kind of spider called the Garden Death Weaver. It is the strongest and lightest material I know of."

"Wow," Carnis gasped, "that's cool."

Harold walked back over to Swiftless to see his fixed wing. A thin cast of translucent webbing wrapped the rip that spanned both left wings. Lifting the wings in his hands, Harold felt that the weight was nearly the same as it had been when the rips had been unbound. There was virtually no difference. But one thing still shimmered beneath the webbing...

"Will he be able to take the cast off?" Carnis wondered aloud.

"Sadly, no," Mr. Porthand replied. "The scar will be with him for life, and if he takes the cast off, he won't be able to fly. I tried to seal it on well, but there is always a possibility it might fall off and need to be replaced. I have extra just in case."

Harold gazed deeper into the cast, seeing the rip's sign plastered underneath. It was clear now—he could see the faint sign of a sideways eight etched into his dragonfly's wing. It was easier to distinguish with the cast on. The webbing magnified the image he hadn't been able to see before. Would he forever see that sign whenever he rode Swiftless? Would he be reminded of who he truly was every time he flew?

"I have a special medication for the wing," Mr. Porthand said. "It isn't the safest treatment, but it will make his wing much stronger and sterilize the affected area."

He pulled a necklace from underneath his shirt, a vial fastened to the end of it. It was small and clear, full of a thick purple liquid that glowed with an iridescence, congealed and bitter like the juice of a poisonous fruit. He handled the glass gingerly.

"Garden Death Weaver poison," Mr. Porthand explained. "They not only make strong web, but extremely potent poison as well."

"Cool," Carnis sighed, fingers tingling for the vial.

"Not as cool as it seems," Mr. Porthand warned. "This poison is the worst known to man. It can kill you within fractions of a second by ingesting it. If you get it on your skin, it will leave a permanent mark. Sometimes, if you get enough on your skin, you can contract a life-long disease. And that's with a drop. If you get it in your eyes, you could go blind. It is extremely dangerous.

"For some odd reason, it has the opposite effect on dragonflies. The poison, for them, strengthens their wings and hardens their skin. It would be foolish of me to give it to you to apply to Swiftless," he said to Harold, "but I trust you will only use it for the right purposes."

Harold gulped. Carrying around poison was not something he would enjoy. But if it would strengthen Swiftless's wing, it was the best option—his only option. He would have to be careful.

"If you're irresponsible, you will be in severe trouble," Mr. Porthand said. "It is dangerous to be carrying it at all. Keep in mind, it glows and is easy to see. You are only allowed to wear it when you are riding Swiftless or are in his stall. Am I understood?"

Harold nodded, eyeing the vial. What if it broke accidentally? What if it shattered while he was wearing it?

"Alright," Mr. Porthand said, looking Harold right in the eye. He handed him the vial, and Harold slipped the necklace around his neck, tucking it under his shirt.

"Apply it once a week until the bottle is empty. And only use a drop each time with gloves on," Mr. Porthand explained. "Never let a teacher see you with it, especially Ms. Dywood. Understood?"

Harold nodded once again.

"So cool," Carnis sighed, eyes the size of dinner plates.

After playing with Swiftless, Harold and Carnis were worn out, and they joined Mr. Porthand, who was standing with his back against the shed wall gazing into the night. The lantern glowed softly next to them as they looked up at the sky in silence, finding patterns in the stars. Not a cloud was in sight.

They talked well into the night. Carnis snoozed for some time, and Harold dozed briefly. Mr. Porthand just sat beside the two of them, as if he preferred staring at the stars than sleeping in his own bed. After a long time, he stood up, walked over to Swiftless, and began saddling him.

"Well," he said, clearing his throat, "I suppose you'd better give him a try before we head back. What do you say?"

Harold gasped, snapping awake from his dozing state. "Now? Me?"

"Yes, you," he replied, "he's your dragonfly, is he not?"

Harold beamed with excitement. He jumped up, running over to Swiftless. Carnis startled awake, stumbled to his feet, and suddenly grasped the gravity of the situation.

"He's so cool! Can I try? Just one ride . . . please?" Carnis begged, rubbing his eyes.

Without answering, Harold leapt onto Swiftless's back, hands shaking with excitement. He had never been so thrilled in his life; he had dreamed of flying since he was a little kid.

"Where should I go?" he asked, looking up and around at the world that enveloped him.

"Anywhere, for five minutes," Mr. Porthand smiled. "I trust you."

Harold couldn't believe his luck. Smiling his thanks, he kicked Swiftless and the two soared gracefully into the sky. The cool night air whipped through Harold's hair and clothes, sending the thrill of lightning through his nerves. He had never felt so free in his life! He was riding a dragonfly!

Up they soared, higher and higher until they reached the tops of the highest trees. Harold could see bird nests and the fresh leaves of spring slick in the moonlight. He could see the moon; it was so big! It felt so close.

Up, Swiftless pumped his wings, higher and higher. They soared above the treetops, where Harold had seen the clouds before. They had been so far away, but now, he felt like he could touch them. The pond below them was a puddle. Orahton, a dot. The waterfall a soft trickle. Harold yelped in happiness. This was freedom!

After a few short moments of gaping at the breathtaking view, Swiftless released his wings into a free fall. It was like he was showing Harold his best. The pair fell, faster and faster, Harold laughing the whole way. He held onto Swiftless with all his strength. The force tugging him off was strong, but Harold felt stronger.

The land came closer and closer, the town becoming a dot, a blotch, a compound of small waterside homes. The pond came so close, Harold thought they might crash. But he was fearless. Just before they hit the water's glassy surface, Swiftless pulled up with all his might, and they sped like bullets around the edge of the pond, past Galidemus and the homes and the reeds and the docks and the boats. Harold could see a small Carnis waving frantically on shore. He could see the stalls, the windows of every building, the ripples of water on the surface of the pond. He could see! He could see the night-fishers, and the farms. Every island, every plant. Everything—

Faster and faster they flew, diving behind the pond's waterfall. For a split-second, Harold was in a world of water. The sheen of the waterfall was magnificent, clear as glass and smooth as a sheet of sapphire silk. So much water falling! It sparkled in the moonlight, spraying flecks and tears at both Harold and Swiftless. For that split-second, Harold was in pure paradise.

They emerged from behind the waterfall, eyes glistening with joy. Harold couldn't believe what he was seeing. As they zipped across the smooth, glassy water, Harold patted Swiftless on the head.

"Thank you," he whispered, eyes bleary from the wind and the freedom.

They landed gracefully next to Mr. Porthand and Carnis. Carnis was ecstatic. Mr. Porthand seemed impressed. Harold hopped off Swiftless, trying to hide tears of joy. He had never felt so happy.

"You were amazing!" Carnis gasped. "Swiftless is really good!"

"I—" Harold gasped, trying to find the words. "I . . . that was amazing!"

"That was," agreed Mr. Porthand, "that was the best performance I have ever seen from a first-time rider. Swiftless is extremely fast for a Sapling."

"I'd say he could contend with the professional racers," Carnis said.

Harold shook his head in humility. "He can't be *that* fast."

"He is, though," Carnis persisted. "You know how I watch dragonfly races so often? If anyone should know, it's me."

Harold couldn't argue any further. Swiftless felt fast, and Carnis knew his dragonflies. He sighed in happiness, wiping away his tears.

Mr. Porthand smiled, "What are the tears for?"

Harold smiled back. "I've never felt so happy in my entire life," he confessed. "I've always felt—I don't know, lonely? All my life. But I'm not alone. I've got you guys and now a dragonfly. It's amazing."

Fresh tears sprung to his eyes, but he tried to hold them back. Mr. Porthand smiled at him.

"Can I give him a try?" Carnis asked eagerly.

Harold nodded and Carnis took off to enjoy his five minutes of flight. He slumped down with his back to one of the stalls, trying to regain composure. Mr. Porthand sat down next to him.

"Quite an experience, isn't it?" his teacher sighed.

Harold nodded, swallowing the lump in his throat. For years and years, he thought he would be alone. He had made some temporary friends here and there. But he never had someone to lean on. Now, during his first year of actually attending Galidemus, he had made three amazing friends. And as if that wasn't enough, he had discovered Mr. Porthand, his uncle and teacher, his family. He had a family—and he still couldn't quite believe it. He wasn't so alone anymore. A sigh of relief escaped from his lips.

"Harold, you know if anything goes wrong, I will be there for you," Mr. Porthand said intently, putting his hand on Harold's shoulder. "I always have. You are never alone."

Harold looked at Mr. Porthand straight in the eye. They were blue, flecked in brown, and damp. He nodded, a lump reforming in his throat. He couldn't cry in front of Mr. Porthand—not in front of a teacher. He looked up and blinked at the stars, gripping the vial of poison on his neck.

"I am always here for you," he continued. "So are Carnis and the Parker twins. You are important, Harold, much more important than you think."

Harold turned to face his uncle, tears welling in his eyes, and chuckled at himself for crying. Mr. Porthand just laughed at him. "It's okay to cry, Harold. It's a normal thing."

Harold nodded, unable to find the right words. He ended up crying and laughing at the same time, tears of joy spilling down his cheeks.

They walked back in silence, the lantern guiding their way. After Carnis returned from his ride on Swiftless, he made his jealousy crystal clear. He claimed it had been the best ride of his life, but comparing Swiftless to Sickworm, Harold couldn't disagree.

Shortly after he had landed, they locked Swiftless back up with gnats for him to eat, and started back toward Galidemus, a huge stony shadow even in the dark. It was well past midnight, and they were exhausted.

Once they retreated safely inside the school halls, Harold and Carnis separated from Mr. Porthand and walked back toward their dormitory.

The dormitory was silent and dark, but the boys didn't dare light a lantern. Harold noticed Snip was still missing.

Carnis flopped onto his bed, falling asleep as soon as his head hit the pillow, not even bothering to take off his shoes. But Harold found it a bit more difficult to fall asleep than Carnis, despite his exhaustion. He couldn't keep his thoughts quiet. He couldn't stop thinking about Ms. Dywood and Stark and about Swiftless's fast recovery. It was like magic. He couldn't stop thinking about his friends, especially the missing ones. He hoped he would find Petunia and Snip in the morning. He missed them more than he expected.

But most of all, Harold couldn't stop thinking about his dream. Ever since the nightmare, things in it had been coming true. Swiftless could now fly, just like in his dream. So what about the rest of the dream? What about the monster? Would it come alive as well? Would it grow into a giant and find its way into the pond?

Eventually, his questions faded into a mist and sleep swallowed him whole.

CHAPTER TEN

The Chirper

Harold awoke to a strange feeling in his eyelids. He tried to open them, but they felt stuck. He tried to close them, but he couldn't. Sitting up in confusion, he blinked and looked around. Carnis was standing right next to his bed, a grimace on his face.

"Carnis?" Harold asked, a bit confused.

"Hi," his friend replied. "Have you ever held someone's eyelids open to wake them up?"

"So that's what you were doing," Harold sighed.

"It's creepy."

"Well, don't do it again," Harold suggested.

"Trust me," Carnis said, "I won't."

Harold laughed. Since when did Carnis have to wake *him* up?

"What time is it?" Harold asked suddenly, remembering his detention with Mrs. Murphy. The dread of the day ahead of him throbbed in his mind.

"Well after breakfast," Carnis said. "You'd better hurry. Mrs. Murphy is waiting for you. As for me, I've got a weekend to enjoy. So hurry up."

Harold jumped out of bed, pulled on his shoes, and combed his green, tufty hair as fast as he could. He hoped Mrs. Murphy wouldn't be too cross; she was nothing to mess with. Trying to push the thought of bothering her to the back of his mind, he laced his boots.

"Have you heard anything about Snip and Petunia yet?" he asked hopefully.

"Nothing," Carnis said. "I wonder where they went? Nobody seems to be looking for them except for us."

Harold sighed in frustration. Where could they be? They hadn't appeared since Harold had shouted at Snip in the meal room the day before. His friends wouldn't just abandon him like that, would they? And even if they wanted to, how were they hiding so well?

"I've got to go," he said, while running down the dormitory stairs. "See you around!"

"See you later!" Carnis called faintly behind him.

The meal room was empty except for a single bowl of oat gruel still steaming on the Algae table. Harold felt a bit guilty, and a bit hungry. It was tempting, but he needed to wait. He had to find Mrs. Murphy as soon as possible.

Taking double strides, Harold marched toward the kitchen door. It was closed, and could easily be opened, but he figured he should knock to be polite. He had been rude enough for one morning. He rapped his knuckles gently on the white double door, waiting for a response. No one came. He tried again, this time louder. Finally, someone came to the door, but it wasn't Mrs. Murphy.

A short, burly man opened the door, copper stubble flecking his chin. His eyes were a solid piercing blue, and his features looked like chiseled in stone. The figure only came up to Harold's shoulders, and he wore a white cook's outfit. His hands were covered in black silt, his expression stern.

"Who're you?" he asked in a growly voice.

"Harold," Harold replied. "Who are you?"

The man shifted uncomfortably behind the door.

"The name's Hargow," he replied. "What're you doin' here? You hungry? We ain't got no food right now."

"Not hungry," Harold lied, "I'm here to have detention with Mrs. Murphy."

"She-Cook?" Hargow asked blatantly. "Everyone knows 'er. Come 'ere."

Hargow opened the doors to reveal a boisterous scene inside. Harold remembered coming to the kitchen a lot when he was younger. When had he last been there? Maybe when he was five or six? It wasn't exactly a social hub in Galidemus.

Hot ovens radiating heat lined the kitchen walls, making the huge room uncomfortably hot. Cooks were everywhere, carrying things, cooking, transferring, talking. Noise was everywhere. The boil of water and the clink of iron grated against his ears. A long table ran down the center of the lengthy room. Smells wafted everywhere, of desserts, main courses and other delectables. A huge corn cob lay on its side in the back of the room, hundreds of chefs plucking off the large kernels and scraping meat from their husks.

Barrels stuffed full of food lay stacked up to the ceiling in the center of the room, balanced against the back wall. Behind it peeked a huge egg, ladders reaching the top of it, with cooks holding buckets and tapping into the thick shell from the top. The atmosphere was lively and loud.

But possibly the most noticeable object in the room was Mrs. Murphy herself. Raising a good head taller than any of the other cooks, she ordered commands center-stage, yelling with all her might. Her large build took up more room than three cooks could possibly fill. Hargow led Harold straight toward her, jostling through the crowd of white-clad people.

"So, what'd you do to get in trouble?" Hargow asked as they walked. "It takes a lotta mischief to get yerself detention with She-Cook."

It took a moment for Harold to realize he was talking about Mrs. Murphy. He shrugged as they wormed past a tight knot of older cooks.

"I caught a dragonfly a little later than I was supposed to," he said, as honestly as he could.

"Ah," Hargow chuckled. "That'll do it to ya."

They reached Mrs. Murphy shortly, where they found her cutting up sugar cane, boiling duckweed, and yelling commands to the cooks around her all at once. Harold was not surprised at her ability to multitask, but he couldn't help being intimidated. She looked up from her work, and noticing Harold, came over as fast as her big behind would allow.

"Harold!" she beamed. "My boy!"

She smooched him on the forehead, leaving a smear of lipstick in its place.

"I haven't seen you for so long. Do come sit!"

Harold glanced behind him as he sat down, looking for Hargow. He seemed to have slipped away when he had the chance. Harold wished he could do the same.

"Harold, my baby!" she gushed, handing him a whole handful of sugar cane for him to suck on. "Relax, darling. I have some work to do. Put your feet up for a while!"

Harold groaned and reclined into a soft chair next to the oven. So far, his detention had been more humiliating than he expected. A whole day of this would kill him.

"Was it you who had missed your breakfast?" she asked, as she turned her back on him to stir some soup in a pot. Harold was about to reply with a lie prepped and ready, but again, Mrs. Murphy cut him off.

"Oh, never mind that," she smiled. "How have you been? Has your first year been going well? Oh, and dear, how does the sugar taste? Does it taste delicious? Absolutely divine? And how is your poor dragonfly? And your friends? Oh, dear, do tell me, please!"

Harold could think of only one word that could answer all the questions at once. "Good," he grunted.

"Oh, how perfectly and absolutely wonderful!" she exclaimed. "And I almost forgot to tell you. You look rather dashing today. That hair of yours can melt a girl's heart!"

"Er. . ." Harold knew this was far from the truth.

"Splendid!" she cried before he could even answer. "The cut on those locks, Harold! It looks professional!"

Harold sighed, trying to put in his word. This was Mrs. Murphy alright. Nonstop flattery and exaggeration. He had always done his hair by himself, and everyone else thought it looked silly.

"Mrs. Murphy," Harold asked politely, "can I help with anything?"

"And *such* manners!" she gushed. "Why girls don't swarm you I don't know. I know of that one—Penny or something—she's a little odd, sure, but that's the only one I see around. Good grief, Harold, you can do *better*—"

"Mrs. Murphy?" Harold interrupted, his ears burning. "Can I help you with anything?"

"Oh, of course, of course!" she sighed. "I see you want to keep her *friendship* a secret." She giggled, winking at Harold. Harold just shook his head in despair. He could never get through to her.

"But, no dear. I think we've got it handled just fine," Mrs. Murphey finally replied. "Just sit down and relax! It's the weekend! Care for some of my worm-enhanced parmigiana Romano?"

She held out a grayish wheel of cheese from a shelf. It was huge, slightly speckled in orange.

"Why, you used to eat this every time you visited me when you were little. Used to down it like water!" she batted her eyelashes with flair.

"Worm-enhanced?" Harold wrinkled his nose, then remembering Mrs. Murphy's love for manners, said, "I mean, don't you know a lot of kids are allergic to that stuff?"

"The cheese?" she gasped.

"No, the worms," Harold lied. "The allergic reactions are pretty dramatic, you know."

"Oh, great gobs of gurgling gizzards! I knew those two were up to something!" she turned around, cupping her hands around her mouth, and shouted with quaking volume. "Stephy! Ry! Get over here this instant!"

Quicker than Harold could have ever expected, two dairy cooks pushed through the crowd to stand right in front of Mrs. Murphy. Stephy had strawberry blond hair and freckles that dotted her face. Ry was muscular, with black buzzed hair. Both looked confused.

"What is it, She-Cook?" asked Stephy.

"*What is it?*" Mrs. Murphy sneered. "You two should know perfectly well! You have been sneaking worm slime into the parmigiana Romano!"

"Under your orders," Ry pointed out. "Worm slime is the main ingredient in your worm-enhanced cheese. You told us to."

"You know perfectly well how dangerous it is," she snapped back. "You're fired!"

Looks of disbelief sprouted on not only Ry and Stephy's faces, but on Harold's, too. He had to say something. This was all his fault.

"Wait!" he protested. "Worm slime, did you say? I've heard it's only the worm meat that is poisonous. But worm slime is perfectly healthy for the body! It has . . . it has vitamins!"

"Vitamins?" Mrs. Murphy asked.

"Oh, yes, lots of them," Harold nodded. "Vitamin A, B, C, D, all the way down the whole alphabet! Tons of them."

Mrs. Murphy raised an eyebrow. She glanced back and forth between Stephy, Ry, and Harold. "I suppose vitamins *are* healthy for the body," she said. "I hire you two again! Now get to work!"

Frozen in surprise, the two cooks turned around slowly to leave. Harold was just glad he didn't get them in worse trouble. Once they left, Mrs. Murphy, still fuming, went back to her work. She mumbled under her breath, then said out loud, "I was about to make them both Venariovums by the way they acted."

Too curious, Harold asked, "What's a Venariovum?"

"Oh, nothing dear," she said, waving her hand as she focused on her duckweed.

Harold paused. "I really want to know."

Mrs. Murphy sighed. She turned around to face Harold. "A Venariovum is an egg hunter. They have the most difficult job of all of the cooks. They have to fly their dragonflies, or find some other way to get to the tops of the trees. Then they have to steal eggs from the nests without the mother bird noticing. Many perish on the job. It is very difficult. In fact, we just got a delivery earlier today. Hargow and his team are working on tapping into it right now. You can go watch them if you'd like, darling."

"Hargow taps into eggs?" Harold asked.

"And finds, too," she said. "In fact, he's my best Venariovum. He's been in the business for over thirty years."

Harold whistled with surprise. "Can I go to watch him tap the egg?" he asked.

"Be careful," she warned.

Harold meandered his way through the crowd toward the half-hidden egg, which towered behind a wall of stacked barrels and crates. Hargow's team laid ladders against the massive egg, and they balanced at the top of each one, a bucket in hand and a small chisel to crack the egg. Hundreds of hairline cracks ran along the egg's surface, and a few places at the top betrayed a few small holes. Most of the men working on the egg looked similar to Hargow—rough around the edges. Some bore eye patches, while some had scars or tattoos.

Harold sat down next to the egg, and focused on Hargow, who was perched at the top of one ladder.

He gazed down at Harold. "You again?"

"Yes, me again," Harold smiled. "Mind if I help you guys?"

"Sorry, squirt, but this project is under construction," Hargow called down, looking back at his precious egg. "I can't afford to get fired today by offending She-Cook."

"I won't get in the way," Harold insisted.

"You would," Hargow countered, "and you might kill yourself in the process. Go find something else to do."

"I won't *kill* myself," Harold laughed. "I'll be careful. I'm on detention, aren't I? But I haven't done an ounce of work yet. This'll *kill* me if I have to sit around listening to Mrs. Murphy all day."

"Well, She-Cook likes it that particular way," Hargow said. "And believe me, I don't care if you die trying to help us. I'm just afraid you'd mess the egg up."

Harold wrinkled his nose. Venariovums were a distasteful lot.

"Hargow, please let me do something," Harold pleaded. "I'll be extremely careful if you let me help you. An extra pair of hands would be good, right?"

"Or the extra pair of hands could get us all fired," Hargow growled. "Go find something else to do."

Angered, Harold decided to give up. Hargow was solid. He wouldn't change his mind. At best, he could watch. In one last hopeful gesture, Harold shouted, "Can I help with anything down here?"

"Harold, I just told ye'—" Hargow began to growl, but was interrupted by his crew member at the base of the egg. He was shouting frantically.

"Sir, sir! I think we've got a chirper, sir! It just drained!"

Hargow slid down the ladder and ran over to his teammate. "How long ago?" he asked.

"Only a couple of minutes, sir," the teammate answered. Hargow immediately turned around to face his men, expression stern.

"Off! Off!" he called. "We've got a chirper on our hands, men! Quickly! Quickly! Get She-Cook and return to your posts! Hurry!"

All in a scuffle, Hargow's team was everywhere, pulling down ladders and scrambling around. Harold jumped up at the sudden commotion, confused at what was happening. In the clamor he was jostled around like a piece of driftwood in a mad sea.

It didn't take long for Mrs. Murphy to arrive on the site. She marched straight up to Hargow without even noticing Harold.

"What is it? What is the matter?"

"A baby bird," Hargow replied. "I'll find out who brought it here immediately."

"Oh, Hargow, what terrible luck!" she gasped. "I'll get my team on it right away! What a horrible inconvenience! I'll clean it up as soon as I can. I—"

Hargow held his hand up to silence her.

"There will be no need," he said. "We can deal with this. You have lunch to worry about. We'll take care of it."

"Well, I—" she began.

"Just prepare for lunch," Hargow urged.

"Thank you, Hargow," she sighed. "Be careful."

She trotted off, ignoring Harold in the frenzy, and disappeared into the crowd.

Harold's eyes trailed after her, then noticed Hargow approaching him. Harold opened his mouth to ask what was going on, but before he could say a word, Hargow gripped his wrist, murder in his eyes.

"You're coming with me," he growled.

CHAPTER ELEVEN

Helping Hargow

"Hey, let me go!"

"Stop strugglin', won't ye?"

Nobody seemed to realize Hargow was carrying Harold away. Either that, or nobody cared. Harold struggled, trying to free himself of Hargow's grasp, but he was just too strong. He yanked Harold farther back into the kitchen until they reached the far wall, where a small back door stood in the corner. He tried to call out, but the bustle of the kitchen overpowered his voice. Finally, Harold was yanked outside. Hargow threw him on the ground, shutting the door behind him.

Outside, Harold found himself in a little neighborhood dotted with tiny cottage homes. Each was modest in size, the names of each cook written on signposts in each yard. Towering flowers in early bloom gathered in clusters, shading the homes. A path wove through the neighborhood like a web.

Harold crawled away from Hargow on his hands and knees as the furious Venariovum approached him. He rubbed his wrist in pain; it had been twisted by Hargow's grasp. Hargow rolled up his sleeves, fists clenched.

"What are you doing?" Hargow growled.

Harold frowned at him. "I'm trying to get away from you! What does it look like? And why are you trying to kidnap me?"

Hargow rolled his eyes. "Didn't you want to help me? Now's your chance."

He reached for Harold's hand, helping him to his feet with ease. Harold stood up, confused.

"You said you wanted to help me, didn't you?" Hargow asked.

Harold thought for a moment. "Yes—wait—is that what we're doing?"

"Of course it is. Good grief, get a head on your shoulders!" Hargow laughed. "Now come along quickly. She-Cook wouldn't like this."

Off he walked, straight through the cluttered neighborhood, leaving Harold behind. Harold scrambled to his feet, running to catch up to Hargow. Even though he was stocky, he was fast. They walked side by side in silence, traveling further down the trail.

"Now see here," he grumbled, "I knew nobody would volunteer, so I figured you could help me. We need to catch the chirper. Usually, She-Cook would have me kill 'em, but I've taken a liking to them— curse my soul—and I hate to see them die. So I bring 'em back to my place and raise 'em until they can be free. Got that?"

Harold nodded, more than a little confused.

"Sure, whatever," Harold said. "Wait, you *keep* baby birds?"

The people of Orahton feared birds as much as they feared lightning. People were often squished, eaten, pecked to death, or even flown away to some high nest, which fostered a healthy fear of all things with wings; that is, except dragonflies.

"I know it's dangerous," Hargow confessed, "but they're so innocent and cute an' all. I can't resist!"

"This is ridiculous!" Harold laughed.

"I tend to see the good in stuff," Hargow said, throwing up his hands in surrender. "Take my first mate for example. He used to be the mos' feared burglar of the century, but now he's as tame as a tadpole. Wouldn't hurt a fly!"

"Well, that's comforting," Harold chuckled. "A villain is preparing my food—"

"Now don't you get all bitter," Hargow warned, "do you want to help me or not?"

"What's the chance of survival?" Harold asked.

"At least fifty percent," Hargow said, grinning.

"Fine," Harold said, laughing at himself. He was too bored to sit by and watch.

The path continued into the reed forest, and soon the cottages that once surrounded them disappeared. Up above loomed heavy cattails, brown crowns waving in the breeze. Some were fluffy and shedding. Others were tightly packed, and yet others were barely ripe, still green or yellow. They cast huge shadows upon the forest floor. Twice, they crossed bridges, mere planks of bark extending across little trickles of water that fed the pond. As they traveled, the path continued, hiding in the undergrowth.

For a while they walked, until Harold could see a splotch in the distance rise, then turn into a small, brown, mushroom-shaped house, complete with a sturdy bark roof. The door was round and short, a bronze knob at its center, just Hargow's size. A huge bean plant towered next to the house, a single pod dangling over the stout chimney that sprouted from the top of the roof. The bean's vines twisted and tangled into the reeds that surrounded the small clearing. Water lettuce and pansies bloomed around the yard, and the path led right up to the front of the house and stopped at the front steps. The wooden steps were rickety and worn, splintering in some places. The few windows that studded the mushroom-shaped house were foggy and crusted in dirt. Harold could barely see through them.

Hargow walked up to his house like a proud rooster. Without unlocking his door, he swung it open, revealing a cozy home inside, complete with a small kitchen and a bed. A comfortable fireplace— more like a pile of ashes—lay off to one side. A small velvet chair stood in front of it, and a collection of cabinets clustered on the other side of the one-room home. A scant bed lay in the far corner of the room, the mattress ripped. An empty kettle sat on the counter, a pile of clothes sat next to the bed, and a bin full of dirty water sat next to the clothes, murky froth coating the top. Chains of beans and corn kernels hung from the ceiling, clinking together as the pair walked past them. A large chest loomed on the far wall, and Hargow marched straight up to it. Using a single key from his belt, he unlocked the chest to reveal an assortment of random tools and weapons.

"Cool home," Harold nodded, watching Hargow gather some instruments from the chest.

"Thank you," he replied. He dropped a short sword and a coil of rope into Harold's arms, then retrieved the same for himself. "We'll use these," he said.

"Wait, that's it?" Harold clarified. A rope and a sword were clearly inefficient to capture a baby bird.

"What do ye' mean 'that's it'?" Hargow asked. He bolted the chest shut, and they walked back outside. Hargow closed the door behind him and they began walking back to Galidemus.

"I mean," Harold said, "that this stuff will not work to catch a bird! We're walking to our deaths!"

Hargow chuckled under his breath. "You mean to say this isn't enough?" he asked. "I've been in this business for thirty years and this is all I've used. Not good enough for you, young chap?"

"Well, *I* haven't been in the business for thirty years!" Harold shouted. "This is completely insufficient—"

"Insufficient!" Hargow huffed, "well, that's what I'm giving you, whether you like it or not. Would you prefer to go empty-handed?"

"No," Harold said, "but how in the world have you been doing this for thirty years with just a rope and a sword? It's impossible, Hargow."

"Nothing is impossible," Hargow said, raising an eyebrow at Harold.

Harold found himself at a loss of words. The sudden calmness in his voice silenced him. He focused on the trail ahead, deciding it was best not to argue with the guy anymore. The road, despite being cleared, was taxing on his legs after they began to jog through the forest. When they returned, the little cook's neighborhood was anything but quiet.

Cooks were everywhere, running to and fro, leaping into their houses and bolting their doors. Some ran aimlessly into one another.

Others cowered behind the towering flowers. The place was in total pandemonium.

For a moment, Hargow stood completely still, staring awestruck at the insanity before him. He didn't move for several moments. Then, as if snapping out of a trance, he grabbed Harold's shoulder and dragged him forward.

"Harold?" Hargow growled. He pointed to the wall of the school where the kitchen was inside. "It looks like the chirper's already hatched. I think it's a hawk. It'll be confused, which means it will be angry. Violent. You need to be careful. Use your rope to lasso its neck. Then I'll lasso its feet. That should pin it up."

Harold nodded, his mind racing and his knees wobbly. *If* he survived, he would have a great story to tell. He chased after Hargow, who was bolting toward Galidemus. They both raced through the back door, shoving through the frantic crowd. The kitchen inside was a complete mess.

The kitchen looked like a silverware drawer shaken by a small child. Ovens were overturned, barrels were split, spilling liquids and food all over the floor, and the corn was left abandoned. In the center of the room, the huge baby hawk raged.

Standing in the crumpled remains of its shell, the baby chick stood, wet and matted and confused. For half a moment, it looked down at them, strutting over with graceful, fluid movements. Both Harold and Hargow stood still, amazed.

"Bless his soul," Hargow whispered.

Harold dove at Hargow and only just in time. The chick's beak came crashing down on them, nearly killing him on the spot. Harold yanked him behind an overturned table.

"Hargow!" Harold scolded. "And you told *me* to be careful!"

"Sorry 'bout that," Hargow said, scrambling to his feet. "I forgot they do that sometimes."

He looked over the back of the table. The chick was coming their way. Hargow leapt from cover and dashed behind an oven. "Don't forget! Rope 'er neck!" he shouted over his shoulder.

Suddenly, Harold was alone.

He reached out of his cover for a ladle, snatching it from the ground, wary of the chick that was now distracted by some boiling stew. He tied it at the end of his rope.

How would he climb on top of the chick? Nothing in the kitchen was tall enough, except. . .

Wait! Hargow's ladders! It might be dangerous, but it was Harold's only option.

Carefully, Harold crept behind overturned appliances, meandering his way toward the ladders. They were sitting on the far side of the room, and he needed to get there undetected. Darting behind ovens, tables, and chairs, Harold crept closer and closer. He was almost there...

Suddenly, a whooping noise came out from behind one of the overturned ovens. Hargow sprang forward, swinging a rope above his head like a mad cowboy. With a crazed expression, he raced toward the chirper's legs, hollering as he went.

The chirper's beak came crashing down, crashing to the floor in thundering rage. Harold winced as Hargow dodged the first blow, then the second. Finally, he managed to sneak beneath the chirper's legs, and the chick began stomping down on Hargow's head.

Like a bullet, Hargow raced around the chirper's legs, the rope trailing behind him.

"Harold!" he called frantically.

Harold snapped out of his trance, sprinting the rest of the way toward the ladders. If he didn't hurry, Hargow would become a pancake. Mustering all his strength, Harold lifted the ladder, swung it over his shoulder, and ran over to the commotion. The baby hawk was so distracted with Hargow it didn't notice Harold coming up from behind.

Harold propped up the ladder, balancing it while the chirper wriggled. After several failed attempts, he managed to keep it still. If he climbed too quickly, he might fall, but if he went too slowly, he might lose his chance. He took a deep breath and raced up the ladder, feeling it wobble under his feet. He jumped . . . and managed to grip some tail feathers!

Harold held on for dear life as the baby bird squawked and screamed, pulling himself onto its back. Then he scrambled onto its neck, barely keeping balance. He swung the rope attached to the ladle under the chick's neck, and caught the ladle with shaky hands from the other side. Then he tied the two together, and pulled hard. The chick reared up, cocking its head left and right. Harold stayed out of its vision, and kept pulling. The chick cocked its head again, and stopped stomping at Hargow.

Harold pulled again. The chick cringed, rearing up and roaring in protest. It tried to take a step forward, but Hargow pulled on the tangle of ropes at its feet, and it stumbled, slipped, and crashed to the kitchen floor. Hargow darted from beneath the bird just before it crushed him. The force of the fall sent Harold flying into the air.

The fall hadn't been too far, but as he fell, his shoulder grazed the corner of an overturned table. Then the blunt force of the impact with the floor slammed into Harold's shoulder. Pain shocked up his arm. Hargow witnessed the whole thing and hurried over.

"You okay, son?" he asked. Hargow himself had a long gash in one arm and a scratch across his face. Harold nodded, clenching his fist. Looking down at the injury, he noticed his shoulder bled through his clothes, and Hargow peeled back the sleeve, wincing at the damage. The table had punctured his skin, leaving a nasty scratch.

"Just a flesh wound," Hargow sighed. "No broken bones. Thank goodness."

"I guess so," Harold groaned, dabbing the wound with his sleeve. He could see the skin around it turning purple.

"That was some quick thinking, boy," Hargow chuckled, "you'll be okay?"

"I think so," Harold said. "How are you going to get the chirper out?"

"I have my ways," Hargow winked. "I 'preciate your help, I will admit. Stop by anytime."

Harold just smiled.

"Now mind you, I don't get days off like you youngins' do, so you ought to be prepared to help. But you'd be welcome."

Hargow helped Harold to his feet, pain searing through his arm. But once he was standing, it wasn't quite so painful. Harold smiled at Hargow.

"Thanks for letting me help you," he said.

"No, thank *you*," Hargow laughed. "You'd best get going now. She-Cook would have a fit if she saw you like this. I'll cover for you. See you 'round."

Even though he wanted to stay, Harold knew he should go to the hospital wing. And Hargow was right. If Mrs. Murphy saw him, she'd have a fit. He waved goodbye and disappeared through the double white kitchen doors, walking back into the meal room.

The room was empty, all except one lone bowl of oat gruel, stone cold at the Algae table. So Harold took a seat, ravenous with hunger, and licked the bowl clean.

CHAPTER TWELVE

The Return of the Twins

Days went by. Harold's shoulder slowly healed, but the injury made completing simple tasks difficult. Soon, the bruise was nothing but a purple splotch, and his cuts no more than thick scabs.

The injury had made riding Swiftless a challenge, but it didn't stop him entirely. Harold tried to visit Swiftless every day. Swiftless's wing still had the cast on, as it would stay for the rest of his life. Harold could still see the mark of the Ferrals under the spider web wrap. But Swiftless seemed much happier now that he could fly.

One thing loomed over Harold heavier than anything else. Petunia and Snip were still missing and Harold couldn't find them, no matter how hard he tried. As the days of the week passed, Harold still hadn't seen them once since he had said all those awful things to Snip. Had he scared them away forever? Had they gone home for some reason?

On several occasions, Harold had searched the whole school, inside and out, but couldn't find them anywhere. They didn't show up for mealtimes, classes, or rest. Snip didn't show up once in the dormitory for five days. Petunia wasn't even in the library, where she usually was, reading up on concoctions and biology. But possibly the strangest part of all was that nobody seemed to notice.

Teachers insisted they were just fine when Harold asked about them. Even Mr. Porthand seemed to think they were alright, though he refused to tell Harold where they were. Other students didn't even notice their absence. But Harold couldn't get their image out of his head. He thought about them all the time. He was worried.

One day, well into the school week, Harold and Carnis were sitting alone at the Algae table, slurping up minnow soup. Both Petunia and Snip's seats were vacant beside them. Harold felt lonelier than ever.

"Carnis?" Harold asked as he poked at his food, "do you miss them? Petunia and Snip?"

Carnis smacked his lips. Salty brine dripped from his mouth. "Sort of," he admitted, "but it's kind of nice to have a break from them, don't you think? I mean, Petunia's not here to fuss over our homework and Snip's not here to whine about his food. It's peaceful."

"You don't miss them just a tiny bit?" Harold asked.

"I didn't say that," Carnis said. "I do miss them. A lot, actually. I hope they're okay. But it is a *little* nice, don't you agree?"

Harold couldn't. He missed them a lot more than he let show. Mostly he missed Petunia. Maybe it was her common sense that none of them had, or just her personality that lightened the room that made him miss her. He didn't know.

"I worry about them," Harold finally said, sipping his soup.

"Don't worry," Carnis reassured. "If the teachers think they're okay, they're probably fine."

"But what if they're just hiding from us?" Harold said. "What if they're mad at us and don't want to see us ever again?"

"You worry too much," Carnis sighed.

"I mostly miss Petunia."

"Why?"

"I don't know. She knows everything," Harold sighed. "She's smart. She knows what is right and wrong. She kind of steers us, you know."

"I think it's just that she is so much better than Snip," Carnis nodded.

"Snip's alright," Harold said. "But I don't know. I just miss her more."

Carnis shrugged. He lifted his bowl to his lips, sipping loudly. Harold wiggled uncomfortably. He didn't have feelings for her, did he? No, they were just close friends. Maybe he was just nervous about confronting Snip.

Suddenly, someone plopped down on the seat next to Harold. Harold glanced over, finding Piggy melting onto the seat.

"Piggy?" he asked, more than a little confused. Piggy was an Algae, though not a very capable one. She usually sat at the end of the table alone. Why was she here? Her bowl was steaming and untouched, and it sloshed as she set it on the table.

"Hey y'all," she warbled. "How's today for you?"

Carnis looked up from his bowl, snorted, and sent fish flying out his nose.

"Er . . . hello, Piggy," Harold coughed. "It's good—great. How are you?"

"Very good," she smiled, nose upturned. "You know, I was just talking to Snip, and he said—"

"Snip?" Harold asked eagerly. "Was Petunia with him?"

"Since when are *they* separated?" Piggy smirked, her eyelashes batting. She thrived on attention.

"Are you toying with us?" Carnis asked, wiping his mouth on his sleeve.

"Not at all," Piggy shook her head, "they wanted me to come and get you."

Harold stood up from his seat, surprised at his own reflexes. "Carnis, let's go," he said.

"Can I finish my soup, first?" he begged.

"No," Harold said firmly. If they didn't act soon, their friends might slip between their fingers yet again.

"You just want to see *Petunia*," Carnis smirked. Harold frowned. He was just eager to see them—*both* of them—again.

"Can I come?" Piggy asked eagerly.

Harold didn't have time to pause for thought. "Fine, but don't be mean to Snip. What happened during the boating lesson was an accident, and you were part of it, too."

"Was *not*," Piggy shot back. Harold just ignored her. He led the two out of the meal room, and under Piggy's instruction, headed straight for the library.

The library appeared to be empty and was silent with tension. Harold could feel his heart racing as they wove between bookshelves, making their way to the back of the room.

"They're over here," Piggy said, leading the boys behind a tall bookshelf. Anticipation filled the room. They seemed to be walking upon the string of a bow; their steps wavered on a tight wire.

They rounded the bend to find Petunia and Snip standing there, eyes glimmering.

There was a moment of silence. Harold glanced back and forth between them, relieved, but feeling the anger building inside. They were unscathed; nothing had happened to them. They had just been hiding. For what? Some ridiculous game? Harold tried hard to bite his tongue. Blood drew in his mouth. What he wanted to say would only make things worse—but he was so relieved to see their faces again. He was glad they were back, glad they were okay. He was so glad they wanted to see him again.

"Petunia—Snip—"

"Hi," Petunia whispered. "I'm sorry. I can explain, I promise—"

"Sorry?" Carnis said. "You disappeared for days!"

"Look," Petunia begged, "Snip was being teased really bad that day, and we had to—"

"Had to take a break from *us*? Had to leave us to worry about you?"

"Give them a break, Carnis," Harold said.

"I guess it's only fair," Carnis grumbled. "Since they gave *us* a break."

Harold frowned at the twins, straining to contain his frustration. "Where were you guys?"

"In a—" Petunia stuttered. "Look, we really didn't want to leave you guys alone. But we had to."

"I'm sure," Carnis growled.

"Okay, let me explain everything before you get angrier," Petunia frowned at Carnis. "That day we disappeared was especially bad for Snip because everyone saw him crying. We had to hide!"

"Big deal!" Carnis went on, throwing his hands into the air with frustration. "He can take care of himself."

"You guys don't understand!" Petunia glared, on the verge of tears. "Snip is different. I have to shield him. He doesn't stand a chance."

"What are you talking about?" Harold asked. "Snip is no different than you and me."

Snip stood in the corner, hunching his shoulders in shame.

"Oh, for heaven's sake!" Petunia sighed. "You guys don't take a clue. Do either of you even know what makes a Ferral a Ferral?"

Harold was taken aback.

"What do you mean?"

"Grey hair," Petunia said softly. "Grey hair is the mark of the Ferrals."

Harold glanced from Petunia's face to Snip's head, where a crown of grey hair quivered.

"But Snip isn't a Ferral," Carnis said.

"I know," Petunia said, "but now do you understand? People hate Ferrals. Half the students in this school loathe Snip, whether he's a Ferral or not. They torment him if I'm not there to help. What you said to Snip that one day spread like wildfire. We had to hide for his safety. People have tried to *hunt* him before. They've tried to take him from our home in the summer, and from school the rest of the year. I have to protect him. It's my duty when our parents aren't there."

All fell silent. Carnis rubbed the back of his neck.

"I'm so sorry, this is all my fault," Harold sighed. "Now it all makes sense."

"Totally," Piggy nodded.

Everyone looked in her direction.

"Why is *she* here?" Petunia asked, annoyed. Piggy crossed her arms.

"Look, I'm sorry, too," Carnis sighed. "I had no idea."

"I should've told you earlier," Petunia said. "It's not your fault."

"But why does Snip have grey hair?" Harold asked, turning to Snip. "You're not a Ferral, but you have grey hair. How did you get it?"

Snip shrugged. "It's a closely guarded secret. Even our parents don't know. But I promise—I swear—I'm not a Ferral."

Carnis chuckled under his breath, "I can't even imagine it."

"How did you hide?" Harold asked. "We didn't even see you once."

"Mrs. Kernester sets aside a room for us when things get really bad," Petunia said. "We sleep there, and do the homework for classes there. We eat there. But we're only allowed to use the room if we promise not to speak with any students while we stay there—you guys included. I don't like it. It's the first time we've had to use it all year. But it was really bad this time. Some kids tried to lock him in a closet until he starved to death and another one had a switchblade. *He* got detention."

Harold furrowed his brow, shocked. He shuddered at all the terrible things that must have happened to Snip. Now he understood.

"I'm really sorry."

"You didn't know, so don't be," Petunia said, resting her hand on his shoulder. Harold cringed in pain.

"What's this?" Petunia asked, peeling up Harold's sleeve. Underneath was his injury, still scabbing and painfully bruised. Snip shriveled back at the sight of dried blood.

"What happened?" she gasped.

Harold shook her off. "A lot has happened since you guys left." Harold smiled, glancing at Carnis. Carnis smiled back.

They told them about how Swiftless had been healed almost overnight; about how they had ridden him, and how fast he was; about how they had overheard Ms. Dywood and Stark again, and about Mr. Porthand. Finally, they relayed Harold's adventure in the kitchen, and soon they were laughing and sharing stories once again. Even Piggy chimed in, the anger and confusion dissolving between her and Snip.

"I can't believe Swiftless can fly!" Petunia laughed.

"And fast, too," Carnis added with excitement. "It's pretty wicked."

"And you lassoed a baby hawk without me?" Petunia chuckled.

"I guess so," Harold smirked. "But trust me, it's not something you want to do on a holiday."

Snip smiled as he listened. Even *he* seemed happy.

The afternoon passed into evening, and soon it was dinner time. Harold, Carnis, Petunia, and Snip sat in their usual places once again, laughing as if nothing had happened.

Ever since the mishap with the chirper, meals had been a little late, so most of the time the students had to wait for their food. But it was slowly returning to normalcy. Now, they hardly had to wait at all for food to arrive. Soon, hundreds of piping hot bowls of water lettuce soup came out the kitchen doors. The soup was just cool enough to drink. Harold ate until his bowl was clean.

It was just as the bowls were being collected that trouble came their way. As snobby and rude as ever, Puella came striding over, decked out in jewels and frills, a scowl on her face.

"I see the Parker twins have finally returned," she laughed.

"Go away, Puella," Harold warned. In truth, he was surprised she had noticed their absence, but he was too irritated with her to care.

"I think not," she snarled. She marched over to Snip's seat, snatching his bowl out of his grasp. It was still full; Snip ate notoriously slow. "What is helpless Snip going to do? Poor baby Ferral!"

Harold stood up with Petunia. Snip showed no objection to losing his dinner. He was used to the harassment. He wouldn't risk a fight with Puella for his life.

"Give it back," Petunia warned.

"Why?" Puella smirked. "I'm only going to give it back if he fights for himself. I'm sick of seeing you protect him. Who protects a Ferral?"

This was getting out of hand. Harold searched the room, trying to find a teacher that could step in. He spotted none. What would they do? Puella was not easily stopped without authority.

"Come on, Snip. Don't you want your dinner?" Puella taunted.

Snip scowled down at the table. He clenched his fists and stood up, limbs quivering.

"Don't do it," Harold urged. Suddenly, Petunia swung an arm at Puella and missed. Puella chuckled.

"You can't touch me," she smirked. "I'm a *Royal*."

Petunia aimed another swing, but before she could even move, Carnis stood up and held her back.

"You'll get yourself in trouble," Carnis grunted. Petunia struggled against his grasp. "Let me go! Don't do it, Snip . . . please—"

Snip turned to face Puella, but couldn't bring himself to make eye contact.

"Come on, Snip," Puella coaxed. "Touch me and you get expelled. Imagine the headline: *Young Ferral Attacks Poor Royal Girl.* But don't touch me, and you'll never prove you're more than a worthless rat. What to do..."

Snip launched at Puella. Everyone in the meal room was watching. But just before Snip could make an impact, Harold stood in between the two. Snip's fierce swing collided with Harold's chest, making Harold stumble. Harold ignored the pain, spun around, and aimed a swing at the bowl in Puella's hand. His hand collided perfectly. The bowl was sent sailing to the floor, sloshing soup into the air. Then it crashed to the floor, sending splinters of ceramic everywhere.

All fell silent after the crash. Snip froze, his fist suspended in mid-air. Petunia gasped, clutching her mouth as Carnis loosened his grasp. Puella smirked, and Harold glared at her, staring right into her eyes, his chest throbbing.

"Idiot," Puella growled at Harold.

Harold didn't move.

"Leave now," he commanded. "You don't belong on this side of the meal room anyway. Take yourself somewhere else."

"Who put the nameless boy in charge?"

"I am not nameless," Harold retorted.

"Oh, yeah? I thought you were too little to tell when your parents dumped you."

Harold's ears turned blood red. "I have a name. More than just Harold."

"Really? Let's hear it."

Harold clenched his fists. If he said anything, everyone would find out his secret—he shouldn't.

"Come on, no-name," Puella sighed, "I don't have all day."

"You wouldn't believe me if I told you," he said, trying to steady himself.

"I probably wouldn't," Puella admitted, "but I *am* interested in hearing your fairy tale. What has the lunatic thought up today?"

Harold swallowed. And swallowed again. His mouth felt dry. He wanted to shout the truth about himself, but he knew if he did, it would be disastrous.

"I can't."

"Why? No name, no dragonfly."

That did it. Harold felt rage bubble up inside of him, erupting in fury.

"My name is Harold Porthand, okay? Now, leave us alone!" he shouted.

Harold clapped his hand over his mouth in surprise. The entire meal room had frozen, eyes locked on Harold. Now they all knew . . . if they believed—

"Porthand?" Puella laughed. "Like Mr. Porthand? That old chimp? I don't know, but if I were you, I'd adopt a name that suits you better. Porthand is a peasant name, but even *that* is too good for you."

"It's true," Carnis gasped. Sweat was beading on his brow from the effort of holding Petunia back.

"Right," Puella smirked, "I'll take the overeater and the psychopath for their word."

She turned to Snip and spat at his feet, glaring into his eyes. Petunia sucked in her breath as she watched.

"You deserve it, Ferral," Puella spat. Then she waltzed back to her Royal table, making sure to kick the Algae table first, sending soup sloshing everywhere. Everybody within a six-seat radius groaned, but Harold squinted after Puella, ignoring the curses around him. Royals rarely got punished for anything. This whole mess would certainly go unaddressed.

After a few moments, Carnis released Petunia, huffing and puffing from the effort. Petunia ran after Puella, crazed with fury. Carnis cursed and ran after her, and Harold and Snip were left alone.

Harold sat back down in his seat, rubbing his eyes in stress, and Snip did likewise. It was silent for some time.

"Are you alright?" Harold asked after a while.

Snip shrugged, "It's fine. I'm used to it."

"I can't believe her."

"I know. I'm sorry I punched you," Snip sighed. "I hope it didn't hurt."

"Not too much," Harold said. "Are you still hungry? I can ask Mrs. Murphy—"

"No, no," Snip said, shaking his head. "It's okay."

Harold wiggled in his chair. It was strange being alone with Snip. Snip was hardly ever alone.

"Snip?" he asked. "I know you answered this before, but... do you know how you got grey hair?"

Snip tapped his shaking fingers on the table while he thought. "I don't know," he replied. "My mom and dad said that when Petunia and I were born, Petunia came first. Only by a couple of minutes, but she was just the way my parents wanted her. Green hair. Plump. *Basically perfect*. A healthy baby. But when I came second, they said I was all shriveled, grey, and half-dead. I almost didn't survive. And I was born with grey hair.

"Most of my childhood I spent indoors. My mom was always fretting about me. Soon, the secret got out that I had grey hair, and I began to get hunted, even as a small child. Good people and bad people went after me. They thought I was a spy in disguise. They hated me. Especially Royals. It was dangerous to send me to Galidemus, but our mom has been ill ever since we were born—we really took it out of her. She couldn't teach me at home. She's always been sick and can hardly take care of herself. So Petunia watches over me. We've kept it a secret between us and Mrs. Kernester until now, but it's hard to hide the color of your hair for too long."

"Wow," Harold said, letting out a long sigh. "So you don't know how you got it."

Snip nodded. "I'm the only person I know of who has grey hair and is not a Ferral."

Harold sighed, wondering how, why—

Just then, Petunia and Carnis returned. Both looked infuriated at each other, but otherwise fine. Harold breathed a sigh of relief.

"Did you catch her?"

"He caught *me*," Petunia said, glaring at Carnis. "If he hadn't held me back again, I would've *beaten* her."

"You would have been in serious trouble," Carnis retorted.

"Whatever," she snapped

The rest of the evening was silent, and Harold's thoughts ran rampant through is mind. How did Snip have grey hair? It wasn't hereditary, because Harold would have received grey hair, too, then. So how did Snip get it? He had been cursed forever, and people hated him as a result.

But Harold was glad they were friends. He didn't care if Snip had grey hair. After all, Harold was half Ferral himself.

CHAPTER THIRTEEN

Juniper

The days returned to their normal rhythm. Harold found himself busy with his school work as the end of the year was nearing, about a month away. He couldn't help noticing that things were strangely uneventful. Everything had been so abrupt and uncertain over the past weeks Harold found it hard to think. But now that things had calmed down, he could breathe. He could finally focus on school and riding Swiftless. Now that his injury was healing, Harold rode Swiftless every chance he could get. The sensation of riding left Harold breathless. Exuberant. It was hard to explain, but it was something like pure joy.

Teachers assigned more and more schoolwork, filling Harold's schedule as swiftly as a squirrel stuffs its hole before winter. Frankly, Harold was glad for the extra work. It gave him little time to think about the Ferrals, Puella, Petunia and Snip, and the secret of his family. It gave him little time to think about summer, too.

Harold hated summer. Most children relished the thought of the warm weather and the free days. But for Harold, it was anything but exciting. Living in Galidemus, he was left to wander lonely halls during the summer. Most of the time, he didn't see anybody other than Mrs. Kernester and occasionally Mrs. Murphy over the hot months. Students came and went throughout the years, but no long-term friends really stuck, and Mrs. Murphey never let Harold go into town alone. Nobody visited him either, and there was hardly anything to do.

School months were so much more exciting. There were people everywhere, and things to do. Old, jaded Galidemus suddenly became fresh and new. And this year, now that he attended Galidemus as a student, it would be even harder to return to living alone with the headmistress. He was almost dreading it. Of course, he would have Swiftless to ride now. But riding all day was hardly a reasonable way to spend time. Eventually such an activity would become mundane.

Harold preferred to focus on the pattern of his current schedule rather than the near future. And now that his schedule had finally fallen back into place, he felt like a regular student once more. There were no monsters beneath doorways. No Stark. No unconscious teachers or Ferral talk. No worries about grey hair. Nothing out of the ordinary.

That is, until one morning.

It was during Home Remedies class, the class Mrs. Kernester herself taught. Each student had taken their seats, and Harold sat with his friends, as usual. He was eager to work on some various concoctions Mrs. Kernester had talked about last class.

Mrs. Kernester stood up at the front of the class, rapping her pointer on her desk. But the moment she spoke, everything changed.

"Good morning class," she said, smiling. "Before we begin class today, I would like to introduce a new student that has joined us for the remainder of the year. I've had the honor of introducing him in *my* classes; he's demonstrated that he is quite adept at concoctions. Come on in, Juniper."

Harold hadn't yet processed his shock; he stared, eyes wide, at the back of the room where the new student was emerging. Juniper stepped from the doors to the classroom, a smirk on his face. His expression was familiar—much too familiar—and suddenly Harold felt his stomach plummet. It was Juniper—one of the night-fishers they had borrowed a boat from to catch Swiftless. Thin and much too tall to be in Harold's grade, Juniper strode swiftly to the front of the classroom. His lips were thin and pale, his skin equally so. His eyes were a piercing blue, like ice shards trapped inside his skull. His ears were slightly pointed, and he wore dark clothing. He seemed much too old to be in Harold's grade. But possibly the most intriguing part about him was his hair: a light grey, slicked back on his head with gel and comb.

Harold could feel the air leave the room. Another grey-hair? What was going on? Harold shared a glance with Petunia, Snip, and Carnis. Snip was so surprised, his mouth hung agape, frozen in position. Harold reminded himself to keep a low profile. Hopefully, Juniper wouldn't recognize them.

With long strides, he strode to the front of the class and took a stand directly in front of Mrs. Kernester. She grasped his shoulder and took a deep breath, a smile on her face.

"Now, class. I know this might seem shocking, but you know firsthand that grey hair is not a direct indicator of the Ferrals." A murmur went through the classroom as she said the word.

"No one truly knows how one gets grey hair, unless of course you are a Ferral yourself," she continued. "I expect nothing but hospitality toward Juniper. If he feels offended by any one of you, it is his right to report the activity to me. And there will be consequences. Am I clear?"

Harold watched as stiff necks complied. This was crazy—another grey-hair. While he believed Snip wasn't a Ferral, Juniper was utterly suspicious. It was lunacy to invite such a person into the school. With Snip, it was different. Everybody knew he was harmless. But accepting Juniper was taking it too far.

"One last thing," Mrs. Kernester added, "Juniper's father is a night-fisher. He will be joining us as one of our own: an Algae."

The class silenced. Two grey-hairs in one class? It must be cursed. Harold felt like a deflated balloon. Things couldn't get any worse. They had just been returning to normal, and now, all of a sudden, they were changing once more beneath Harold's terrified eyes.

Juniper strode to the back of the classroom to take a seat. As he passed Harold's desk, he felt Juniper's cloak brush his face. He tore his eyes from Juniper's gray hair and noticed the cloak he was wearing—it looked familiar.

How had he not noticed it before?

It was the cloak he left in the boat.

Harold gasped, then trying to hide his surprise, ducked his head. Juniper only tipped his face to the side, locking his icy eyes with Harold's, a glimmer of irritation within.

He knows, Harold thought. *He knows*.

"It doesn't make sense," Petunia said, waving her fork in the air. She was chewing something made of potatoes, thinking aloud.

"Another grey-hair?" Carnis asked, scrunching his nose.

"Hey, Snip isn't even close to resembling Juniper," Petunia smirked.

"Of course not," Carnis shrugged, "but I'm just saying the hair is a dead giveaway."

"People are going to start thinking they're brothers," Petunia frowned, "which means I'll be the sister of two lunatic cannibal creatures. At least that's what everyone will say."

"That's a bit dramatic," Harold pointed out.

"Yeah, well, all of this is a bit dramatic, don't you think?"

Harold chuckled. "I guess so."

Snip shook his head. "I never thought I'd see another normal, civil grey-hair in my life."

"I agree," Petunia nodded, taking another bite.

"Well, he definitely knows about *me*," Harold groaned.

"What do you mean?" Carnis asked, cheeks bursting with potatoes.

"Do you remember how I left my cloak in the boat when we were going to save Swiftless?"

Petunia gasped, putting her hand over her mouth. "Oh no!"

"Oh, yes."

"Why do these things always have to happen?" Petunia cried.

Snip and Carnis looked as if they had just received a death sentence.

"Okay, no offense," Carnis said. "But I think I'll keep my distance while you're being hunted down by a teen Ferral."

"I won't be hunted," Harold reassured, not feeling very assured himself. "I'm one of many. There are obviously other Harolds in Galidemus."

"Not many. I've never met one. He'll find you."

Harold shuddered. Juniper was bigger than him, taller than him, probably had a grudge against him, *and* shared a dormitory with him. It was a recipe for disaster.

He fingered his hair in frustration. Things had just been returning to normalcy. He'd been busy with normal responsibilities again, and he almost enjoyed it. But now. . .

"So he has grey hair. He looks old. He looks mean. He's joining at the end of the year," Harold assessed. "But he could be like Snip. Friendly, not dangerous. He could just be poor, and that's why he was wearing my cloak. He might not have even looked at the tag yet. He could just be . . . normal."

"Why is he so old, then?" Petunia asked. "He looks at least two or three years older than us, and that's being generous."

"Growth spurt?"

"Harold, be serious."

"Fine," Harold sighed, "I don't know. He could be a spy. A Ferral spy. Mr. Porthand said the Ferrals would come after me at some point."

"Maybe he's after all the food," Carnis said. "That would be the end of the *world*."

They all looked at Carnis. There was a long moment of silence.

"He's going after the food? Really?" Petunia asked, rolling her eyes.

"We have some good food here at Galidemus," Carnis said, throwing up his hands. "That's all I'm saying. And food is vital. At least, I think it is. Food is the reason I wake up every morning."

Harold stared, bewildered, at Carnis. How could they be such good friends when they were so different? It was a mystery.

"Carnis," Petunia began, but she was interrupted by her own laughter. She chuckled hopelessly until everyone was laughing, and in Carnis's case, choking on the large amount of potatoes in his mouth.

Harold rubbed his temples in giddy desperation. "Yes, food is vital!"

Petunia smiled, "It's literally the reason we *all* wake up every morning!"

Juniper's appearance was so baffling, he could be after the food for all they knew. But after they had their laugh, the question still remained: Who was Juniper?

"Do you think he's up to something?" Carnis asked.

"I think so," Harold answered, "but what, I don't know. I mean, Mrs. Kernester wouldn't invite a villain into the school willingly."

"I don't know, mate," Carnis shrugged.

"Wait, you don't think Mrs. Kernester would—"

"No, nothing like that," Petunia said, putting her hand on Harold's arm.

"But you can't deny she's been acting kind of strange lately," Carnis sighed.

Harold couldn't deny it. "I'm sure we can trust her, guys. I've been living with her all my life."

"I don't know," Petunia said. "It's hard to know who to trust these days."

CHAPTER FOURTEEN

Slug Slime

Harold skidded across the dormitory floor, soles squeaking on the oily surface. His shoes slipped and slid as he tried to gain his balance. He gritted his teeth, clenched his fists, and waited until he skidded to a halt. He looked ridiculous. Thankfully, nobody was in the dormitory except him. He would just have to be patient, or he would fall onto the slicked floor, covering himself in slug slime.

Ever since Juniper had enrolled at Galidemus, he proved to be a slippery criminal; committing petty crimes almost every day and slipping between the teacher's fingers like sand every time. He was a trickster that had gone one step too far, to the point where what was annoying had become dangerous. It had only been a dozen days since the mysterious figure had joined the Algaes, but in that short time, he had gotten away with several pranks, mostly aimed at Harold, for some reason.

This was not the first time slug slime had coated the floor. Juniper had also stuffed Harold's boots with mud and dipped his socks in toilet water. He had even gone as far as to put ice in all the dormitory drawers, soaking everyone's clothes.

The most annoying thing about him was that he was as slippery as a slug himself. He always got away. There was no way to prove Juniper had done any of it. He acted like a studious angel in front of the teachers. Most of the time, the mayhem was blamed on other boys in the dormitory; they seemed more likely suspects than *Juniper*. Harold hadn't been blamed for anything yet, being the one targeted half the time, but it was only a matter of time.

It was obvious Juniper was targeting Harold for *some* reason. He took every chance he could get to make Harold's life miserable. Today it was slug slime. His least favorite.

If anything had improved since Juniper arrived, it was that Puella seemed to lie low. Juniper was cunning, quick, and slippery. He out-bullied her ten times over. Harold couldn't tell if she kept her distance out of shy admiration or vengeful contempt, but frankly, he didn't care.

Harold slid across the floor for several long moments, his legs tense with impatience, and finally bumped against the wall. He then carefully guided himself across the room, using furniture to direct him. It was a tedious process, but at least it wasn't as bad as the last time when the whole floor had been coated before sunrise. The other Algae students had been slipping around all morning, scrambling to get to class in time, feet covered in thick slime.

Juniper was unpleasant to sleep with, too. He didn't snore; in fact, he was completely silent, but Harold found it hard to rest with him in the same room. He only talked to teachers, avoiding fellow students like they were vermin. He was perfectly respectful to his elders, but didn't even acknowledge the boys in his dormitory, and was quiet— eerily quiet.

Juniper also wore Harold's cloak wherever he went. It was as if he was rubbing it in Harold's face. He didn't even take it off when he slept, which made stealing it back difficult. But what would it prove if Harold stole it? Juniper had targeted him so much, it was obvious he knew it was Harold's cloak.

Stealing it back would be a foolish risk, too. Juniper had fully taken advantage of Mrs. Kernester's protection. If anyone lifted a finger against him, he would report the incident. And Mrs. Kernester wasn't light on punishment. Of course, she was gracious, but less so than Harold had ever seen before. Many students had been punished when they hadn't done a thing, and sometimes the entire dormitory faced the consequences. Carnis had been in trouble more than a few times, having to clean toilets and write apologies and mop up slug slime for things he never did. Harold felt bad for him.

And to make matters even stranger, nobody knew where Juniper found all the stuff he was using. Where did he get three buckets of slug slime when everyone was confined to the school property? Where did he find so much ice? And how in the world did he coat the entire floor before sunrise? It was baffling.

Harold slid into the dormitory's shared desk, taking a seat. He examined the bottoms of his shoes, which were slicked in gooey slime. Now his feet would squish every time he walked. He cursed under his breath, then tried to focus on his studying. So far, he knew there was biology and boating homework left, and a little math. He hadn't even started.

He groaned, looking up at the ceiling to clear his head. He couldn't focus under these circumstances. In his frustrated state, every word and number blended together. He slapped his books closed, packing up his things. Then he swung his book bag over his shoulder, and stood up, knees shaking.

The ground swam beneath him, a great thick pool of slime. He took a cautious step forward, but the action sent his foot skidding along farther than he intended, until he was nearly doing the splits. Harold was *really* glad he was the only one in the room, now. Trying to stabilize himself without falling into the huge puddle of slime, he stepped again. His sole slipped, sending him sailing to the floor, and before he could blink, he was sitting in the goo, despite all his efforts. Harold groaned. Now he would look like he had just wet his pants.

Seeing the dormitory stairs three strides away, Harold decided getting his hands messy was inevitable. He smacked them down on the floor and inched his way across the commons.

Finally, Harold reached the door to the stairs, hands, pants, and shoes coated in gel. Trying his best to stand up, he turned the doorknob with some effort, and swung the door open. Slicked stairs, greased in slime, cascaded before his eyes. He cursed again, not caring who heard anymore. Juniper had gone too far this time. Some unfortunate student really would get sacked for this one. Maybe Carnis.

Harold grabbed the handrail and began his slow descent.

Harold peeked into the Animal Studies classroom. The rest of the students were already seated, spraying their maggots in defuming solution. After sleeping in and getting sabotaged with slime again, he was painfully late and frustrated.

He quietly slipped through the door and sat at his usual place, pants still wet. His maggot, Lard, was already writhing on his desk.

"Why, hello there, Peter!" Mrs. Vera smiled at Harold as if he was right on time. "We're just giving them a good scrub now. There's a brush on your desk."

Harold picked up his brush, and with a grimace, started scrubbing dead skin off of Lard. The maggots would be mulching soon. Carnis scooted his desk closer to Harold's, and Petunia and Snip did the same. They were already scrubbing their maggots, trying to hold their breath.

"Harold," Petunia scolded, "you're nearly half an hour late! What happened?"

Harold sighed. "It wasn't my fault. Had an incident with you-know-who."

"Oh, no," Petunia exclaimed. "Not the slug slime again."

"He even greased the stairs!" Harold growled, but not too loudly; Juniper was seated just across the room.

"Great," Carnis mumbled. "Now *I'll* get in trouble again. You said the stairs, too? I'm in for it."

Harold exhaled in frustration.

"You look like you wet your pants," Snip said.

"Thank you, Snip, for pointing that out!" Harold said.

"What? I'm just saying…"

There was a long moment of silence, filled with the constant rustle of the students scrubbing their maggots. Cleaning maggots seemed wrong, more wrong than naming them. The creatures were already so filthy, cleaning them didn't do much good.

Harold sighed. "Taking care of these things makes me sick to my stomach."

Petunia and Snip began to chuckle at their predicament. Harold just laughed, shaking his head.

After a while, they continued to scrub in silence and their smiles wore off.

"I wish Juniper wasn't here," Harold whispered after a while. "He gives me the creeps."

Carnis shrugged, still in a funny mood. "We don't *always* get what we want, Harold. Like at lunch yesterday. Did I want the whole pie to myself? Yes, I did. Did I get it? No, I didn't."

Petunia rolled her eyes. "Carnis, that pie was meant for half of the Algae table, including us. And it was a massive pie."

Carnis twirled his thumbs. "Just my size," he nodded. "I'm a growing boy."

"Maybe you're growing a bit too much," Petunia smirked, "at least horizontally."

"Hey, I'm skinny as a chicken!" Carnis said.

"Chicken aren't skinny," Harold pointed out.

"Fine," Carnis smirked, "I'm as skinny as a *skinny* chicken."

"That's still not very skinny," Harold chuckled. "How skinny are you thinking? Is this chicken anorexic?"

"Fine, an earthworm. Whatever."

"That's better," Petunia approved.

Harold chuckled under his breath. Even when the world seemed to be crashing down around them, they still managed to laugh at it.

Harold liked to practice early on Swiftless before riding class began. With his own key, it was easy to visit Swiftless during his free hours. Of course, Ms. Dywood disapproved of him even owning a key, but Mrs. Kernester wasn't bothered. It was one of the few things Harold looked forward to every day. Flying Swiftless offered another world at his fingertips. It was his favorite pastime, and he made a point to ride daily.

Harold jogged up to the stalls, whistling down the path and into the little clearing where the sheds were lined up. Usually no one joined him when he practiced, so he never expected to see anyone. Today, however, a figure riding a silver dragonfly was flying where Harold usually did, zipping around cattails and reeds.

Harold had never seen such precision. The mysterious rider was not only fast, but so accurate it gave Harold chills.

A bit curious, Harold crept behind some grass, watching as the rider spun and sped across the skies. It was rare to find another rider out practicing, especially in the middle of the day. The rider could even be a professional racer, for all Harold knew. The thought made Harold quiver with excitement; Swiftless could wait a moment or two. Maybe he could glean some riding tips if he watched. He often heard that professionals liked to keep their training methods secret. So he laid down in the grass, watching the strange figure intently, eyes glued to the silver dragonfly.

After a few minutes had passed, Harold noticed the rider was practicing a certain routine. He even memorized a bit of it. The rider first shot into the sky, nearly to a point where Harold couldn't see him anymore. Then he would dive down, a sort of fake sword or stick in his hand, thrusted in a fighting stance. After he reached a certain point on the attack, he would pull his sword up and turn back down into the reeds. He disappeared in the reeds for a while, shot out farther North, and did the pattern over again. The precision was so sharp, it was almost identical every time he repeated the loop.

Harold was at first mesmerized with the performance. But after a few runs, he realized it would be smart to write the pattern down. He wanted to record the movements so he could try them on Swiftless later. He hastily pulled out his notebook and pen, and scribbled down the pattern as best he could. The second he was finished, he gazed up into the sky where the rider was still practicing. He wanted to watch until riding class began, if he could. The athlete would surely be scared away by the class on the ground when the other students arrived.

A few minutes went by before the rider broke his pattern. He appeared to have finished, and descended to the ground, toward Harold and the stalls. Harold wanted to stand up and wave the pro away, to tell him this was school property, but curiosity held him firm. He ducked his head so only his eyes were peeking above the tall, green grass.

Down the rider came, landing on the far side of the stalls, face obscured by shadows. He was too far away for Harold to tell what he looked like, but he was tall and draped in a black cloak.

Then Harold realized who the rider was. He was frozen with shock.

The rider was Juniper.

Juniper stepped off his silver dragonfly, grey hair slicked back in the wind. With a grimace, he kicked his dragonfly back into his shed, slamming the door behind him. Harold winced for the dragonfly. But this didn't make sense at all! Juniper had flown so well, it *couldn't* be him—yet here he was, strutting between rows of shacks, stripping off his riding gloves in irritation.

Suddenly, Juniper started coming his way. Harold ducked even further into the grass, trying to hide as best he could. He was glad for his green, tufty hair; it looked much like grass itself.

Juniper didn't even look his way, and strode past unknowingly. After he had disappeared up over the hill, Harold crept out of hiding. He was still so baffled he nearly forgot about Swiftless. Juniper was a professional rider! Now, Harold was even more skeptical of his character. Why had he been riding in those patterns? And why was he so good at flying? Who had given him his own key to practice just like him? And why had he done the whole thing in secrecy, coming during the hours Harold came, the hours Harold knew to be the calmest of the day?

Shaking his head, Harold headed for Swiftless's shed. He could hear his eager buzzing inside, and the noise made him smile. While he fished in his pocket for his key, he noticed movement out over the hills. It looked like the rest of the students were on their way over. Class would start as soon as they made it down the hill. Swiftless would have to wait.

CHAPTER FIFTEEN

Punishment

"**H**arold, can you please tell me the difference between a Sapling and a Bogbug?"

Harold snapped back to attention. "What? Oh, right. Er—one is smaller than the other?"

"Precisely," Ms. Dywood said, flashing a tight smile. She had just arrived at the stalls for riding class and started firing random questions at the students as a sort of pop quiz. The students sat on the squishy mat of moss next to the stalls, huddled together in the chilling breeze. Ms. Dywood liked to have a quick lecture and discussion before her students actually got on their dragonflies. The routine annoyed Harold most days, but today he was glad for the lesson.

He had been focusing on the flight pattern scribbled in his notebook ever since he had seen the class coming, hoping to uncover some secret, but he remained stumped. With class in session, he hadn't been able to tell Petunia, Carnis, and Snip about it, so he studied it on his own during class, taking the risk of being caught in the act.

"Now, Saplings are definitely the slowest of the dragonflies," Ms. Dywood droned on, "and Bogbugs are the least pleasant. They stink like garbage, and nobody rides them. Only a few ride Saplings; they're so slow and *clumsy*, but they are a bit more pleasant than Bogbugs. Am I right, Harold?"

Harold looked up and nodded. Ms. Dywood seemed to be focusing on Harold a little more than usual this class. Hearing her chatter about slow and clumsy Saplings stung Harold's ears. But he didn't say a word. She continued her rant, until Juniper stuck up an arm. He had apparently returned to the stalls with the other students.

"Yes, Juniper?" Ms. Dywood responded with a smile.

"Not to bother you," Juniper said in his poisonous, silky voice, "but Harold doesn't appear to be taking notes."

"Dear Harold," she said yet again, sweet like rotten fruit, "are you taking notes?"

Harold inhaled sharply. He tucked his poison deeper into his shirt. He hoped no one could see it glowing through his shirt. Couldn't they just leave him alone?

"Yes," he lied, averting his eyes from her.

"When you talk to me, you look me straight in the eye," she snapped.

Harold focused his gaze on her. For several moments, no one said anything as the two glared at each other. All fell silent; even the wind seemed to stop whistling.

"Let me see," she finally said, walking over to Harold. She yanked the book from his grasp and began thumbing through the pages.

"What's this? Up, down, reeds, up. Gibberish." She continued to look through the pages while Harold held his breath. Hopefully Juniper hadn't heard what she had just said. Or if he had, hopefully he thought it was gibberish, too. "I don't see anything about dragonflies or riding at all in here," she finally said. "But look here, this must be some sort of diary!"

Harold knew this notebook was definitely not a diary. He'd never kept a diary in his life. So why was Ms. Dywood toying with him?

"It says here," she continued, "'I think Ms. Dywood is the best teacher I have.'"

Harold's cheeks flushed. He'd never say anything like that. He could hear chuckles throughout the clearing, including Carnis's voice. What was she doing?

"And look here," Ms. Dywood said, "I think her hair is so pretty I wish with all my heart I could comb it myself! And her voice is so soft—"

"I *did not* write that!" Harold yelled, standing up and glaring into her face.

"Oh, lying now, are we?" Ms. Dywood smiled. Harold glimpsed a pen in her hand. She always had one in her ear; it must be convenient in times like these. He clenched his fists.

"*You* wrote that in there!"

"Look, students," Ms. Dywood smiled, holding open his notebook for everyone to see, "right here. Who do you think wrote that? Not me, so who else?"

By now, the whole class was doubled over laughing. The only people quiet were Petunia and Snip. Petunia gave Harold an apologetic smile. Harold couldn't stand it anymore. He raced over to Ms. Dywood and snatched the notebook and the pen right from her hands. He yanked the cap off the pen and wrote furiously inside while saying it aloud, "Ms. Dywood is ugly! Ms. Dywood is horrible! She's a slug with a dress on! She's a Bogbug herself! She smells like garbage, and she's so disgusting, she could be a Slug-Spotter!"

The class was howling with laughter. Petunia and Snip were chuckling by now. Everyone but Ms. Dywood was smiling. Her hair turned the deepest, darkest crimson Harold had ever seen.

"Harold, you'll get detention for the rest of the year! You'll get expelled! You'll . . . you'll—" She took a deep breath that threatened murder, calming her hair to a slightly lighter red.

"You will be scrubbing the saddles today, Harold," she said through clenched teeth. "And Carnis will join you. The Parker twins too, I believe. You seem to enjoy their company. I will see you four after class."

The class fell silent. Carnis grumbled loudly so both Ms. Dywood and Harold could hear. Petunia and Snip's faces fell. Harold sat back down, ears bright red. He still clutched his notebook, holding it so tightly his knuckles turned white.

"Now, who remembers the typical Lightning Back colors?" Ms. Dywood continued, her voice clipped, but Harold heard no more. He covered his ears and ignored the rest of what Ms. Dywood had to say. He didn't look at his notebook, either.

After Ms. Dywood had finished her lecture, they mounted their dragonflies and practiced independently. Harold couldn't believe what he had just been assigned. There were *hundreds* of saddles in the stalls, one for every person who attended Galidemus, except for the Royals. He was upset about having to clean so much, but he was even more upset that his friends were being punished, because they didn't deserve it. Although secretly, he was glad they were coming. This way, the work could be done faster, and he would have company, even if they were upset with him.

No words were exchanged between him, his friends, or Ms. Dywood for the rest of the class. Harold tried to apologize to his friends, but they just ignored him. This wasn't his fault, was it? Ms. Dywood had provoked him, and he had retaliated. He knew he had probably been stupid in the heat of the moment, but Ms. Dywood couldn't just get away with false accusations like that.

Yet Harold knew there would be no consequence for her. Anger boiled inside of him until class was finally dismissed, and everyone left except for him, his downcast friends, and Ms. Dywood. All fell silent as she picked up her things, a fraudulent smile on her lips, going at a painfully slow pace. When she was finally done, she gestured the students over. Harold responded with rigid obedience.

"Now, you little rats," Ms. Dywood growled, "you have the rest of the afternoon to scrub every saddle in this complex until they are spotless. You have until dinner time, and because of your audacity, I won't be excusing you from class so you will be marked absent. I'll come and fetch you when your time is up."

Carnis moaned, "That's impossible! We've only got a couple of hours!"

"Not my problem," she snapped. "You have a deadline. So get moving. And one more thing," she smiled, pointing to the scrubs and buckets full of water and soap she had supplied for them. There were only four. "If even *one* saddle isn't clean, I will notice. And if the job isn't done in time, I'll have you scrub the bathrooms of the entire school later. Am I understood?"

Harold nodded stiffly. This was ridiculous, impossible. They had just over three hours, and they had to clean at least five hundred saddles. If they were lucky, they could get maybe a third of the work done. But what she was asking for was ridiculous. It looked like they would be scrubbing toilets over the weekend.

Ms. Dywood nodded, raising to her full, wiry height, like a great spindly spider, and walked away over the hills back to Galidemus. "I'll be back," she called over her bony shoulder.

Harold shuddered, picking up a bucket and scrub. His friends did the same, and they all began scrubbing, each picking a saddle. Ms. Dywood had conveniently dumped all the saddles. with the help of the class, in a huge pile in front of the stalls. It towered inches above Harold's head, and spread at least four times his height in diameter. Harold began to scrub a simple one with teal embroidery. He wished he could lighten the mood. His friends looked miserable.

"At least Royals don't have dragonflies," he said, forcing a smile. "And a lot of students don't even have saddles."

Petunia nodded faintly.

"That woman is evil," Carnis grumbled.

"Carnis, shut up," Petunia frowned. "It's already miserable. Don't make it worse."

Harold exhaled; this was all his fault.

"I'm really sorry," he tried to apologize. "I had no idea she would do something so *severe*."

"Next time, don't get distracted in class," Petunia said.

"Look, Juniper was flying in the strangest pattern, and I was trying to find out what it meant," Harold protested.

"Right that instant?" Petunia asked. "You couldn't wait until class was over? You know how cruel she is. And you *still* risked it!"

"I know," Harold admitted. "I said I was sorry."

"What if it gets cold out here?" Snip asked. "Will we be stuck out here?"

"Only until dinner," Carnis reminded him, "which isn't nearly enough time to finish this job."

"Well, let's focus," Harold said, tired of listening to their griping. "We might be able to get this done. We can't just give up."

So they scrubbed. The sun sank lower and lower in the sky as the friends cleaned. They cleaned a lot faster than Harold had expected. He could clean a saddle in one or two minutes, as could his friends. It looked like the saddles had been recently washed, so they weren't too dirty. But after an hour and a half, they were not yet halfway done scrubbing.

No one spoke as they cleaned. Harold's hands quickly became pruney and wrinkled like pale raisins. The extra texture helped him grip the slippery leather easier, but his fingers soon lost feeling in the cold soapy water. It didn't take long for his pants to get soaked, and then his shoes, until his feet lost their feeling, too. A steady cool breeze blew from the pond, making him shiver. Soon, everyone was freezing cold. Snip began to shake. Petunia's hands quivered.

But still they scrubbed, stacking their cleaned saddles in a neat little pile behind them. Eventually the sun sank down below the horizon, and Harold knew they didn't have much time left to work. They had about fifty saddles left to clean, maybe a little more. But they also didn't have much more than half an hour to complete their task. He scrubbed as fast as he could, digging hard into the seams of the saddles to get rid of the grime. He couldn't believe how much they had already achieved in the time they had been given, but finishing in time looked bleak. They would have to clean double time. Still, they scrubbed tirelessly, never pausing for drink or rest. The muscles in their arms seared with pain and their hands ached from holding the scrubber in the same position for so long. Harold's injured shoulder was throbbing as he pumped his arm back and forth. Ten minutes left. Twenty more saddles.

"My hands look like sausages," Carnis whined, "*and* I'm starving."

"Don't even think about eating them," Petunia chuckled, "you'd regret it later."

Carnis paused his scrubbing and inspected his hand. He took a cautious lick. "Tastes like blood."

"Told you so," Petunia rolled her eyes.

"My fingers look like tiny earthworms," Snip said.

"Gross, Snip," Petunia said.

"What?" Snip retorted. "That's what they look like."

"Guys, focus," Harold said, eyes glued to the saddle he was cleaning.

They had ten saddles left and just under five minutes. Could they do it? Harold risked a peek over the hill to see if Ms. Dywood was coming. He could spot her wiry figure creeping over the hill like a vicious feline. Harold gulped.

"Hurry," he gasped, "she's coming!"

The conversation had ended. Everyone continued to scrub, focused on their work like eagles. Back and forth. Back and forth. Keep going. Ms. Dywood rounded the bend. She would enter the stall grounds any moment. She would see they hadn't finished. Four saddles left.

They each grabbed one last saddle, scrubbing as hard as they could, nearly to the point where the seams ripped. Any moment she would round that bend. Could they do it? Snip and Carnis had finished theirs, and they came over to help Harold and Petunia. Back and forth with dirty scrubs. Petunia finished. They all raced to Harold's and reached down to scrub the last saddle.

"Yoo-hoo!" Ms. Dywood called. She was rounding the bend. Snip hastily tugged the saddle from beneath their grasps and flung it to the top of the clean pile. It tottered precariously on the precipice.

Ms. Dywood came into view, her hair a silky purple. Harold guessed she was anticipating the pleasure of condemning the four students further, of course—until she saw their clean pile of saddles, sparkling in the evening sun. She froze for a moment, hair turning into a deep, evil green.

"How did you finish in time?" she demanded.

Harold was so tired he felt it difficult to respond, "We just cleaned fast."

"You cleaned fast, eh?" Ms. Dywood came closer, inspecting the tower of saddles. She marched around the glistening heap and circled back to the students.

"Impressive," she smiled, but it was not a smile of happiness or pride. It was a scheming smile. Swift, like the tail of a snake, she tapped the bottom of the pile with the tip of her boot. Harold would have missed it if he hadn't been paying such close attention to her. But that little tap, that small kick, sent the tower teetering, swaying back and forth above their heads. There was a moment when time seemed to stand still as they stared in horror at the falling tower. Then...

CRASH!

Down came the pile into the dirt, every saddle skidding into the earth and mixing with the mud. All their hard work gone to waste, stranded on the ground. A cloud of dust billowed up around the destruction, and when it cleared, Ms. Dywood's eyes gleamed at them.

"Unfortunate," she shrugged, "unfortunate indeed. Maybe next time you won't be so hasty to stack them so high, will you now?"

Harold was frozen in fury. He stared at the riding instructor with fury in his eyes.

"You *liar*! The pile was just fine—you kicked it, I swear!"

"Harold, you know it is rude to swear," she chuckled.

Petunia waved the dust from her vision and glared at Ms. Dywood. "You sicken me," she growled. "You're abusing your power!"

Ms. Dywood clutched her chest as if it were a personal insult. "Petunia! Such rude words. No teacher would do such a thing!"

"You just did!" Carnis growled. "We played your game. We did your punishment. What more do you want from us?"

Ms. Dywood snickered. "I'll see you next Monday," she purred.

"More detention?" Carnis howled. "We finished the job like you asked. You kicked that pile, not us! Why are you so . . . so . . . evil?"

"Evil!" Ms. Dywood smiled, "no, not evil. Just strict, yes, strict. You children need to learn a thing or two about punishment. I'm sick of you getting away with things when you deserve much worse. Harold especially. Just because he's a teacher's pet doesn't mean he can't get in in trouble."

Harold glared at Ms. Dywood. He *hated* her. He wanted to punch her in the face, or swipe at her feet, but he knew if he moved a finger, she would just punish them more—or even expel them. He restrained himself, staring at the ground. Ms. Dywood chuckled at their dirty faces.

"You may go and eat your dinner, now, if there is any left," she spat. "I'll see you on Monday. . . Don't be mistaken. You deserve punishment. And you will get punishment. Harsher than you've ever experienced in your soft, little lives."

And with that, she marched away, back up the hill, toward Galidemus. Harold didn't move until she was out of sight.

"Soft little lives," he spat as they marched back home. "She knows nothing about me."

CHAPTER SIXTEEN

The Monster Returns

The castle was so quiet, Harold could hear his own breathing. He chose to skip dinner, even though he was starving. He needed to find a quiet place to think.

The halls were mostly abandoned during the dinner hour, so Harold decided to think while he meandered around. As he walked, he noticed he still hadn't unclenched his fists. He opened them, his nails leaving little crescent-shaped impressions in his palm. His hands ached and his palms were raw. The parts that weren't still wrinkled had dried into tough, pink skin that cracked when he moved. It was painful to do little more than wriggle his fingers.

Why did Ms. Dywood hate him so much? He hadn't done anything to her. So why was she so cruel and ruthless? She got away with humiliating him in front of the only people he knew—*and* she punished them for no reason.

And why was Juniper now the center of attention? Harold's ears reddened at the thought of Juniper's tricks and schemes. Mrs. Kernester only stood on the sidelines, almost silent and distracted on the matter, as if she didn't know what side she was cheering for. She completely ignored Harold most of the time. Harold knew she was busy, but now—now, it was like she was purposely avoiding him.

He took a sharp turn into a long hall. The wall at the end seemed so far away. Harold sighed as he started down the chamber, feet dragging as if he were walking through mud.

He was mad. He was tired of hiding behind a facade, pretending all the changes around him weren't infuriating.

He was mad at Ms. Dywood and Juniper. He was mad at Mrs. Kernester. He was even mad at his friends for being so unforgiving of his mistakes. He was mad at Mr. Porthand for keeping the truth about his life hidden for so long. The very things that defined him had been secret for *years*.

He wished he knew nothing about the monster beneath the door or about Stark. He wished he wasn't related to Golgothar, and he wished he didn't have to put up with Puella and Juniper and all the confusion of grey hair, of who he was, or who he was supposed to be. He wished he could just ride Swiftless in the wind, carefree, never having to worry about detention and secrets and confusion. He felt hopelessly incapable of fixing things and hopelessly confused.

Harold swung a leg at the stone wall, stubbing his foot. He cursed aloud, kicked again, and stubbed his other toe. Couldn't he just stop? This was ridiculous; it was a child's tantrum. He kicked again. Hot tears stung his eyes. He thought of everything he was mad at. He was mad at everything.

He ran down the long hall, coming to a set of stairs. Through his tears, he couldn't see where the stairs led, but he didn't care. He climbed them anyway. There was no one in the hall at the top. The castle was empty.

Empty.

Wasn't there anyone in the whole world he could lean on? Not just school friends, but deeper than that. Could he lean on his friends, Carnis, Petunia, and Snip? Probably. But he was so mad and frustrated he didn't think so. He knew lots of people loved him and cared about him, but. . .

Where was his mother? Gone forever. His father was evil. He had killed her. He had left Harold with the sting of being an orphan. He had been abandoned with an aging headmistress too busy to do anything with him. Too busy to understand him as a mother would understand her son. They were more like teacher and student. No family bond bridged between them. He was alone. He sat down on the cold stone floor. It was so cold. He looked around. Walls everywhere. Why so many walls? To keep him in. . .

Sobs racked his chest. In all of the world, was there anyone? Was he alone? Curling up into a tight little ball, he lay there, crying for everything. He was spiraling into nothingness. No mother. No father. No home.

Harold glanced up and down the hall. It went on for a long way. He couldn't remember how long he had been crying, but no one had passed by. That made him feel even more alone. Why was he here? Why was everything so confusing? Or was he just crazy?

He buried his head between his knees, staring at the cold stone floor. That was when the words entered his mind. It was Mr. Porthand, the night he had first flown Swiftless. He remembered what he had said:

"Harold, you know if anything goes wrong, I will be here for you. I always have. You are never alone. I am always here for you. So are Carnis and the Parker twins. You are important, Harold, much more important than you think."

Harold brushed his eyes with his sleeve, his breath shaking. He wasn't alone. He had Carnis and Petunia and Snip. He had Mr. Porthand and Swiftless.

Standing up to a dark hallway, Harold felt refreshed. His anger evaporated and the confusion melted. Now he felt stronger than ever before.

Looking around with puffy eyes, Harold finally recognized the hallway he was in. It was close to Mr. Porthand's old classroom. He remembered it vaguely, but it was no different from the other classrooms in Galidemus. It wouldn't hurt to explore, would it? He would just peek inside to see what was going on in the abandoned classroom.

Harold marched down the hall, keeping his bloodshot eyes to the floor, glad no one was on the other side. He reached the door in a few moments, but it looked different from last time.

As he got closer, Harold noticed that the door had grown. It reached to the ceiling and was twice his arm's span in width, made of solid oak.

Why had they changed the door? It smelled terrible farther down the hall. Familiar, yet strange. What was that awful smell?

Harold crept closer. The smell was repulsive, like the salty reek of something that had died. He could feel his stomach churning. But he was too curious to turn away. He stepped closer and closer until he was standing right in front of the huge door. The reek was almost unbearable. He was just about to look inside, when something rose from the dust.

A voice.

"*Death . . . Bloooood . . .*"

All of a sudden, Harold was on the floor, retching dry heaves. He tried to claw himself back to his feet, but his legs wouldn't respond. He tried to grasp the handle on the door above him, but his arms were rigid. Sweat began to bead on his brow. Terror clung to his eyes.

"Stop it," he growled, nearly whispering. "No!"

"*Human Bloooood . . .*"

The voice was louder than before, more penetrating than when he had last heard it. His mind was on fire, searing every neuron, every nerve. Harold wanted to scream, but nothing came out but a faint whisper. Was this a dream? It was real, indeed. He could feel the cold stone floor beneath his palms, the sticky sweat smudging on his legs and mixing with the dirt on the floor.

"*Kill . . . Come to me—*"

"Cut it out!" Harold managed, trying his best to force a bravery he didn't feel. But it was like everything was drained from him, like he was nothing more than an empty shell. He cried out in agony, staggering to his feet. He wouldn't—couldn't—it was the monster again—

He slumped against the opposite wall, using his hands to steady himself.

"*Harold . . .*"

"Go away!" he shouted.

"*Kill . . . time.*"

Harold forced his legs into a forward motion. They responded suddenly, powered by terror. His own limbs felt foreign, like they belonged to someone else. But they were taking him away, and that was all that mattered. He ran faster and faster, not daring to look back.

He climbed some stairs, entered several new hallways, took some turns, but never stopped. He didn't pass anyone.

He entered a hall lined with doors, but he was too shaken to recognize it. He could still hear the voice, whispering in his ears, calling out to him.

Harold risked a glance back to see if the monster was following him. The hall was empty, yet Harold could sense it wasn't. He glued his eyes to the path behind him, legs running . . . running . . . mind racing . . . racing. . .

SMACK!

Harold fell to the floor, rubbing his forehead. He ran right into the end of the hall, and a humble door stood in front of him. It was normal-sized, but Harold still scrambled away from it in terror. He was still on his back when the door was answered by a half-shaved Mr. Porthand, standing in striped pajamas.

"Harold!" Mr. Porthand said, startled. "What are you doing here? You look terrible!"

All Harold could do was claw his way inside the room, still on the floor. Mr. Porthand helped him to his feet and led him inside, setting him on the bed. Harold sat, afraid his legs might collapse. He was safe.

"What happened?" Mr. Porthand asked, handing Harold a glass of water. Harold accepted it eagerly, but found he could only sip lightly before feeling like he was going to get sick again. His hands trembled.

"The monster," Harold managed to respond. His lips tasted salty and his breath felt cold.

"The what?" Mr. Porthand said, gripping Harold's shoulder.

Harold swallowed, suppressing the urge to vomit. "The door," Harold whispered.

"Take a rest," Mr. Porthand ordered, laying Harold's head down gingerly on the pillow. Even though the bed was scanty, it felt like a heavenly embrace. He nodded his thanks, though he was doubtful Mr. Porthand even noticed the faint gesture. The last thing Harold saw was his frowning face looking down at him.

Harold's eyes flickered open. Where was he? He was drenched in sweat and lying in an unfamiliar bed. He tried to sit up, but found it difficult, so instead, he propped himself up on one elbow. He gazed around the strange room. Mr. Porthand sat in a chair with his back to him in one corner of the small room. He was dozing, head cocked to one side of the wooden chair.

What was he doing here? He looked at the full glass of water on the nightstand, a faint candle glowing on the floor. It cast eerie shadows on the sparse furniture, quivering back and forth like cackling monsters.

Suddenly he remembered everything. A fresh wave of sweat engulfed him as he gasped for breath. He tried to remind himself he was safe here, but the voice still rang in his ears. It made him shudder; he grasped the thin sheets of the bed in fear.

"Mr. Porthand?" he whispered. His voice felt weak and cold. Mr. Porthand startled awake and stood up, rubbing his eyes. He walked to the side of the bed, frowning in worry.

"Thank God, you're awake!" he breathed a sigh of relief. "You were moving around and mumbling in your sleep. What happened out there?"

Harold managed to sit up, and Mr. Porthand sat beside him.

"Your old classroom is being used for the monster," he gasped.

"Why don't you start from the beginning," he suggested.

Harold nodded. "We were having detention with Ms. Dywood, and—"

"Who is 'we'?" Mr. Porthand interrupted.

"Me, Carnis, Petunia, and Snip," Harold clarified. He waited a moment before continuing. "After that, she gave us more detention. It was evil. We—" He paused as a wave of nausea seized him. His stomach wretched, and he leaned over the side of the bed, but nothing came up. His stomach was completely empty, which almost made it worse. "We finished our work—" he panted, "and she said we didn't."

"I see," Mr. Porthand frowned.

"I was mad," Harold explained, "and I skipped dinner to take a walk around the castle. And that's when I ran into your old classroom door. It was twice its normal size."

"Really?" Mr. Porthand asked. "Strange."

"I was curious," Harold continued, "so I thought I'd take a look, and I was about to open it when the monster started speaking to me again. *Again.* And I reacted so much stronger this time. I nearly threw up. I was on the floor. My mind was on fire. It was horrible. So, I—"

"Monster?" Mr. Porthand asked, cocking his head.

"You know, the one in Mrs. Vera's cottage."

Mr. Porthand frowned. "What are you talking about?"

There was a long moment of silence.

"I didn't tell you, did I?" Harold asked, afraid he was right.

"I don't think so."

For the next half hour, Harold told Mr. Porthand about the monster beneath the door in Mrs. Vera's cottage. Mr. Porthand was shocked about the secret Harold had hidden from him for so long. When Harold protested, saying *he* had kept secrets from *him* for his whole life, it only made him angrier. Once Harold had finished, Mr. Porthand was furious.

"So *this* what you've been keeping from me?" he asked when Harold had finished.

"Yes. I'm sorry, I really am," Harold said. "I didn't think it mattered, and I didn't want you to think I was crazy."

"Well, now I do!" Mr. Porthand said. "I think you're crazy for not telling me! This is vital, Harold! Do you know what this means?"

Harold shook his head.

"It means you're in trouble. Big trouble. And worse than detention."

There was a moment of silence.

"Look," Mr. Porthand said, "let's figure this out. The door in Mrs. Vera's cottage was small?"

"Only up to my waist, really," Harold explained.

"And the new door is big?"

"Yes," Harold shuddered. "Huge."

"Then there's our first clue. Maybe . . . this creature is growing quickly," Mr. Porthand deducted, "and it all makes sense, because I heard some construction going on down at her cottage earlier this year. It all fits. You said the creature talks to you?"

"Sort of," Harold said, not knowing how to describe what he experienced. Thinking about the voice made him shudder.

"Define 'sort of'."

"Well," Harold explained, "it doesn't have a conversation with me. It just talks to me through my mind saying stuff like blood and kill and awful things. When I plug my ears, it doesn't go away. It paralyzes me. I can't move when it's close. I can't shut it out. And it smells awful, like something died in there. It makes me sick."

"I noticed," Mr. Porthand said. He held his hand to his freshly shaven chin as he thought.

"This is not good," he finally said. "I've noticed nothing has been done to block that hall from wanderers. It's probably locked, and nothing more. And I have a feeling if other students had the same reaction to that *thing* behind the door as you did, there would be pandemonium. Yet there isn't.

"Harold, I think this monster is linked to you in some way. It's the only thing I can think of. You seem to have reacted worse the second time than the first, so the monster is getting stronger and bigger. This is no doubt an act of the Ferrals. They are going in for the kill."

"But if it is the Ferrals, how did they sneak that thing in here undetected?" Harold pressed. He didn't appreciate how Mr. Porthand had said 'going in for the kill.'

"There has to be someone among us—a Ferral. Maybe more than one. That's the only way they could have pulled this off."

"Do you think it's Ms. Dywood or Juniper?" Harold asked.

"I think it could be anybody," Mr. Porthand said. "Grey hair is not the only mark of the Ferrals, Harold. A darkened heart is the true identity, something one cannot see with eyes alone. You, of all people, should know that. But listen to me. You are the main target of the Ferrals and probably will be for the rest of your life, if you live that long. You must be extremely careful. The next couple of weeks, possibly days, could become dangerous. It's only a matter of time before the monster reaches maturity. Be prepared to run. But also be prepared to fight. Am I getting through to you?"

Harold nodded, overwhelmed. He was being hunted. He was going to die.

"Shouldn't I just leave?" he suggested, hoping he didn't have to. "If I'm the source of all this danger, why don't I just leave to save all of you? Why don't I just give myself to them?"

"I admire your bravery," Mr. Porthand said, "but your blood is much more valuable than any of ours. And this is the safest place for you right now. It would be worse for all of us if you turned yourself in. You are much more important than you could believe."

Harold nodded. He felt terrible.

"What do you think the monster is?" he asked finally. "How is it talking to me?"

Mr. Porthand ran his fingers through his brown hair. "I don't know," he admitted. "It's most likely a creature from beyond the pond, from the east. I've heard of such creatures that grow larger the more they ingest. The problem is, the more they eat, the hungrier they get, and although they love blood, they'll eat anything on hand. I've never seen one, though."

Harold gulped.

"And as for it being able to talk to you through your mind," Mr. Porthand continued, "your father is strong. Some say he is involved in dark magic, which I don't doubt. He is extremely powerful, and probably linked you and the monster together—somehow. He's done worse. Like I said, be careful. Don't pass that hall again, and don't go back to Mrs. Vera's cottage. Stay away from the smell as well."

Harold nodded again, trying to find something to say. He was at a loss of words. His mind was whirling. How had he gotten into this mess? He hadn't chosen this, but here he was.

"I can tell you're still struggling to wrap your head around it all," Mr. Porthand observed.

"A little bit," Harold admitted.

"Make sure you tell your friends about the danger," he advised. "I mean Carnis and the Parker twins. But keep it a secret from others. I don't want to cause an uproar, and I definitely don't want to be overheard by some disloyal ears. Hopefully nothing comes of this. I'm shocked the Ferrals are striking so soon. I thought they would wait until you were at least fifteen, but I suppose not. Your father is determined. I will try to stay as close as I can to protect you, but you need to be doing your part as well. If things start to look bleak, run to the north. You should find some safety there. And Harold?"

Harold lifted his eyes to Mr. Porthand's.

"Please be rational. We will be going on our first dragonfly-back hunting session tomorrow with Ms. Dywood and the entire class, and I want you to stay close. Do not wander far from the pack. Your actions could be critical to you and everything you love. I am serious. Do you understand?"

Harold nodded and tried to talk, but he felt so weak, he couldn't speak. Mr. Porthand just nodded back and patted Harold on the shoulder.

"Alright," he said, "you should get some sleep now. It's late. You might not get enough of it for the next couple of days, and rest will do you some good. Do you need help finding your way back?"

"No, no," Harold said, finding his voice. "I'll be fine."

Mr. Porthand escorted Harold to the door. Just before he left, he grasped Harold's shoulder.

"Harold, don't be afraid. Your father fears *you* above all things. Don't forget that. Sleep well."

Harold nodded and tried to smile, but his face refused to respond. So he departed on jelly legs, walking as fast as he could back to his dormitory, not even looking back at the dark corridors he traversed.

His mind raced as he lay in bed, shoes still on and clothes unchanged. How could he sleep after all that? Worries sieged his mind. How could his father fear *him* above all else? It was an impossible notion. Yet it was the one thing that kept him awake.

Finally, after what felt like hours of thinking and suffering, Harold's eyes drooped and he gave way to exhaustion. He let his seared mind rest, and slept fitfully until morning.

CHAPTER SEVENTEEN

Pagaroo

Harold slept well into the morning. He woke up confused, but eventually discovered he'd slept in when he opened his eyes to an empty dormitory. At first, he was mad that Carnis had failed to wake him up earlier, but as the day wore on, he was grateful for the extra sleep.

Morning passed uneventfully; no one bothered to ask why he had slept in so late. At lunch, Harold told Petunia, Carnis, and Snip about the night before and Mr. Porthand's warning. Harold watched as fear crept over their faces. The entire day, they kept close to one another. They stayed far away from the hall with Mr. Porthand's old classroom, and walked in groups to their classes. In class, they were quiet and distracted.

Snip was the most nervous of them all, and by the end of the day, every one of his nails had been reduced to nubs. He was so quiet and shaky that when one teacher called his name, he jumped right out of his seat. As if the day couldn't get any worse, it began to rain heavily, the kind of rain that was dangerous to the people of Orahton.

The streams of rain would have easily flooded entire towns, but Orahton had taken precautions against such things. Because of this, they only built homes on lofty places that couldn't flood. Homes had been fortified to withstand all kinds of weather.

It was damp in Galidemus. The floors were slick and the halls were humid. Not only was it uncomfortable, it was dangerous. The air was cold even inside, and dampness clung to Harold's clothes. Harold felt as if he would never be dry.

Mr. Porthand and Ms. Dywood admitted that if the rain didn't let up, there would be no dragonfly-back hunting lesson that evening. It would be unfortunate; everyone had been looking forward to their first big trip.

The field trip was supposed to start at six-thirty, and it was six o'clock now, but still pouring. Harold and his friends waited in the meal room, being one of the only rooms that had windows facing the pond, peering out at the unrelenting rain. The four of them had agreed to stick together, and the meal room was the only place they could watch the rainfall over the water without being separated.

It was unbearably chilly, and Harold sat shivering on the bench, unsure of how he wanted to spend his time. It was dark and gloomy in the whole castle from the cloud cover, and they had a single candle burning between them. Everyone else had left for the warmth of the dorms.

Everyone except Juniper, that is, who was fiddling with a dagger in the far corner of the dark room.

Juniper was deep in concentration, as if he knew something bad was about to happen. The dagger he fiddled with was a sign of danger, it seemed, and Harold's instincts tugged at him as he sat still at the table. Juniper didn't speak to them, but the fact he was there was unnerving in itself.

"Do you think the rain will ever stop?" Carnis wondered. They had all agreed to talk about trivial topics while Juniper was in the room.

"Weather like this will probably keep going well into the morning," Petunia shrugged. "But I could be wrong about the weather."

"Petunia being wrong about something? *Right.*" Carnis smirked. "That sure gives me hope." No one appreciated the sarcasm. Snip began to drum his anxious fingers on the table.

"Snip, stop that," Petunia ordered. "It makes things seem so eerie, like we're about to be attacked or something."

"We just *might* be attacked," Carnis said in a low voice, glancing at Juniper. Juniper took no notice.

"Well, *thank* you for pointing that out," Petunia grumbled. "All I'm asking is that you guys don't make this creepier than it already is."

"I don't think it can get creepier," Harold smiled. "Dark room, candle, rain, creepy guy that might kill us. The creepy guy tops it."

"Shut up!" Petunia whispered, nudging Harold in the shoulder and pointing in Juniper's direction. But Juniper was still as distracted and doleful as ever, facing the wall.

"It's also kind of damp in here," Carnis added after a pause, "and misty. Makes it hard to see. I bet anyone could creep up on us in these conditions. With a dagger, like that one he has over there."

Petunia glared at him, clutching her arm.

"Or a failed exam," Snip chuckled. "Those can freak her out sometimes. Especially if they're her own. But I've seen her flip out with mine, too."

"Wait, are you telling me you're afraid of failed tests even if they're not your own?"

Carnis laughed. "You must be terrified of me and Harold!"

"Hey," Harold protested, "I don't fail nearly as much as you!"

"Guys," Petunia frowned, holding out some cards she had pulled from her bag, "you are not entertaining in the slightest. It drives me crazy when you get like this. Grow up and play some Pagaroo with me."

Carnis and Harold usually hated Pagaroo, but they didn't have anything else to do. And so Petunia fooled them again, and they all prepared to play Pagaroo, the card game for kindergartners.

Pagaroo was a simple game of luck. The deck consisted of cards bearing the four occupations in Orahton: the Farmers, Reeds, Algaes, and Royals, all with increasing value. To win, it was the player's task to find those cards in that order out of a random pile. It was quite difficult to win, but if the player managed it, he was to yell Pagaroo so as to make his success public. This element of the game seemed too childish for the four of them though, so they decided to forfeit it.

Almost as soon as they began, Harold lost. It didn't take long for Snip to lose as well, and soon only Carnis and Petunia remained, drawing cards like their lives depended on it. It was now the fourth round, and both Carnis and Petunia had drawn every card they needed, except the Royals. The deck was almost gone. It was only a matter of time before one of them won, or both lost.

They agreed to draw their cards at the same time for the finale. After a dramatic pause, Carnis peeked at his card, slammed it down on the table, and shouted "Pagaroo!" triumphantly. He sounded childlike in his excitement. Petunia giggled across the table, and Harold and Snip moaned. Carnis *always* won, and Harold had no idea how. It was getting tiresome. He began to collect the cards for a new round, but before he could do anything, Petunia held her card high in the air. She gazed down at Carnis, slapping her card down on the table.

"Whatever are we going to do with a tie?" she smirked, revealing her shiny Royal card.

Carnis inhaled as if he had been shot. Harold and Snip smiled with glee. Finally, some competition. Harold even felt tempted to say, 'the lady wins' to avoid a conflict, but he knew Carnis wouldn't stand for it. The problem was, they had never tied before, and didn't know what to do with one.

"Well, *I* certainly can't live with a tie," Carnis said, arms crossed, "and I said Pagaroo first!"

"I thought we agreed not to say that?" Petunia smirked, hands on her hips.

"Well," Carnis mumbled, "the rules say what the rules say. I won't take a tie."

"You're acting terribly childish."

"Are you calling me a baby for wanting to win something?" Carnis growled.

"No," Petunia smiled, "but why don't you grow up a bit and just call it a tie?"

Carnis growled, resting his fists on the table.

"Guys," Harold interjected. "Stop arguing. Let's settle this like adults. I'm thinking of a number between one and ten."

"One and *ten*?" Carnis chuckled.

"Oh, for heaven's sake, Carnis!" Petunia sighed. "Let's just do this to get it over with."

"Fine," Harold said. "One in one hundred."

"I say one in one *thousand*," Carnis said, puffing up his chest.

"Good grief, Carnis!" Petunia frowned.

"You're just afraid you'll lose!" Carnis said, pointing a finger at Petunia's nose. She pushed it away like it was coated in some vile substance.

"Fine," she said with irritation in her voice. "But Snip gets to choose the number."

Carnis rubbed his hands back and forth like a child on Christmas. "Fine by me."

"Okay," Harold said. "Snip, are you ready?"

Snip shrugged, sinking back into his chair.

"Alright, I'm thinking of a number between one and one thousand," he squeaked.

"Okay," Carnis smiled. "I say 276."

"Alright. I say seven," Petunia smirked. Carnis grinned at her modest choice.

"The number was four," Snip shrugged. "Petunia was the closest."

Carnis shrieked in agony, "FOUR?"

"Yes," Snip said.

"You cheated!" he yelled, pointing at Petunia.

"What?" she shrugged. "Snip is afraid of big numbers."

Harold couldn't stop laughing.

"You knew that already, you cheater!"

"A win is a win," Petunia shrugged.

"Not if you didn't deserve it."

"I did deserve it."

"Didn't!"

"Did!"

"DIDN'T!"

"DID!"

"GUYS!" Harold yelled above all the shouting. "This is *Pagaroo*. Calm down!"

Petunia smiled, and Carnis just rolled his eyes. Snip had been laughing to himself the whole time, shaking his head in dismay. But they started a new game anyway, and it was all soon forgotten.

During all the commotion, the four had almost forgotten about Juniper. Distracted, they didn't see that he finally decided to move from his spot in the dark corner. He crept over undetected, dagger in hand. The students were too distracted to notice him, though, until he was standing right behind Petunia in steely cold silence.

Petunia squeaked at his sudden appearance, but Juniper merely stood there, staring at their fun.

"Juniper?" Harold said, his hands frozen under the table. The laughter came to a halt, but his good mood hadn't worn off just yet. Under normal circumstances, he would have wanted to punch Juniper in the face. This was one of his few interactions with Juniper that didn't entail slug slime.

"It's six-thirty now," he stated. "The rain is gone."

"Okay…" Harold barely had time to respond before Juniper walked out of the meal room as abruptly as he had arrived, his black cloak trailing behind him.

"Well, *that* was weird," Petunia said as soon as Juniper had gone.

"Juniper or the rain?" Harold asked.

"Both. I don't think he's ever said a word to me before."

"He's an odd one," Carnis agreed. "But the rain is gone, which means we can go hunting after all."

Juniper was right. Out the open window, Harold could see the rain had stopped, and the sun was even winking through the clouds down on the pond. He stood up and laced his boots, tucking his knife inside while Petunia gathered the cards. Then they left Galidemus, and headed for the dragonfly stalls below.

The air was heavy outside, pressing on Harold's shoulders, sticking to his hair and his clothes. The rain had cleansed the air, making it smell pure and crisp. Moisture softened the ground, making the trail to the stalls a mud wallow. Harold's shoes were soaked by the time he entered the clearing with Ms. Dywood, Mr. Porthand, and the rest of his classmates, and his toes became numb in the cold.

Standing in front of Swiftless's stall, Harold tried to unlock his insect friend. The rusty iron key slipped in his damp fingers. Unlike the other students, he didn't have to wait for Ms. Dywood to make her rounds to unlock his stall. The extra key proved very useful, as Mr. Porthand said it would be.

The stall door swung open to reveal Swiftless cowering in a corner. He always hated rain, but he seemed more anxious than usual. Harold stepped inside, grabbing the vial of poison and fastening it around his neck, carefully tucking it out of sight beneath his coat. Then, coaxing Swiftless with some gnats, Harold carefully fastened his saddle and harness, and led him out into the open. Ms. Dywood was just approaching his stall, glaring down at him as she passed.

"You don't deserve that key or that dragonfly," she spat.

Harold knew she would take his key and even Swiftless if she could. It was good she wasn't the headmistress.

Changing the conversation, Harold asked, "Are we actually hunting today?"

"It's only a demonstration," Ms. Dywood said tightly. "You won't be hunting until next school year. You'll want to memorize what we do tonight, though. It will come in handy when you have to test next year."

Harold sighed in frustration. Of course, he could have guessed they wouldn't actually be hunting yet, but it disappointed him anyway.

Closing the stall door behind him, he tugged on Swiftless's leash to line up with everyone else in the clearing next to the stalls. He steadied Swiftless behind Mr. Porthand, who sat on a beige dragonfly, as he had been instructed earlier that day. Mr. Porthand turned around to face him.

"Harold," he whispered. It was difficult to hear his voice above all the clamor the other students were making.

"Yeah?"

"Remember, be careful," he said, stretching so he could look Harold in the eye. "Stay close, and please don't do anything unexpected."

"I know," Harold muttered. "I'll stay close."

"No exceptions, Harold," Mr. Porthand pressed. "If you wander off track for any reason, you will be in grave danger. *Any* reason. I'll try to keep an eye on you, but I have thirty other students under my supervision, so I need you to be responsible. Do you hear me?"

Harold nodded.

"Do I have your word?" Mr. Porthand asked, his expression stern.

"You have my word," Harold said.

"Good."

Harold glanced down at the ground. "Mr. Porthand, why aren't we hunting today? It seems like an awful waste of time to just sit here and watch you and that old bug do all the work."

Mr. Porthand frowned. "Ms. Dywood is not an old bug, Harold. And they were Mrs. Kernester's orders. You're not allowed to hunt until your second year."

"Right," Harold said. They sat in silence for a few minutes before Mr. Porthand spoke again. He shouted in a loud, commanding voice so all the students could hear him. "Do we have everybody?"

Ms. Dywood, who sat on a sleek grey dragonfly from behind the students, signaled a thumbs up. Slowly the caravan rose and began drifting forward into the reeds above a little river that branched from the pond. It was hard to follow in a straight line at such a slow pace, but Swiftless stayed focused, as did all the other dragonflies—that is, *most* of the other dragonflies.

Carnis came barging through the line toward Harold, shoving other students aside as he tried to control his dragonfly. Sickworm flew clumsily and bounced off the other dragonflies like a marble in a pinball machine. When he reached Harold, Carnis nearly toppled over him.

"Whoa! Carnis, slow down! Get control of Sickworm!" Harold said, afraid he would slam into Mr. Porthand's dragonfly like a domino. Carnis yanked on his leash and slowed down enough to stop.

"Sorry!" Carnis apologized, calling out to the students behind him. "She's just so terrible! I hate her so much!"

"Oh, she can't be all that bad," Harold said.

"Really?" Carnis challenged. "Every time I try to slow her down, she speeds up. And every time I try to speed her up, she slows down! It's absolutely awful!"

"You should try reverse psychology," Harold said, laughing at his own humor.

Carnis rolled his eyes. "Right," he groaned. "Harold, I have to coax her out of her stall using a bit of Scandinavian slug. *Scandinavian slug*! Do you know how expensive that stuff is? My parents are going to kill me!"

"Scandinavian slug?" Harold exclaimed. "That *is* expensive. But at least she flies. Swiftless can barely get off the ground."

"Oh, quit humbling yourself to make me feel better," Carnis sighed. "I've seen Swiftless fly before. He does *not* 'just barely get off the ground,'" he said, mimicking Harold's voice. "That thing can fly faster than a Sapling ever has!"

"I guess so, but—"

"You know so yourself," Carnis interrupted. There was no use in arguing with Carnis, so Harold sighed and gave up.

"I guess you're right. He's pretty fast. But something's been bothering him today. I actually had to coax him out of his stall this time."

"It might just be the rain," Carnis suggested. "You know how that can scare them."

"Well, it might be that, but I have a feeling there's something more," Harold said. He thought about it for a while before he spoke again. Swiftless had seen rain before. Surely he wasn't this bothered from a few raindrops.

"Where are Petunia and Snip?"

"They're back a ways," Carnis replied. "Snip's not handling Bott well. The thing's a living lightning bolt."

"That's for sure," Harold nodded. "I don't see why you two can't trade. It seems like Snip would like Sickworm so much better, and vice versa."

"After begging Ms. Dywood and Mrs. Kernester, I asked Mr. Porthand, and he just said it was better this way!" Carnis whispered, eyeing the back of Mr. Porthand's head. "He told me to be patient, irritating stuff like that."

"Well, maybe Sickworm just hasn't reached her full potential yet," Harold suggested, trying to make him feel better.

"What are we, dragonfly masters?" Carnis asked. "Sickworm will never be more than a heap of deflated balloon."

Harold shrugged. "Well, you might be right. But keep in mind, many people thought Swiftless would never heal."

"Whatever," Carnis mumbled. "Listen, Mr. Porthand's speaking."

The two watched as Mr. Porthand demonstrated how to notch a bow correctly. Unfortunately, the teachers were the only ones who carried bows, but it was exciting anyway. They continued to drift on as he lectured, and Ms. Dywood interjected as they went. Harold tried his best to pay close attention, but after a while, he noticed a faint whispering behind him. It became distracting.

"Carnis, cut it out," he whispered.

"Cut what out?" Carnis whispered back.

"Quit whispering my name," Harold insisted. "It's distracting. I mean, a couple of jokes I can take, but—"

"I didn't say a word to you!"

Harold frowned, his irritation mounting. The whispering started up again, this time a little louder. He whipped around to Carnis, ready to shove him backward, but he wasn't speaking. He looked back at every other student behind him, but none of them had their mouths open. Suddenly, he felt adrenaline coursing through his veins. And still, the whispering persisted, faintly calling his name in the back of his mind.

Trying to ignore the voice was even harder. It sapped his focus so intensely, he could barely hear Mr. Porthand speaking. And it was getting louder. He could now tell the voice was a woman's voice, and it was very familiar. He didn't know where he had heard it, but he *knew* that voice. He just couldn't put a finger on it.

Harold weighed his options. He had promised Mr. Porthand he would stay with the group. But this voice wasn't dangerous. Carnis couldn't hear it, so the message was definitely intended for him. What if the voice was a possible ally? Mr. Porthand would be *glad* he went. But he would also be angry with him for disobeying his instructions.

What if the voice was a trap? What if Ferrals were making the noise to lure him into peril? He had his knife, but that wouldn't keep him safe against an entire tribe. He could try to ignore it. But it was so tempting, so unrelenting…

"Carnis?" Harold whispered.

"What now?" Carnis groaned.

"I think someone wants to see me," he said.

Carnis rubbed his temples. "Harold, not another weird voice."

"This one isn't evil or anything! I can tell," Harold insisted. "It's just really distracting, and I think someone needs me. I'm going to check it out."

"You can't," Carnis shook his head. "It's probably dangerous, Harold. Voices in your head always lead to mishaps. Just ignore it. I don't hear anything."

"I can't just ignore it," Harold argued. "It's really hard to focus. And what if it's someone who needs help? What if someone is in trouble?"

"Mr. Porthand warned you," Carnis insisted. "It doesn't feel right."

He felt the voice nagging at him, pulling at his conscience. Curiosity lulled him out of logical thinking.

"Please," Harold pleaded.

"Could you just distract Mr. Porthand for a moment so I can investigate? I can tell it's not coming from far. This could be important. Someone is calling me, and it has to be for a good reason."

Carnis hesitated. "I don't like this," he said.

There was a long moment of silence, filled with the muffled sound of Mr. Porthand's droning voice.

"Okay, fine. I'll distract him for a moment," Carnis sighed. "But don't get yourself killed. If you're not back in five minutes, I'm telling Mr. Porthand."

"Thank you, Carnis," Harold sighed.

"Go!"

Carnis pulled sharply on Sickworm's saddle and went plummeting down to the creek below. Mr. Porthand immediately chased after him, while Ms. Dywood watched in utter irritation. Carnis pulled up at the last second, but it did look as if he was going to crash. This was Harold's chance.

Harold nudged a reluctant Swiftless toward the noise. No one noticed him leaving. He could feel he was getting closer to the voice. Was this the right thing to do? Mr. Porthand would be so disappointed if he found out. He was breaking his promise to him. But he was so curious…

Gathering up his courage, Harold parked Swiftless on the brink of a tight cluster of reeds, not far from the caravan behind him. He couldn't see inside—the stalks were too dense. But he knew the voice was within. He pushed Swiftless into the reeds. They seemed to go on forever.

Finally, Harold felt cool air fall on his face. He opened his eyes to see where he was. Suddenly, a swift hand shoved him off Swiftless and sent him plummeting to the ground below. He landed on the hard ground, hands reaching out in the dark, but his vision was blurry from shock and confusion. Dark walls began to close in on him and his consciousness was slipping.

Everything faded to black.

CHAPTER EIGHTEEN

Golgothar

Harold groped around in the dark. He had been shoved off Swiftless in the confusion, and was now lying on a hard, matted substance. It felt like moss, but Harold couldn't see what it was; he couldn't even see his hand in front of his face, it was so dark. The whispering had stopped, but he could feel it was cooler in the enclosure than it had been outside. He could breathe now, but he supposed the wind had been knocked out of him when he fell. He felt fear settling in and he became more aware in an instant. Something wasn't right. Why had he been such a fool? Why had he followed that stupid voice? He hadn't been in his right mind.

He sat up and began to fumble for the knife in his boot. If danger came his way, he would have to fend for himself. He had his knife and his glowing poison to protect him. It wasn't much but it was something. The setting sun that had been shining outside was gone, and everything was dark. He could feel it getting colder, the air shifted by some unseen force, and he began to shiver.

Where was he? Where was Swiftless? He called out for his dragonfly, but to no avail. There was no reply in the utter blackness. Should he try to fight his way through the reeds again? He had no sense of direction whatsoever, so that would be useless. Depending on where he was, he could fall straight into the pond. But where was the pond? He couldn't hear the bubbling water or the breeze above him. The silence sent chills up his spine.

Suddenly a voice spoke behind him. It was not the same voice that had called him. Harold spun around, but the darkness stifled his sight. It was a male voice this time, deep and dark. It sounded like poisonous webs were being spun with each thick word.

"Harold Porthand, my heir," the voice chuckled. "I haven't seen you with my own eyes for such a long time. You have grown."

Harold's eyes widened in panic. He knew this voice. He heard it before, a long time ago. It had been so peaceful then. But this was the voice that had taken that peace away…

"Father."

"I'm surprised," Golgothar said, "that you still think of me as Father. Please, call me Golgothar. It has a ring to it."

Harold clenched his fists, fury tensing his muscles. He tried to step forward but his knees buckled beneath him. He kneeled on the hard, mossy ground.

"You killed her," he growled. "Why did you kill her?"

"Yes, I killed her," Golgothar said, with what sounded like a haunting smile. "It had to be done."

"You took everything away from me!" Harold screamed in anger. Years of pent up sorrow came flooding out. He didn't even care if he was in danger anymore. He had been longing to hear this voice again. He had been longing to speak to *this* person, the one who had taken everything away.

"What are you doing here?" he asked.

"What am I doing here?" Golgothar asked. "Relishing the inevitable. Eventually, you will die, Harold. Not right now, but soon. That is what I'm doing."

"Why do you want to kill me?"

"Harold, you will always be my offspring. You will always be my heir. Always. Often, I wish it wasn't so. And there is only one way to fix it. So I eliminate as needed."

Harold felt a wave of nausea seize him. He fell on all fours, wheezing. When he gained his composure, he lifted his head and glared into the darkness where his father stood. He still needed answers.

"Who was whispering to me?"

"I have powers, Harold. Powers none can master but me. I can conjure shadows and harness darkness. I can also reanimate memories. You recognized that voice because it was your mother's. I knew you wouldn't be able to resist."

Harold felt his fists clench in fury, in grief, in hatred. He had heard his mother's voice. Tears sprang to his eyes, falling on his cheeks and making cold little tracks on his face. Where was his mother? His family? Gone forever. He could never get her back. He gripped his head and sobbed.

"I'm disappointed," Golgothar remarked. "I thought you were stronger than this."

Harold clenched his fists and rose to his knees. The only thing that was powering him was pure hatred. He wished he could see him and spit in his face. He wished he could watch him humiliated, ruined, killed. His face hardened into stone as he glared into the dark.

"Where's Swiftless?"

"Good," Golgothar said, "there is some spirit in you after all."

"Where's Swiftless?" Harold repeated.

"Here and there," he replied evasively. "He is fine. You will get him back soon."

"Show yourself!" Harold yelled, "I want to see you!"

Soft chuckles echoed around the room. If anything, the place got darker.

"Harold, I am constantly enveloped in darkness. My shadow and I are one. I can see you, but you cannot see me. That is because I *am* the darkness. I can blot out the sun, erase the stars. I dwell in my own shadow, because the shadows of others are not good enough for me, not dark enough on my skin. I am no longer living, but live in the night. I am he that is hate."

Harold shivered. The words were poison in his ears, trickling deep down inside him. He wanted to escape and run far away, he wanted to soar into the skies with Swiftless and never return. And yet, he wanted to stay and hear more, the sound of his father's voice, the secrets it held.

"What do you want with me?" Harold asked weakly.

"Now we're getting somewhere." Golgothar said. "I am here to give you a message, Harold. Tonight, you will die. The Ferrals will overtake Galidemus, and at this point, there is nothing you can do—except worry. Worry is the most potent of weapons. Blood will be spilled tonight. Orahton will be smitten, and there is nothing you can do to save it. So get ready, Harold. This is the end. Farewell."

And then, in a great flash, the darkness was lifted and a piercing light sliced through the darkness. Harold shielded his eyes from the light. It was blinding, though it came from a fading sun. His eyes dilated in panic.

When he could finally see properly again, Harold noticed he was lying on an outcrop of moss surrounded by tall reeds. He could see the stars beginning to appear above him. Swiftless was lying on the far edge of the outcrop, cowering against the reeds.

"Swiftless!" Harold called. He raced over to his dragonfly on weak legs, collapsing beside him. They lay there side by side, gasping the steely air. Harold felt so weak. His hands and arms were shaking and his stomach churned. It was hard to believe that only two hours ago, he had been playing Pagaroo with his friends.

The moss was so soft beneath him, and he was so exhausted. He had encountered his father and heard his mother's voice and had survived without a scratch. But he had to get up. The others would be worried about him. He had been gone far longer than five minutes. He had to warn them; they needed to prepare for the Ferral attack.

Harold stood up, steadying himself on Swiftless. The dragonfly quivered with effort, but buzzed his wings with anticipation. Feeling dizzy, Harold climbed onto Swiftless's back, nearly flattening Swiftless under the pressure. They slowly drifted out through the reeds the way they came from.

They emerged into a world of cattails and streams and hazy sky. Harold could see the path they had been traveling earlier, the water, and a dragonfly with a rider hovering right in front of him. Suddenly, someone was hugging him and voices were shouting. Harold recognized Petunia, her cheeks streaked in tears and her hands shaking.

"Harold!" she cried. "How could you *do* that? We couldn't get in! We couldn't even hear you!"

"I'm okay," Harold breathed, tears beginning to form in his own eyes.

A disheveled Mr. Porthand approached from behind Petunia, followed by Carnis and Snip. The rest of the caravan had left.

"Harold!" he cried. His face was lined with worry, but Harold expected that now he was safe, he would be furious with him. "Where have you been?"

"I'm sorry," Harold mumbled. "There was another voice and Golgothar and—"

"We must go to my room immediately," Mr. Porthand ordered. "It is unsafe to speak out here. Now."

Harold nodded and peeled away from Petunia, straightening himself on Swiftless's back. How could he leave his friends like this? How could he break his promise? He kicked Swiftless forward and the group gathered speed as they flew back to Galidemus. Nobody said a word as they returned. Harold felt sick to his stomach. He tried to remind himself to enjoy the silence, but he couldn't. Golgothar's deep, evil voice filled his mind.

Mr. Porthand slammed his bedroom door and locked it, throwing the key on his bookshelf. They had returned to Galidemus after locking the dragonflies in their stalls. It had been tiresome and tense, and Harold still felt weak. He had even forgotten to return the vial of poison and his riding gloves to the stall in his hurry. Now the poison was in the school, yet another dangerous situation.

He knew he was in trouble. Mr. Porthand pointed to his rug and demanded they sit. Soon, they were sitting in a circle on the floor, sullen and quiet.

"Harold, it takes a lot to make me angry," Mr. Porthand finally spoke. Harold kept his head down. "You could have been killed! I gave you one *simple* instruction that you failed to follow. I would like an explanation immediately."

Harold detailed all the events as quickly and precisely as he could. He told them about Golgothar and their conversation, the cold darkness and his mother's voice. After Harold began to speak of Golgothar, Mr. Porthand's anger towards Harold redirected to his brother. He was disgusted and furious at what his Golgothar had become. By the end, Mr. Porthand was barely holding onto composure.

"He dared use your mother against you," he seethed, teeth clenched. "Your mother would never have wanted to be used like that," Mr. Porthand continued. "He has crossed a line. I'm so sorry you had to go through this, Harold." He reached out and put his hand on Harold's shoulder. "You were lucky you came out alive. You'll be even luckier if you can make it to tomorrow. Flint is determined to end our lives by the morning. I shouldn't have been so hard on you. You haven't learned to deal with your father's dark magic and manipulation like this. What happened was inevitable."

Harold appreciated what Mr. Porthand said, though he wasn't much relieved at the resolution. Were these really his last hours?

"I need to warn you," Mr. Porthand continued. "It has been reported this evening that Juniper and Mrs. Kernester have gone missing. I don't know the extent of Mrs. Kernester's involvement in any of this, or if she has been taken by Juniper as hostage, but nobody knows where they've gone."

Harold shuddered. "Do you think she'll be okay?"

"I don't know, Harold. She may be held as a prisoner to be used against you. Don't worry," Mr. Porthand said. "We need to prepare as quickly as possible. We don't have much time. I think I may be able to provide some protection . . . here."

Mr. Porthand stood up and walked around the rug to his bed. He pulled a large chest from beneath it, grunting with effort. Then he pulled a key that was hanging from his neck out of his shirt and unlocked the chest. He dragged it over to the rug in between the students. He then began to pull out various items from the chest.

"Carnis," Mr. Porthand said, handing him a short spear. It had a sharp black tip that swelled with a red liquid and a sturdy wooden handle. Various beads dangled from it, hanging down in an ornamental design. Carnis's eyes bulged.

"This has saved more than one life, including my own," Mr. Porthand explained. "It's made from chestnut and hardened coal. The tip contains poison, so be careful. It would do well to carry it close, just not *too* close," he winked.

Carnis stared at the spear, hands shaking. He couldn't speak, couldn't move. He just nodded and mumbled something, though Harold wasn't sure what.

Mr. Porthand retreated to the chest again, this time pulling out three little bottles of colorful liquid. He handed them to Snip, who was more scared and surprised than ever.

"Snip, these vials will help your friends in danger." Snip was frozen in fear as he looked down at the three bottles, glinting in the candlelight.

"The green vial can heal any wound, but you have to use the whole bottle only once. You must be wise about when to use it. Only use it on fatal injuries.

"The pink vial will put anyone in the vicinity to sleep, *if* it is poured on the ground. Be careful with this one. It will also put *you* to sleep when you use it, so only use it as a last resort.

"And lastly, the blue vial. If you drink it all at once, you can breathe underwater for up to three hours. It can also be used only once, so choose wisely when to use it. You may not need to use these at all," he warned. "They are extremely rare and expensive. If you don't need to, don't use them. You must be brave, Snip. No one can protect, so you must be smart and quick. I know you have it in you."

Snip nodded, accepting the vials. They clinked together in his clumsy arms.

Mr. Porthand returned to the chest again. This time he pulled out a wooden bow with twelve arrows, studded with beautiful little shells and gold flecks. He knelt next to Petunia, handing her the bow. He draped the arrow pack around her shoulder, full of golden arrows. Petunia gasped at how it sparkled.

"Petunia, this is my bow," Mr. Porthand smiled. "It nearly always finds its mark. Be smart; there are only twelve arrows. Use it in emergencies, and collect the arrows after you use them, if you can."

Petunia gave a steady nod, flexing the bow's taut string. It made a faint twanging sound.

Mr. Porthand stood up for the fourth time and went to the chest once more. He withdrew a short sword, gold and silver, and incredibly sharp.

"Harold," Mr. Porthand said sternly, "this is my most prized possession. It is part of a pair. I inherited it from my father, and its twin is your father's. They match perfectly. It's the sharpest sword I've had the privilege to wield, but I know its true potential is shown in the hands of a hero. I am no such thing. But I believe you are."

He handed the sword to Harold, but Harold politely pushed it away.

"I can't," Harold said, shaking his head, "It's so important to you. I can't just take it. You should use it."

Mr. Porthand smiled down at Harold. "Look," he explained, "I was never fit to have it anyway. I knew it was meant for you. You can use it so much better than I could. And plus," he added with a wink, "you don't have a choice."

Harold smiled slightly as his uncle thrust the sword into his lap. It shined as he stroked the blade.

Mr. Porthand then sat back down, looking at the four with concern. "You are in terrible danger," he said. "You must be fast and quiet. I plan on evacuating the school while you flee."

"Flee?" Harold asked.

"Harold, I know you would rather fight, but trust me. You would do best to live another day."

Harold shook his head. "What does that mean? That if I don't flee, I'll die? Doesn't that mean you'll die, too?"

Mr. Porthand frowned. "I don't know, Harold. But your life is far more valuable than mine. This is the only way."

"I can't leave you if I know you might die!" Harold protested. "That's ridiculous—you know that!"

"You have no choice, Harold. You need to run. I will come and find you after everything settles. But you must keep running north. North is the safest way, and you will find refuge there. Ferrals scarcely venture there. North, north, north. Do you hear me?"

They nodded slowly, but Harold refused to look up, glaring into the stone floor.

"Move fast, but keep low to the ground. Take your dragonflies. Do not return until I come and find you, or some other trusted person does. Do not return if they say they will kill me, all of Galidemus, or even all of Orahton. Do not return if I am calling for you, screaming for you to come back. Harold, you are much more important than me. Please listen—you have no idea how important this is. I need your word."

Each gave their word until it came round to Harold. Harold shook his head.

He could feel hot, angry tears brimming in his eyes. "I can't lose you," he said weakly. "I can't. I can't lose you after losing so much."

Mr. Porthand's eyes squinted as they began to fill with tears. He smiled at Harold, squatting down beside him. "Harold, I would want nothing more than to go with you. But it is my duty to stay, and yours to flee. I've been protecting you my whole life. I can't fail now. I won't throw my life away—trust me."

He gave Harold a hug. Tears streamed down Harold's cheeks. He couldn't lose the only family he had ever loved. But now he was being asked to leave him behind?

Mr. Porthand finally pulled away. Harold wiped his eyes with his sleeves, gazing around the room. Petunia was biting her lip, and Carnis and Snip were averting their eyes, lumps in their throats. He didn't want to leave, but the time had come. It was almost night and they needed to hurry.

"Be careful," Mr. Porthand said, patting Harold on the shoulder.

They stood up, gripping their new weapons with white knuckles. Mr. Porthand helped them to the door. Harold looked back at his teacher as he walked down the hall. Would it be the last time he saw him? Harold fastened the sword to his belt, waving a shaky hand behind him. Mr. Porthand waved back.

"We'll meet again, Harold!" he called down the hall. "We'll meet again."

CHAPTER NINETEEN

Running

The stalls lay silent at the bottom of the hill, casting moon shadows long and dreary. The world at night was peaceful for that moment, but Harold could hear faint shouting behind him as students evacuated Galidemus. Candles were lit in houses along the shore and people strayed from their homes to see what all the commotion was.

A great darkness had been cast over the pond, and before long, the moon was obscured by the clouds. Harold could see the water in the pond churning and frothing like the sea. The gentle river that fed the pond was now gushing, stirring the water into foam. But the most active waters of all lay in the center of the pond. They were bubbling up and releasing steam and fog. It looked as if something was breathing beneath the waters.

The stalls were still locked, but Harold could easily unlock Swiftless on his own. Swiftless lay alert inside, and Harold was surprised at how eager he was compared to earlier in the afternoon. Watching the light of Harold's swaying lantern, he was charged with electricity, tense with anticipation. Harold saddled him as fast as he could and ran to meet the others.

He helped Snip lock pick his door and saddle Bott. Carnis broke into his and Petunia's stall with the tip of his spear. It took some effort, but soon they were saddled and ready. They silently hopped onto their dragonfly's backs and flew toward the north as low and swift as possible, each second drifting farther away from Galidemus.

Harold clenched Swiftless's saddle, the reality of the situation gripping him, and looked up to the sky for comfort. The few stars that remained were swept away by a dark cloud, and soon they were traveling in deep darkness, having left the lantern behind.

They pressed their dragonflies forward relentlessly. Sometimes Harold dared to look back at the darkness behind him. Most of the time, he did not.

The reed forest lay in the north, and Harold had a hard time steering Swiftless through the stalks. But it provided good cover and an accessible view of the pond to the left of them. He could see a cloud of black fog rising above the water from his vantage point. A figure stood on the fog, straight and tall, barely decipherable in the shadows. Harold could guess who it was, but he hoped it was not...

Other Ferrals were approaching; they were coming in numbers and hordes. After a while, Harold spotted dark figures bounding beneath the reeds. Huge shadows with long legs bounded in the distance, leaping high into the sky and crashing down again with such violence, it shook the ground. Harold knew they were grasshoppers, and he could see riders on them. He nearly choked in fear; he had never seen a Ferral in person before.

It was insanity to ride a grasshopper; they were so erratic and untrainable, only the Ferrals were insane enough to try it. Hardly landed before jumping again, they took no notice of what they crushed beneath their feet.

The riders were converging on one location, and Harold felt a rush of adrenaline as he recognized the solemn spires of Galidemus in the distance behind them. Some were entering the forest behind them and some were spreading out over the terrain. Even though they were hidden among the reeds, it was only a matter of time before they were spotted.

Harold thought of splitting up, but they had little chance of defending themselves alone if they encountered a Ferral. They would have to stick together. Could they hide? There were scant places big enough to disappear within the forest, and it would be a chore finding somewhere to keep all the dragonflies. Harold hoped they wouldn't be spotted; their best option was to keep going.

There were noises in the forest, twigs snapping and bounding feet and the wind rushing through the cattails above. Harold could feel the eerie cold clamping onto his skin.

Suddenly, a grasshopper leapt through the shadows and crashed right in front of them, blocking their escape. Petunia screamed, and they scrambled off their dragonflies, drawing their weapons. The grasshopper was huge and dark, its black eyes round and violent. It was armored in a thick, brown shell. The rider was smiling on the grasshopper's back, with sharpened black teeth that sparkled in the moonlight. He wore dirty rags and wielded a large black axe.

"Three, no four tasties!" the rider exclaimed. He spoke with a rasp, like something was caught in his throat.

Carnis hurled his spear at the grasshopper, aiming at its hide. While the spear did find its mark, it merely bounced off and clattered to the ground. The grasshopper's exoskeleton was too hard.

"Ooh," the rider snarled, "the bitsies carry stingsies! Tsk, tsk."

The grasshopper leaped in the air and landed behind them with a crash. The rider flung his axe into their huddle just before they could turn around. They shoved their dragonflies aside to avoid the blow, but the axe snagged Harold, leaving a long gash in his forearm. It began to ooze blood that turned black when it rose to the surface. Harold let out a yelp of pain, clutching his arm.

Taking the distraction as an advantage, Petunia notched her bow and sent an arrow flying at the rider. The golden arrow buried itself into the rider's chest.

The Ferral fell off the grasshopper to the ground, and the insect bounded away into the night. After some stunned moments of silence, they rushed over to the Ferral, who was slumped in the mud. He was dead, his eyes wide and white. Harold felt his stomach churn.

"I killed a Ferral . . . I killed someone—" Petunia whispered, on the verge of tears.

"He attacked us first," Carnis panted. "We need to hurry."

They collected Petunia's arrow and Carnis's spear, glancing into the woods around them. Reeds towered above them, cold, dark pillars framing the sky. They hopped on their dragonflies and dove deeper into the forest. For several minutes, they kept weaving through the reeds, stomachs still knotted.

Suddenly a yelp rang through the foliage. It was a man's voice, familiar and urgent. Harold blinked into the darkness, but all fell silent.

"What was that?" Petunia asked, looking around for the source of the noise.

"I don't know," Harold said.

"We need to keep going," Carnis said. "It was probably just a random noise."

Harold doubted the noise was so random, but Carnis was right. They needed to keep going.

They kept flying through the forest. It was then that Harold noticed the painful stinging in his arm. He tried to wrap it with some of his shirt, but the grass-woven material leaked blood just as bad as his severed skin did. He bit his lip and tried to focus on his breathing.

Finally, when they were sure they were alone, Petunia whispered into the dark. "Harold, your arm!"

Harold nodded, then shook his head. The forest floor swam beneath him. "I'll be fine."

"It looks bad," Carnis warned. "It might be poisoned."

Harold's head was reeling. It took all his concentration to reply. "Might be. It hurts really bad."

"Snip, should we use the healing potion?" Petunia asked.

Harold's hand slipped in his saddle. He fell off Swiftless to the ground, clutching his arm. Although they had been hovering just above the ground, it still hurt. The dragonflies froze.

"Harold!" Carnis called.

Harold was vaguely aware of Carnis and Petunia hopping off of their dragonflies and hunching over him.

"It's poison," he heard Carnis say. "We need to wash it out. We may not need to use the potion. Hurry, the water is right over here."

Harold was dragged to the pond's edge a short distance away, his muscles locked and frozen. He could feel his vision closing in, and the voices were melting into the distance. He tried to focus, but it took all his willpower to stay conscious. He heard splashing water and a shriek. He tried to open his eyes to see what was going on. Through cracked eyelids, he glimpsed a rubbery hand reaching out of the water and clamping onto Petunia's arm. Another hand reached up and grasped Carnis's leg. Petunia was being dragged into the water. Snip reached down to help, but another hand clamped onto his shoulder. Harold tried to call out but his voice didn't respond. His mind was slowly slipping. Was this the end? The pain in his arm melted away. A hand grasped his foot and began dragging him under the freezing water, but his leg felt so distant, it didn't feel like his own. He was going under. He was going to drown. This was it. Finally, Harold slipped into unconsciousness.

"Hold on, hold on! He wants him alive! We found him!"

Harold awoke to strange voices surrounding him. He couldn't open his eyes or move, but he could hear people speaking.

"Should we take him now?" one voice rasped. It sounded much like Stark, but younger.

"Not yet," another responded, this time a woman's voice.

"Let us go!" a girl's voice shrieked—Petunia's. There was more splashing and grunting. "Let us go! He's hurt!"

Harold became aware of what he was feeling. His arm was throbbing horribly, but it didn't sting anymore. His head was lying on a sandy bank. He was still immobile, but he began to crack his eyelids, squinting at his surroundings.

Carnis and Snip lay frozen on the shore, pinned to the ground by two strange figures. The creatures had their backs to Harold, and he could see fins protruding from their spines and gills carved into their throats. Sharp horns extended from their skulls. Their skin was wet and rubbery.

Another strange figure was pinning Petunia to the ground, clamping his slimy fingers around her wrists. Harold saw their faces resembled Stark's, and panic began to clench his throat. They were somewhat amphibian, somewhat human. They wore ragged clothing, made of seaweed and water foliage. Another one was sitting next to Harold, a woman, he supposed; she had long dark hair flowing down to her waist. Harold had never seen such dark hair before. It was nearly black.

The woman didn't pay much attention to Harold, so he focused on cracking his eyes so she would think he was still unconscious. He noticed one of Snip's vials lying on the ground next to him, empty and discarded. They must have used it on his wound. He noticed his friends were disarmed, but he could feel his sword still resting on his hip. He could take them by surprise—could he escape these water people?

"We found him so soon," the woman remarked. "It was almost too easy with the injury."

"Is he okay?" Petunia called out. "He's hurt!"

Harold could see her struggling.

"He'll be fine," grunted one of the men. "We used the healing potion. Quite a find, I'd say. Those kinds of potions are rare these days. He would've died within seconds had you just washed his arm with water. But he's wanted alive."

"Indeed," the woman said. "He'll be fine. As for you three—"

"What are you people, anyway?" Carnis interrupted.

The woman snorted. "Foolish boy," she spat. "We are the water dwellers. We serve Golgothar, for a duration."

"Why?" Snip called out. His voice was small and strained.

"Why?" the woman retorted. "We have no choice. The water dwellers are in a severe famine right now. Golgothar offered to save us if we caught *him*." She glanced down at Harold. "He rewards generously."

"If you just asked Orahton, we could have given you food," Petunia said. "All you had to do was ask."

"Who are you to say what the town will and will not do, little girl? Do you run Orahton?"

Petunia wiggled under the water man's grasp. "There's plenty of food in Galidemus. We can give it all to you, I promise—"

"Foolish child," the water woman snarled. "As soon as your little friend wakes up, we will take him to Golgothar ourselves. We'll give him exactly what he wants, and he will feed us."

"Golgothar is a liar!" Petunia said. "Don't trust him!"

"We have to," the lady said. "Betrayal results in death. Do you really think I'd rather die than to turn you in?"

Petunia didn't answer.

"That's right," the woman said. "You see the dilemma we're in. I'm sorry if he is your friend, but it must be done. We water dwellers are a peaceful people and would not do such a thing under normal circumstances. It's just business."

That was when Harold sprang up.

He grabbed the knife from his belt and snapped it into the air, slashing the water lady's arm. Then he jumped to his feet, holding the knife to her throat. The men rustled, but didn't leave Harold's friends. One grunted. Harold pressed the blade into the woman's neck, making her gag.

"Please," she begged, gasping for air. "Help!"

The water men did nothing to respond. Her eyes filled with fear as she stared at Harold. Harold knew he couldn't do it. He lessened his grip ever so slightly, but still held the knife firm.

"Let us go," Harold demanded.

"You'll have to kill me first," she spat. "If I let you go, I will not only die by the hands of Golgothar himself, but I will have betrayed my people."

"Then join us," Harold insisted. "You probably want to get rid of Golgothar as badly as we do. Why not join us?"

The woman's eyes squinted.

"You wouldn't understand. There is nothing that can be done to oppose Golgothar. I know this. Surrendering would mean giving up."

"You already surrendered," Harold said. "The only difference is that with us, you have a chance to live."

The woman looked at Harold for a long time. It was then that Harold noticed it was taking all his strength to restrain her. He was weak, and getting weaker. If she didn't make a decision soon, they were all doomed.

Finally, the woman spoke.

"Let go . . . now," she whispered, her voice steely cold.

Harold shook his head.

"Trust me," she whispered.

Harold was prepared to shake his head again, but he paused for thought. Could he trust her? No. But something was telling him he should.

He bit his lip in frustration. Was it instinct? Or pure insanity?

Without thinking, Harold pulled his knife from the woman's throat, jumping back so he could escape. Like a loaded spring, she leapt to her feet, tackling one of the men.

Harold was stunned. For a moment, he stood frozen. Then he sprang into action, tackling the man holding Carnis. The water dweller whirled around, punching Harold in the gut. Harold was sent sprawling in the shallows, clutching his stomach. His breath left him and he began to wheeze. He was too weak to stand up—he lifted his head to see the water woman killing one of the water men with Carnis's spear, which had fallen to the ground, and advancing to the next. They began to brandish weapons as the fight escalated. Petunia was free, Carnis nearly there. Petunia sprinted over to Harold, kneeling in the water and placing her hand on his forehead. He was still gasping for breath. Black walls were closing around his vision. He heard some muffled noises in the distance, and then everything returned to darkness.

A buzzing noise startled Harold awake. Like the flapping of wings, the flickering of something surfaced in the pool of his consciousness. This time, Harold wasn't paralyzed; his muscles tensed suddenly the second he was awake. He jerked his head up abruptly, heart pounding. He was on a dragonfly, with three others surrounding him. He could see Carnis and Snip flying beside the dragonfly he was on, with Swiftless following behind them. Sitting up, he noticed Petunia sitting right in front of him.

"Petunia?" he asked. Petunia turned around, her eyes filled with relief.

"You're awake!" she gasped. "Carnis, Snip, he's finally awake!"

The group halted and they jumped off their dragonflies. Harold gingerly stepped onto the floor, feeling a stabbing pain in his side.

It must have been where the water man had punched him. What had happened since then?

"What's going on?" he asked.

Petunia smiled. "That water lady, you convinced her. She's on our side now."

Harold looked around at his friends in disbelief. "I thought I was dead. Multiple times."

Petunia chuckled, biting her lip.

"I thought you were a goner," Carnis admitted. "Without her, you would be."

"After that, she returned to the water, but she said she would stay hidden until things blew over," Petunia explained. "She was really thankful for whatever you did for her."

Harold shook his head. "I didn't *do* anything, though. This is crazy."

"I know," Snip said as he twitched nervously.

"If it weren't for her, we'd *all* be dead," Carnis said.

"What did she do with the guys who attacked us?" Harold wondered.

"Dumped them in the water," Carnis said.

Harold felt nausea seize him. "This is insane. I hope she's okay. Did you catch her name?"

"No," Petunia said. "I wish I had."

There was a long moment of silence.

"Harold, I'm so glad you are okay," Petunia said. "That poison worked faster than I thought it would. Well, actually, I didn't even think the axe was poisoned in the first place. You blacked out, like, three times."

"I only remember bits and pieces," Harold chuckled, but stopped abruptly when the jabbing pain in his side flared.

"We'd better get going," Snip said, noticing Harold wince. "They are still after us, and we can't take much more of this."

Harold nodded and started over to Swiftless.

"Harold, are you sure you can ride?" Petunia called from behind him. "You still look a bit pale."

"I'll be fine," Harold tried to reassure her. "I *think* I'll be fine," he added, remembering what happened the last time he said *that*.

Petunia smiled weakly as they hopped onto their dragonflies. They sped up, swerving through the undergrowth, cattails flying by. Harold felt his strength returning, but still felt an intense fear gripping him— would they make it? Was Galidemus evacuated yet? And was Mr. Porthand still safe? *North*, he reminded himself. *North*.

The further they flew, the more Harold worried. He wasn't worried about himself, but he was terrified for his friends. And he couldn't get Mr. Porthand out of his mind. Was he safe inside Galidemus, or out wandering in the dark? Had he been captured?

They hadn't traveled far due to the chaos, and they could still run into another grasshopper rider any moment. If one of them got poisoned again, there would be no way to cure it. And if more of the water dwellers found them, it would be difficult—virtually impossible—to escape. As they marched northward, the pond remained to their left the entire time, and it gave Harold an unsettling feeling.

Harold still felt weak, his bruises throbbing. His arm, at least, had been restored to full strength. The potion had worked so well, not a trace of the wound was left. But his side flared with every gentle movement and his head still felt like it was swimming.

He noticed his friends were tired, too. They all had scratches on their wrists from being pinned to the ground, and Petunia had an abrasion on her forearm from releasing her bow without a guard. Was this all his fault? And how far north would they get? What could possibly save them from this mess?

They traveled a few minutes in silence. It got quieter the farther they traveled, which seemed both a good thing and a sinister thing. Their dragonflies began to grow weary, and despite the adrenaline, the four of them were slowing down. They hadn't been traveling very fast, but maneuvering around all the reeds taxed the dragonflies. Harold could feel Swiftless slowing down, and Sickworm began to fall behind. How long would they last?

Harold was nearly out of hope when they reached a clearing, barely decipherable in the darkness, opening up to a cove and the pond. A clearing that was shockingly familiar.

In the center of the cove was a small island, crowned with nothing more than a few tufts of grass. There was nothing unique about it; there were many of these coves along the pondside. But something struck Harold with fear when he saw this island. He knew this island. It nearly brought him to a stop.

This was the island in his dream.

The nightmare flashed before his eyes, echoes calling from the night he cleaned Mrs. Kernester's office. Everything was becoming frighteningly clear. Everything up until now had happened just as he dreamed it. Swiftless had been healed. He had encountered the monster beneath the door—twice. What was to happen next? Was his dream foretelling his fate? Was he supposed to face that—that—creature out there *alone*?

The thought made him suck in cold air, which he felt sharp as a knife in his lungs. He didn't want to do it. He just wanted to fly on and ignore the impulse to go out to the island. But it felt like something he needed to do. It was like a needle in his mind, penetrating his thoughts. It reminded him of the voice from when he had tried to catch Swiftless. That quiet whisper. *Choose wisely.*

That quiet whisper had told him to trust that water woman and release her from his grasp. He had known it was the right thing to do, but he had no idea why. He pondered how his life had changed dramatically in the last few weeks. Swiftless had become a great dragonfly, he had become a great rider, and the water woman had saved their lives in exchange for nothing but moral justice.

At first, Harold clenched his saddle in anger. He didn't want to keep following that little voice in his head because it grated against his natural instincts. But he knew he needed to. It was infuriating.

The cove was passing by. If he left, he would be leaving his friends behind. He would be ditching them to fend for themselves, to worry about him. If he went to that island, he might come face to face with the monster beneath the door as his dream had foretold. Even in his dream, Harold had been terrified. He clenched his teeth. They were about to pass the cove.

If he went on without going to the island, he would be safe. If he stayed away, he would be keeping Mr. Porthand's promise. He would be with his friends, and they might make it out alive. But—

Harold groaned in frustration. He pulled Swiftless to a halt, causing his friends to stop as well, piling up behind him like dominos.

"What's going on, Harold?" Petunia called from the back of the pack. Harold gestured his friends over as he hopped off Swiftless.

"I think I have to go to that island," Harold said when they had gathered around.

Petunia shook her head as if he were joking.

"I'm sorry it's all so abrupt," he continued. "But that island was in my dream. I know I might sound crazy, but I just know I have to go out there. I don't know why. Please trust me."

"Harold," Petunia said, fear flashing in her eyes, "now is not the time to be stupid."

"I'm not being stupid," Harold reassured. "I know what I'm doing."

"You can't be serious," Carnis said, resting his hands behind his head in frustration.

"I am."

A few moments of stunned silence followed.

"Harold, please," Petunia pleaded. "Don't go. We've come all this way, and you can't just leave us."

Snip shook his head as he stood beside his sister, nerves making his hands tremble.

"Look," Harold said, "you guys are great friends. I may never see you again, but I just want you to know I really appreciate all of you. I know I have to go out there. Say goodbye to Mr. Porthand for me."

"Wait, we're saying goodbyes now?" Carnis asked, angry sarcasm tainting his voice.

Petunia began to cry. "Stop, please. This is stupid."

Carnis looked Harold square in the eye, and the anger and stress dissolved.

"You're serious," he confirmed.

"Yes."

"Harold, don't," he pleaded, grasping Harold's arm. It was the first time Harold had ever seen him completely stricken with fear.

"Keep going north," Harold told them, trying not to let his voice waver. "You guys are the greatest people I've ever met. Thank you for being a family to me. I hope to see you again.

Then, refraining from looking back for fear he would change his mind, he pushed Swiftless out onto the pond toward the small, dark island.

CHAPTER TWENTY

Poison

The wind blew strong and cold against Harold's face, as if urging him to turn back, trying to make him see reason. But he pressed forward into the unrelenting headwind. The tall field grasses that clustered on the little island whipped violently in the dark. Murky water was shoving up onto the shores, turning the sand dark and cold.

Swiftless shivered in the breeze, as if shaking off the fear of the moment. Harold placed a reassuring hand on his dragonfly's back. They were one, together in mind, one lone star in the night.

Harold drew his sword from his belt, and it caught some wayward glint of light in the darkness. Everything was still and silent. He didn't dare take his eyes off the black fog that hung over the water. Teeth clenched and eyes set firm, Harold knew Golgothar could hide no more.

"Come out!" he shouted, trying to keep his voice from shaking. "I'm not afraid of you!"

An eminent chuckle pierced the fog. Harold shuddered as it drew near. It felt as if he could touch the voice, as if it was a solid thing.

"You . . . you said you were darkness itself. But do you know why?" Harold swallowed. "Because dark things *hide* in the darkness. Dark things hide because they are afraid. Admit it! You're afraid of me!"

Golgothar snarled, stepping from the fog so Harold could see him—for the first time.

Behind ragged, pale skin, Harold could see his father—still young, but old, appearing human, yet not human. His father could have been handsome. But his eyes were full of evil—sunken in, catlike, with black pupils thin as slits that cut through the milky whites of his eyes. His hair was tufty like Harold's, though gray and frosty instead.

As Harold peered through the shadows, he noticed pale arms that looked weaker than they were. Golgothar didn't slouch, but stood straight and strong, as if he was standing on the earth rather than a dark fog. What startled Harold the most was the resemblance to himself. Harold could guess Golgothar had looked just like him in his youth. It horrified him.

"Harold," Golgothar smiled slickly, "*you* are afraid of *me*. Not the other way around. You've already proven yourself an unworthy disappointment. I thought you were quicker—stronger. No, it is you who fears *me*."

Harold didn't move. He knew Golgothar was trying to intimidate him. But if he was so powerful, he didn't need to do such a thing. Taunting was only a sign of his weakness. He stood firm with Swiftless, jaw clenched in concentration.

"I thought you would be interested to know," he continued in his deep, deadly voice, "I finally found that imbecile, Mr. Porthand. You two have grown close. I haven't yet decided if I should kill him now, or if he should be forced to watch your demise. What do you think?"

Harold clamped his mouth shut. How had Mr. Porthand been captured so quickly? And how could Harold save him? A thousand questions and emotions overwhelmed Harold's mind. He squeezed Swiftless's saddle until his knuckles turned white.

"Don't make him suffer," he said. Harold was surprised at how quiet his voice sounded.

"Suffer?" Golgothar chuckled. "Do you realize who I am? I haven't killed someone kindly since your mother."

Harold swallowed hard, trying to block out his voice. His side was still throbbing, but Golgothar's words stung worse. He closed his eyes for a split second, opening them in a flash.

"All the things you've done are nothing," he said, glaring with laser focus. "You can taunt me all day, but it will do *nothing* to me. You're procrastinating. And you're doing it because you're afraid of me. You don't want to fight me."

Golgothar's face flashed annoyance, but a look of amusement quickly followed. "You think you are braver than you are," he spat.

"No," Harold insisted. "You could have killed me many times. You could have killed me when you killed my mother. You had plenty of opportunities with all the henchmen you have around. So many missed moments. Yet, you held back. And you waited to get a huge monster and a slew of men and grasshoppers and water dwellers all to kill a single person. It shouldn't be that hard. But you did all of *this* because you are afraid of me!"

Harold knew he was right as he saw Golgothar's face flinch. Rage flashed in his father's eyes. He clenched his fists, eyes gleaming.

"Do you not know who I am?" he shrieked. "I am Golgothar. I am chief of the Ferrals! Dare you challenge me? You know how this will end, Harold . . . you know you will die—"

"No, I don't," Harold said. "I don't know how it will end. *You* don't know how it will end, either. That's one thing you can't do. You can't predict the future. That's why you're so scared; you don't know any better than I, and you're terrified."

Golgothar squinted, his expression torn in fury. "You think you're so clever," he nearly whispered. "So brave and quick. So special. But you know you are nothing, Harold. You are *nothing*. And you've irritated me too many times..."

Like a great, sickly raven, he withdrew into the fog in a great swoop, a black hole drawing everything into itself, disappearing into the darkness. Everything fell silent. Swiftless and Harold were left alone, hovering above the island.

Harold tried to let his father's words fall at his feet, but he could feel them crawling through his ears and into his mind, burrowing deep down inside. He shook his head as if to toss them aside, furrowing his brow with effort.

He tried to focus on the silence, listening to the things he could just barely hear. For a short moment, Harold could hear the buzzing of

Swiftless's wings. He could hear the water lapping onto the shore of the small island, and the wind shaking the reeds and field grasses. He could hear his breath, unsteady and rapid from adrenaline. He could feel his heart beating, fast and throbbing. Would these few moments be the last it would beat?

Harold glanced up at the sky, black with a thick layer of clouds. For a second, the moon peeked through the clouds, shining a ghostly glow down on Harold and Swiftless. Then it disappeared into the stratosphere again. The shimmer was heartening—a light winked behind the storm. He clenched his sword tighter, preparing himself to fight. Swiftless coiled into a spring.

The world ceased to breathe—

Quiet.

Quiet.

Quiet.

Then something.

Voices.

Loud voices.

Harold covered his ears as the voices got louder. They seemed to echo around him as if he were in a closed room.

They were calling someone.

They were calling *him*.

And the voices were coming from underneath the water.

They were so loud, Harold could feel his chest pulsing with the voices. They rattled his bones. He looked down into the depths of the water—

Then suddenly the voices ceased. The water stilled. The wind calmed. Harold's heart was beating so loudly, he could hear it.

Silence—

SPLASH!

A massive creature leapt from the depths, sending water into the air like a firework. It was so huge, so massive, it completely filled Harold's field of vision.

It was like a snake, but with four short legs, short like tree stumps. Its eyes gleamed a neon yellow, piercing the dark like daggers. Its tail was colossal, with a spiked fin on its spine. Black scales, sharp like spades, covered every square inch of the monster's body, hiding its clammy skin. A smell, like salty, wet death plumed into the air. Harold swallowed his dinner for the second time that day. He gripped his saddle tighter, for fear his sweat would make it slip in his hands. He hadn't been able to withstand the awful stench the first two times, and he worried he would succumb again. He tried to hold his breath, but his stomach churned.

The creature bared its huge teeth, rearing its head at Harold. Harold could feel its hot breath on his face—it smelled like stomach acid and rotten meat. The monster coiled back at the sight of him, reptilian head ready to strike. Harold trembled under its terrifying eyes.

"*Death . . .*" the creature spoke. Harold swallowed his fear. He could stay in control. He would have to stay in control. His life depended on it. "*Death . . . bloooood—*"

Then it struck.

With lightning speed, Harold and Swiftless dodged the monster. The anticipation had prepared them to move quickly. Harold swiped at the creature's snout, but missed by too much. He would have to get closer, risking death, just to give the beast a paper cut. Harold pushed Swiftless up, climbing higher and higher to put some distance between them.

The creature spun around to attack again, but Harold and Swiftless were already too high for it to reach. For a split second, Harold felt relief flood through him. He was safe at this height. But not for long.

An arrow whizzed past Harold's cheek, just nearly missing him. Then another flew by, but Harold dodged it. He gazed down to where the shots were coming from, and found Juniper riding his sleek silver dragonfly, hiding among the shadows. His dragonfly gleamed in the pale moonlight. Harold could just make out another arrow notched, the bow lifting toward him, aiming—

He dove beneath Juniper's arrow, realizing he couldn't go much lower if he wanted to avoid the monster. He would have to charge his enemy head on if he didn't want to be eaten alive.

Harold dove down to meet Juniper, and the two clashed swords mid-flight. Juniper had switched from his bow to a long silver blade, much longer than Harold's humble short sword. But Harold held firm.

He slowly pushed Juniper upward, staring straight into his ice-cold eyes with fury.

"You'll never be his heir," Juniper spat.

"You don't have to worry about that," Harold replied with some effort.

Juniper pressed him harder, and Harold could feel Swiftless sinking. He gazed below him, the black monster rearing furiously in the water. It was only a matter of moments before he would be within the monster's reach. He juked Juniper and surged up into the night. When he was high enough, he whipped around, expecting Juniper to be on his tail. Instead, he had disappeared.

At first Harold was confused. But then he remembered the pattern he had witnessed Juniper rehearsing a couple of days ago. He strained to remember the pattern. First, he had gone up. What was next? He had swerved a bit below again, and then he would disappear into the reeds. That was the pattern, which meant Juniper was hiding in the reeds. After a few moments, he would sneak out and charge Harold from above again. He had to surprise him.

Harold pushed Swiftless down toward the monster. It was against all instinct, but it was his only option. Down they streaked, whizzing past the monster's snout. The monster roared and chased Harold as he sped downward, doubling back onto itself. The pond surface was getting closer and closer by the second, the glass wall that separated two worlds. Closer—closer—

At the last moment, Swiftless pulled up and soared across the pond, redirecting their path, right through the monster's squat legs. The monster's momentum sent it sprawling into the water, but not for long. The monster jerked its head up again and continued to chase Harold underneath its own limbs, coiling into a tight kink. It was unnaturally flexible, and Harold began to panic as he glanced at the monster's raging face not far behind them. The monster had wound its enormous head through its own short legs.

It followed Harold all the way through, up the tail and into the sky, jaws snapping. Waves surged up around Harold and Swiftless, nearly pulling them into the frothy depths. Swiftless pumped higher and higher and Harold watched for Juniper.

The monster roared behind them, again, too far below to reach them. But they kept climbing. He spotted Juniper emerging from the reeds, speeding—unaware—toward him in the dark. Harold braced his sword, racing right at Juniper. Just before the two collided, he dove beneath him, slitting his silver dragonfly's belly.

Down Juniper spun, shrieking as he fell. His dragonfly spiraled to the ground, crashing into the water. Harold watched as Juniper emerged from the ice-cold water. He swam toward the shore, sputtering and gasping, struggling to reach land. Harold felt a stab of guilt for killing a dragonfly, but he hadn't had a choice. Right now, his main focus was to stay alive, to keep Swiftless alive, and to keep his friends alive.

With Juniper no longer an immediate threat, Harold and Swiftless were left alone with the monster. It was thrashing down in the water below him, generating massive waves. At the moment, Harold was safe. But the monster would soon figure out how to reach him, or do more damage to Orahton below. His friends were down there. Mr. Porthand was down there. He had to get rid of it. But how?

Harold took inventory of the weapons he had at his disposal. He had his sword. He also had the dagger in his boot.

Harold searched himself. His eyes caught a glimmer reflecting off the vial of poison hanging around his neck. He must have forgotten to take it off when he had finished riding Swiftless earlier—but he was glad he forgot. The poison might do some damage. If one drop could kill a man, maybe the whole bottle could kill the monster. But what if the monster was immune to venom? What if it didn't swallow it, or the vial fell into the pond? It was risky. But it was better than scratching the beast to death with his sword.

After some quick thought, he decided to try the sword first. If it failed, he would use the poison, but only as a last resort. It was dangerous enough wearing it under his shirt while he flew. Gathering his courage, Harold dove down again, his blade ready at his side.

The second the monster was within range, it struck like lightning at Harold and Swiftless.

Swiftless dove down just as quickly, barely missing the huge mouth. But Harold reached up, tearing a cut into the monster's enormous neck. He could feel the blade slice, but not deep. Thick, maroon blood oozed from the wound. Harold gasped in relief, even if he had only scratched the monster, and they began to climb to safety again. But there was little time to celebrate.

The enraged beast roared so loudly, Harold nearly dropped his sword to cover his ears. Then it stretched like it had never stretched before, gaining on Harold and Swiftless double time, fury powering its stride. Suddenly, the monster's jaws snapped down and a huge tooth gouged Harold's leg with tremendous velocity, tearing all the way down his calf and across his ankle, piercing skin and clothing. Harold shrieked in pain. The cut was deep, nearly to the bone. Nausea seized him and he vomited over the side of his mount, partly from the pain but mostly from the monster's sickening smell. The searing pain in his calf was so excruciating, he could barely breathe. He had never felt pain like this before. He clutched Swiftless's reigns until his knuckles turned white. He had to continue. He had to push the pain away. He had to focus.

He took a deep breath, and the pair zoomed down beneath the monster's legs a second time. Through the watery cathedral they sped, the monster's huge head chasing them not far behind. Harold gazed down at the white, frothy water raging below him.

Through the back legs they raced, up the tail and higher into the sky. He had to find a way to get the poison into the monster's mouth. His sword just wasn't good enough. He would have to try his last resort.

They soared up, Swiftless tirelessly pumping his wings, the monster chasing them from behind, jaws gaping. Harold rocketed up until he was just out of reach and whirled around, waiting for the monster to open its mighty jaws again. But this time, it kept its mouth closed.

Instead, it shrank back into the water, a rumble in its throat, hatred flashing in its eyes. Only its snout was visible—and then it disappeared. A deafening quake rumbled the ground and reverberated through the air. Harold could feel the atmosphere quivering around him. Ripples throbbed on the pond's surface. Screams sounded underwater, echoing out into the night. Harold tensed, frozen mid-flight.

Then, suddenly, the monster rose again, murder in its eyes. Water cascaded off its scaly back in torrents. It rose higher and higher, higher than before. A mighty span of bat-like webbing spread out from its sides. Its wings, which had been concealed against its body, unfurled. Then they started flapping slowly, and the monster miraculously rose into the air. The rush of wind from the flapping wings was so terrific, Swiftless careened in the wind.

Like a cloud of smoke, the beast rose higher into the night. Its head leveled with Harold and Swiftless, eyes piercing like needles.

"*Bloooood...*" It called. "*Thirsty... Blood...*"

The monster beat its wings and roared in fury, blasting Harold and Swiftless with its hot breath. Its roar almost blew them away. The pair rocked and spun in the wind like tumbleweeds in a tornado—spiraling down toward the water. Harold knew if they went under, Swiftless wouldn't be able to fly again until his wings dried, and then they would both be doomed. But the pond surface got closer and closer...

Harold doubted Swiftless could resist the force of the wind. The water was inches away—Harold braced for impact—

With superhuman strength, Swiftless charged the wind head-first. It felt like slamming into a brick wall, only a hundred times worse. The monster's hot breath stung Harold's eyes. The force nearly peeled him off of Swiftless's back. But Swiftless refused to relent. Harold was shocked at how vigorous and determined he was. The monster's breath and beating wings were impossibly strong. The blast of wind was relentless. Swiftless wouldn't be able to hold on much longer—

Just when Harold was about to give up hope, the air current slowed to a stop and Swiftless was finally given a short rest.

But it didn't last long. Instead of catching its breath after roaring, the monster began to inhale with the same amount of tremendous force, sucking everything within range into its massive mouth. Swiftless was yanked toward the monster's gaping throat, and Harold watched in horror as teeth the size of javelins got closer and closer...

Swiftless was exhausted, but he charged the wind in the opposite direction with every ounce of effort he had left. They weren't gaining ground; in fact, they were just prolonging their deaths. Every few seconds, Harold glanced back at that gaping maw, studded with huge, ivory teeth, sharp as razors. It came closer every time, and Harold clung to Swiftless, knowing they had only moments left—

Then Harold felt the vial of poison cold on his neck, throttling in the wind—

It was just waiting to be thrown.

Harold had only a matter of seconds. He yanked off his necklace with shaking hands, almost dropping it into the frothy currents below. When the thread tangled in his trembling grasp, he gazed back, down into the monster's throat. Harold was so close he could see deep inside the monster.

This was his chance.

Harold uncapped the vial of poison. Then, with all his might, he flung the bottle straight down, hoping his aim was right. The small container tumbled through the air, carrying all his hope with it. The monster didn't notice the faint tickling in his throat as the vial cascaded down his esophagus.

There was a pause.

But nothing happened.

Harold felt a sinking feeling in his stomach. They were so close to the monster's teeth, he could see the serrated edges. Yet Swiftless still pushed on through the wind, unrelenting, less than an inch away from death.

Harold closed his eyes, expecting teeth to tear him apart at any moment. At any moment everything could disappear—

A faint shudder quivered up the monster's spine.

It was ever so faint, so slight, only an alert eye would have noticed it. The monster kept inhaling, and Swiftless held onto his tiny thread of hope. Then. . .

The monster coughed.

Harold and Swiftless were sent hurling into the air like autumn leaves in the wind. The force was tremendous; they had been saved by the biggest cough Harold had ever seen.

Swiftless nearly collapsed from exhaustion, and he spun like a rag doll in the wind. Harold almost fell off, they spun so violently. They were inches from the water before Swiftless finally gained control. They swooped into the air, and Harold could see the monster from a distance.

The creature had landed in the pond, thrashing in the water, tossing huge waves on shore. Harold watched the beast's eyes gleam in fear. It began to hack and sputter, whipping its tail around in fury. It folded its wings, trembling in the water. Harold couldn't believe what he was seeing. Was this the end of it all? He glided closer to gain a better view.

The poison spread through the monster's body so fast, a glowing purple gloss crept up the monster's neck, slowly expanding across the rest of its armored body. It gasped for breath and began to contort in frustration. Harold cringed as the creature let out a blood-curdling roar.

In one last attempt at revenge, the monster planted its feet in the water and rose up to Harold and Swiftless's height. Directing all its fury at them, it lashed out its claws from the depths, spraying water high into the sky. It reached and stretched; Harold felt panic grip him as they dove out of the way.

Suddenly, the monster could reach no further and he froze in midair. It teetered there for a moment, silent and still in the water. The life left its eyes, and Harold knew they had won; the monster was dead.

Then it tipped, a frozen carcass of death falling down on Swiftless and Harold.

Swiftless dove as fast as his exhausted wings would allow out from under the beast. Massive waves rose up around them, blocking their escape from either side. Harold ducked as they skimmed across the water, squinting into the dark. They were beneath its belly.

They were so close. . .

They were almost to the tip of the tail.

An arrow tipped with poison zipped through the air.

Harold saw it out of the corner of his eye, saw it release from out of the thick reed forest. A dark figure cocked a second arrow, and Harold recognized the figure.

Mrs. Kernester stepped from the shadows, a smirk on her face, a smirk he had never seen before. It didn't register. He saw her, but he couldn't believe it was her, actually her.

They were running for their lives, and he had almost made it!

His own teacher, his headmistress, his guardian. His mother.

The betrayal numbed him. Harold didn't feel it, and didn't want to. He could see her face, see it like the shining surface of the moon, all empathy drained from her complexion. Who was she? Harold almost didn't recognize her; it was horrifying.

She hadn't been aiming for the monster.

She was aiming for *him*.

And that's when he felt it.

The arrow pierced his shoulder, near to his heart. Harold shrieked in pain. It was worse than the gash in his leg; the gash was only a paper cut compared to the fatal wound in his shoulder. It was poisoned— Harold could feel it seeping into his bloodstream. It was only a matter of time before the poison got into his veins and pumped into his heart—it was so close to his heart! He could see black creeping up his shoulder and neck. The pain was excruciating. He forgot everything— all he could feel was pain.

Startled by the impact, Swiftless faltered and nicked against the monster's tail.

They crashed into the water.

Harold looked around frantically for help. His arm would not move, so he could not swim. He choked on water as he flailed and struggled to keep his head above the surface. He was vaguely aware as his sword slipped from his fingers and sunk down, down. . .

Someone called out.

Then everything faded away.

CHAPTER TWENTY-ONE

Bruises

Harold's world was pain.

He could feel it in his bones, his skin, his arms and hands. He could feel pain searing his shoulder. There was pain down his left leg, deep and stinging. His eyes were squeezed shut, and when he tried to open them, they wouldn't respond. When he tried to wriggle, the sizzling pain intensified.

He was alive. What had happened? He remembered the monster, he remembered falling into the water. He thought he had died.

Harold strained to remember details. Bitter memories trickled in like molasses.

After some effort, he could recount a few events. He remembered Juniper and the monster, Golgothar's hair, which looked like his own, and the poison cascading down the monster's throat. Then he remembered he wasn't safe anymore. He remembered Mr. Porthand was in danger—and his friends were lost in the north—and the Ferrals were still out there, hunting and killing. It still looked bleak—the thought sent chills up his aching spine.

He could hardly move. Was he dead? He didn't think this much pain was possible in the afterlife.

Finally, after concentrating, he peeled his eyelids open to reveal the scene before him. He was lying on a bed, soft and white. He was in a room. It was in Galidemus. Other beds lined the walls, and other people were lying in them.

The long, cascading curtains were open, and Harold squinted as sunlight assaulted his retinas. A large, plump lady in white was tending to him, stirring something in a bowl on a nightstand next to his bed, bent in focus. Harold could see he wasn't covered in blankets. He could see his leg bandaged in thick white wrappings, and still more binding his shoulder where it hurt the most. The wraps were stained dark. The rest of him was still in tattered, muddy clothes, damp with pond water.

Harold saw other figures around his bed. He recognized Carnis, slumped in a chair that was propped up next to Harold's head. He looked more worried than Harold had ever seen him, but he was alive. He was safe.

Then his eyes wandered to Petunia and Snip, who were sitting at the foot of his bed. Petunia had tear tracks covering her face, shining in what seemed like morning light. She had a bandaged arm and was holding a tissue in her hands, knuckles white, eyes bloodshot. Snip sat beside her, clutching his knees. He had claw marks on his face and arms and hands.

And then Harold saw Mr. Porthand, expression sober, leaning up against the wall. His arm was in a cast, and he had a long gash running up his cheek and down his jaw. He would have that scar forever. But all Harold could do was blink in relief that they were alive—they were all *alive*.

Harold tried to prop himself up with one elbow, grunting in pain, but the nurse hastily set him back down, relieved he had woken up. Her sigh of relief made the others lift their heads, and soon Harold was surrounded. Petunia nearly leapt to her feet and threw her arms around his neck, sobbing. It hurt terribly, but it was worth the pain. He forced a smile as Petunia cried tears of relief.

"Harold!" she gasped. "You're awake! You're okay—"

"Harold!" Carnis shot up out of his chair like a lightning bolt, followed in suit by Snip. Mr. Porthand straightened like a bean pole, a look of relief spreading across his face.

"Harold, thank God you're awake!"

Harold smiled. He didn't trust his voice; it felt bogged down in his throat.

"What in the world happened to you?" Mr. Porthand asked.

Harold tried to speak, sending tendrils of pain through his chest. "A lot . . . a lot happened . . . and what happened to you? You're *alive*—"

Mr. Porthand traced the gash on his face with his finger. "He got me," he chuckled, "but I'm still here. Snip saved your life, you know."

Harold looked up at Snip, face was covered in scratches. His ears turned red from embarrassment.

"When you fell in the water, he dove in to save you," Petunia explained. "We weren't far away—there were water dwellers everywhere, but he got you out alive. They nearly drowned him."

Harold furrowed his brow, looking at the claw marks on Snip's wrists, palms, up his arms and onto his face, his skin red and swollen. *Snip saved him? Snip??*

"Thank you," Harold said simply; he couldn't think of anything else to say.

Snip just smiled.

"What happened to the water dwellers?" Harold asked. "Why have we never known about them before?"

Mr. Porthand shrugged. "Apparently, they've lived around here longer than we have," he replied. "I talked to a few a while ago. They were suffering a bad famine underwater for several years. I have a feeling Golgothar caused it, and used it as leverage to force their participation in this scheme. They were at the point of starvation and they didn't really have a choice in joining the Ferrals. They're normally quite peaceful; they didn't desire to come out of hiding at all, especially not to harm us."

"So are they free now? Were they given food?" Harold confirmed.

"Yes," Mr. Porthand replied. "I suppose you deserve a bit of a summary. I apologize. It's been a rough night."

"You can say that again," the nurse grumbled. She marched to another patient, leaving Harold behind.

Mr. Porthand chuckled and cleared his throat. "After I sent you four off," he explained, "I went to evacuate the school. I knew it would be hopeless to send the students to their homes, so I planned to gather everyone and take them to the basement. Unfortunately, the moment I told another faculty member about the mess, she began to panic and—"

"Was this Mrs. Murphy?" Harold interrupted.

"In fact, it was," Mr. Porthand chuckled. "She refused to send her Venariovums out the day before; said she heard strange noises.

"Anyway, she panicked," he continued. "She was terrified. Told the whole school about the Ferrals, and in a matter of minutes, everyone was outside running around like a bunch of headless chickens."

Petunia snorted a laugh.

"It's true," Mr. Porthand insisted. "It was complete pandemonium. I couldn't do anything about it. So instead of gathering the entire student body, I focused on several small groups. The first group had about fifteen students, and I began to bring them to Mrs. Vera's cottage. It was isolated enough, I figured.

"I was successful in getting them there, but on the way back several grasshopper riders arrived. I found myself surrounded by about three of the brutes, alone, unarmed, and sandwiched between Galidemus and the cottage."

"They caught you then," Harold deducted.

"It was inevitable," Mr. Porthand said. "They took me to a small clearing in the reed forest. It was a long walk, and we had to circumvent Galidemus, so it took even longer. They refused to let me ride their grasshoppers to pick up the pace.

"On the way there, I could guess you had already confronted a rider yourselves. Shortly after that, I saw a dead rider on the forest ground without his grasshopper, shot by an arrow. The other riders were furious about it."

"Petunia shot him with her bow," Carnis said, "but the rider struck Harold's arm. His axe was poisoned, and we didn't know it until Harold was already nearly unconscious."

"I know," Mr. Porthand sighed. "I figured."

"What do you mean?" Harold asked.

"I knew you were probably hit by an axe, any one of you," he explained. "Ferrals have good aim. I know those axes are poisoned, and so I called out to try to warn you."

"So that was that shout we heard!" Harold said, remembering the odd noise in the forest. He thought nothing of it before, but now it made sense. "You weren't far behind us—"

"Not at all. In fact, I even glimpsed you once," Mr. Porthand said. "After I called out to warn you, the riders broke my arm. It snapped like a twig—hurt terribly. Then they hustled me along and told me to be quiet or they'd snap something else; I could tell we were close when we saw you from a distance at the water's edge."

Harold squinted. He strained to remember the three water dwellers, the woman that had saved them, and falling unconscious time and time again.

"We hid in the undergrowth," Mr. Porthand continued. "They said the *others* would deal with you." He paused as he recalled the scene. "We watched from a distance—and it was one of the worst things I've had to watch. I couldn't call out. I couldn't help you, and they pinned me down so I couldn't struggle.

"So I watched. I saw Harold go unconscious, saw the water dwellers attack. I saw the whole thing. But you surprised me."

Harold smiled.

"I didn't believe you would escape," he said, "but I was wrong. That water woman saved your lives. I expected the riders who were holding me hostage to go after you, but they didn't. After you disappeared, they brought me to a clearing beside the water and tied me to some reeds. I couldn't move, so I waited."

Harold thought back to the night before. They must have been close to separating near the cove at the time.

"I waited a long time," Mr. Porthand said. "I stood there, watching the dark, cold water. When I got tired of standing, I tried to sit. Not the most comfortable experience."

Petunia chuckled, "At least you got to rest."

"I would hardly call it rest," Mr. Porthand admitted. "After some time, Flint showed up himself."

"Really?" Harold said. Golgothar must have gone directly to Mr. Porthand after talking to him—right before the monster attacked.

"We had quite the reunion," Mr. Porthand frowned. "Of course, he wanted to toy with me first, so he talked for a few moments. Then he cut to the chase. He told me Harold was about to be attacked by that . . . that . . . *creature*, and I would have to watch."

Harold frowned. So Golgothar had chosen to make his uncle suffer. He felt guilt weigh on his shoulders, yet immeasurable relief flooded his mind. Mr. Porthand sensed his thoughts.

"It was difficult to watch," he admitted, "but we're both alive. And you put on quite the show, Harold."

Harold laughed, shaking his head.

"I sat through the whole thing," Mr. Porthand continued. "It was the best riding performance I've ever seen. I've never seen such ingenuity and bravery. I was stunned. After you killed that monster, I saw it fall, and if it weren't for Mrs. Kernester, you would have made it."

Fresh flashes of betrayal and horror haunted Harold's vision. He remembered seeing Mrs. Kernester on the shore, aiming an arrow into the night. He remembered looking down and seeing the arrow protruding from his shoulder, shirt darkened with blood. He gazed down at the wrappings that bound it now. A little bit lower, and it would've taken his life. He still didn't fully believe it.

"You saw Mrs. Kernester," Harold said, his voice soft.

"Yes," Mr. Porthand said. "Harold, I didn't know. I didn't even see it coming."

Harold shook his head. "I still can't believe it."

"What are you talking about?" Carnis asked.

Harold glared down at his shoulder. "I was almost there, almost free. Did you see the arrow?"

Carnis nodded.

"Mrs. Kernester fired it at me."

"I thought it was Juniper," he said. "We saw him crash. We were too far away to catch him, but we cheered for you, Harold. It was epic."

"Juniper did not surprise me, I must admit," Mr. Porthand said.

Harold nodded, eyes glossed over. His mind was still on Mrs. Kernester. She was no longer on the sidelines. She had chosen her side.

"Harold," Mr. Porthand said, putting a hand on his good shoulder, "I would never ask you to forget Mrs. Kernester, but she made her decision. I know she raised you, but she's gone now. She's always treated you more like a student than a son."

"I guess so," Harold admitted.

"Look around you. There is no reason to miss her," he said. "Look at the friends and family you have now."

Harold looked at the group of people surrounding him. He saw friends who had risked their lives for him. He saw an uncle who would stay by his side no matter what. He saw he was not alone. He saw he was loved.

Then he remembered Swiftless. The dragonfly had saved his life.

"Wait," Harold said. "Where is Swiftless?"

Nobody spoke.

Mr. Porthand sighed. "Harold, we haven't been able to find him since you crashed. I'm sorry."

"What do you mean, you haven't been able to find him?" he demanded, trying to suppress the panic in his chest.

"He's missing," Carnis said. "There are people looking for him right now. But we can't find him."

Harold's heart sank. His dragonfly was probably dead. He tried to remember the last moments he had seen him, sinking in cold, black water. His memory was so foggy.

"He saved my life too many times to count," he said hopelessly.

"I know," Carnis nodded. "We'll find him. I promise."

Harold nodded, wishing he could have faith in his promise. But hopelessness spread inside him like a disease. Swiftless was gone.

There was a moment of silence. "So you didn't go north, did you?" Harold asked his friends. "You waited around to see if I would die?"

"Basically," Carnis chuckled.

Petunia frowned at him. "We couldn't just *abandon* you," she insisted.

"I know," Harold smiled. "I would've done the same. But how did you get me here—I mean, into Galidemus?"

"It happened rather quickly," Mr. Porthand said. "I saw you fall into the water. I thought you were dead. But Golgothar insisted you weren't, yet. Carnis, Petunia, and Snip were close to your landing spot, and we saw them drag you out of the water. You were drenched in your own blood, and I was terrified even looking from a distance. But Flint was convinced you were still breathing—his plan was ruined, and he was furious. He contemplated killing me, but he claimed one without the other was pointless. So he slashed my face in his anger— marked me for the slaughter, or so he said. Then he left me there untied and gathered the rest of his Ferral army. I don't know how, but they disappeared as quickly as they had arrived. In the short time they were in Orahton, they did little damage. There are several houses crushed and some minor damage to Galidemus, but nothing serious. Nobody died, thankfully."

"How did you get me all the way to the school before the poison killed me?" Harold asked.

"Mr. Porthand helped us," Snip said.

"I carried you home on my dragonfly," Mr. Porthand said. "Fortunately, I had some healing herbs with me from Galidemus, and one proved to work well on your wounds, at least in postponing the effects. I'm glad I remembered to grab them before leaving Galidemus. You really beat yourself up, let me tell you. The poison was working so fast, your entire chest was black by the time we applied the herbs. The medicine held you over until we got here, but just barely. The nurses took over by then and I will admit I'm glad they did. My broken arm hindered me greatly."

Harold was in shock. "I can't believe I'm still alive. How long have I been out?"

"About ten hours," Mr. Porthand said. "The nurse warned us you might never wake up. Now you know why it was such a long night."

"Horrible," Petunia agreed. "I haven't eaten a scrap."

Harold frowned, "And you stayed here for ten hours, just to see if I would wake up?"

They all nodded. Harold felt a lump form in his throat. "You didn't have to . . . I'm s-s-sorry!" he stuttered.

Mr. Porthand smiled down at Harold. "I would have had it no other way," he said.

Harold just smiled, blinking up at the ceiling.

"And since most of us haven't had a scrap to eat in the past twenty-four hours," Mr. Porthand smiled, "I think it's well past time to eat. I hope you don't mind, but I think we'll head to breakfast now, Harold."

Harold didn't mind at all. He wasn't hungry anyway.

"We'll visit after brunch," Petunia promised. She kissed his forehead as a goodbye. Carnis and Snip were so hungry, they barely waved goodbye. They filed out of the hospital wing until only Mr. Porthand was left.

"Get rest," Mr. Porthand said as he gave Harold a gentle hug. Harold nodded and Mr. Porthand rose, pressing a worn piece of folded paper into his hand.

"I found this in Mrs. Kernester's office," he explained. "I figured I would take up the responsibility, now that she broke her promise."

Harold accepted the paper, frowning in curiosity. Mr. Porthand left the hospital wing for breakfast, and Harold was left alone to read what was inside. Carefully unfolding the yellowed paper, he read the message:

> *To you I leave this child, whomever you may be, in full possession. His name is Harold and his parents are Flint and Marigold. Wherever he may be, give him the love I, as a parent, would have given him. Give him a good home, and please take care of him. He is more important than the stars.*
> *Deepest regards,*
> *Marigold*

Harold felt tears spring to his eyes. He traced the handwritten letters with trembling fingers, feeling the warmth, the love within. Tears of joy trickled down his face. The nurse returned, surprised to see him alone and crying.

"What in the world are you fussin' about?" she asked, giving him a glass of warm, green tea while she prepared a salve.

Harold smiled at her abruptness, chuckling. "Just reading a note from my mother," he said.

CHAPTER TWENTY-TWO

Home

It took several weeks before Harold gained enough strength to walk outside again.

The cut in his leg healed quickly, and he had been able to walk inside Galidemus for some time, but the nurse refused to let him go outside until his shoulder had mostly recovered.

It was near the end of spring now, almost summer, and the days had gone from chilly and wet to warm and windy almost overnight. A gentle breeze blew through the long, green grasses that flourished in the fields beyond. The long, ripe cattails swayed, furry brown tufts bent in prayer. The pond was peaceful, swollen from the melting snow. Water lettuce and algae spread and slug-spotters quickly became busy. Baby birds screamed in their nests high in the trees, and small minnows shimmered in the shallows. Insects of every kind buzzed in a chaotic symphony, and dragonfly larvae were wriggling in the depths.

Orahton was lively and noisy during the short spring months, and Harold loved all the commotion. After weeks of waiting, he finally convinced the nurse to set him free, and he couldn't wait to clear his head and get some fresh air. He sat in Swiftless's empty, open shed, thinking, listening to the water and the life around him.

A few days before, Mr. Porthand told Harold he could stay with him over the summer. Naturally, Harold was overjoyed. He couldn't dream of anything better. Summers had been lonely and boring, and he was thrilled he would finally be able to enjoy the warm months.

Mr. Porthand was now Harold's official guardian, and Mrs. Kernester's betrayal was viewed as a formal abandonment. She had vanished; nobody had seen a trace of her since that dreadful night.

Because Mrs. Kernester had disappeared, the position of principal was still vacant. Mr. Porthand served the rest of the year, but he wouldn't stay for any longer. It wasn't his forte. Harold was disappointed; Mr. Porthand was much better than Mrs. Kernester had ever been.

Home Remedies class had been taken off the schedule for the rest of the year, but would resume the following year with a new teacher. Harold didn't miss the class. He enjoyed having an off period more than anything. And as for the rest of the classes, they resumed as usual.

Animal Studies was the worst class of all at the end of the year. Each of their maggots mulched, and they got the pleasure of releasing them into the wild as their final project. Lard turned out to be a nasty, oily fly, with no talent for flying at all. Carnis's maggot, Matt, however, was actually quite the opposite. He had been the strongest flyer, and Carnis could hardly bear the irony of the situation.

The school year ended just yesterday, and students were now slowly trickling out of Galidemus and back to their homes. Today was Harold's last day at Galidemus. Tomorrow, he would move into Mr. Porthand's pondside home out east. In fact, Harold should have been packing. Mr. Porthand lived fairly close to downtown Orahton, and not very far from Carnis and Petunia and Snip's houses. He was thrilled.

But something was holding him back from all the excitement.

Swiftless was still missing. After all this time, no one had found him.

Harold tried constantly to recall those last moments in the water, but his mind was foggy, and he couldn't remember any details. And now he was leaving and it seemed as though he would never see his dragonfly again.

Desperation crept in. He hoped against hope Swiftless was somewhere out there, still alive. His friends had searched the spot Harold and Swiftless had crashed numerous times, and each time had found nothing, not even an antenna.

The monster that had once fit in a small room was now decaying on the pond floor. The water dwellers slowly began to pick apart the monster so it would decay faster. Every now and then, random scales coated in purple gloss floated to the surface, bobbing in the currents. Harold had salvaged a couple of them with Carnis's help. They were still shiny and as big as his face, covered in the gloss from the poison.

Since the water people were no longer in Golgothar's grasp, they returned to a secretive and guarded lifestyle. The people of Orahton supplied them with enough food to last for years, and in return, the water people agreed to remain loyal to Orahton.

The monster had been a creation of the water dwellers themselves. After examining the waterlogged carcass, they admitted such monsters were difficult to breed, and it appeared Stark had done so secretly. Apparently, he bred the egg himself and helped raise the creature in Galidemus—buckets of fish and corn were found hidden in another one of the classrooms, used for feeding the massive beast.

And as for Stark, he had escaped with the Ferrals as well. There was no sign of him; it was as if he had turned into a vapor and vanished, just like the rest of the Ferrals. Harold wasn't complaining—he would much rather have them gone than present and looming.

Stark had also been meeting with Mrs. Kernester in her office for some time towards the end of the year. He had broken into her office and destroyed it as a distraction to hide what was really happening in Galidemus. Harold had guessed correctly that the muddy splotches in Mrs. Kernester's office were Stark's footprints, but he hadn't known that Mrs. Kernester was in on it.

Ms. Dywood was questioned for her secret meetings with Stark as well, but she pleaded innocence. She was set free and returned to Galidemus as a teacher once again. Harold was frustrated with the verdict. She never paid for her abuse and treachery.

Poor Mrs. Vera was so shocked from the ordeal, it took a while to coax anything out of her. When she did manage to speak, she swore she hadn't intentionally brought the monster into her cottage. She claimed Mrs. Kernester organized it herself, and all she could do was stand by and watch. *That* had scared her out of her wits. It frightened her even worse when Mrs. Kernester claimed that if she ever touched the beast she would be fired or murdered. Mrs. Vera left the thing alone like it was made of toxic waste, and tried to keep it a secret, as she had been instructed. Thankfully, she wasn't found guilty and kept teaching Animal Studies, to Carnis's great disappointment.

Lastly, Juniper had also vanished like a cloud of thin smoke. No one had seen him since, and he wasn't really missed. Many students claimed he was just a wayward youth, misled by Golgothar and his influence, but Harold still kept his eyes open for that telltale silver hair.

Much of the student body finished school early after the fateful night when the Ferrals attacked. Their parents were so frightened for their children that many took them out of school even before finals—Petunia and Snip included—to Petunia's disappointment. Carnis returned home the day *after* finals, to *his* disappointment, and now, it was Harold's turn to leave. But where was Swiftless?

Harold sighed, bringing his knees up to his chest. It smelled musty in the stall, like dust and mushrooms. Evening sunlight streamed in through the doorway, casting a fiery light on the paneled wood wall. Outside the air smelled fresh, like rain, but Harold didn't mind standing in the musty, abandoned stall. He hoped that maybe, if he waited inside, Swiftless would come home.

The setting sun had turned the sky into a painting. Reds and oranges gleamed at the horizon, while yellows melted into pinks and purples higher up. Finally, at the pinnacle of the sky, blue hazed into the black of night, and faint stars were finding their way through the darkness. Billowing clouds shaped like mushrooms bloomed in the sky, shaded in the evening colors.

Harold always preferred sunsets over sunrises. The sky was so much more colorful, so peaceful and calm, like the last breath of a day bloom flower.

It was still warm out, and would be until the sun set entirely, but Harold intended on staying until the last minute. It mattered little if it rained or hailed or turned cold outside. Harold would wait.

But what if Swiftless never came? Several weeks had passed.

Harold bit his lip in frustration. He knew deep down that Swiftless wasn't returning because he couldn't. And that meant he was dead. He had to be. But some part of him just wouldn't believe it.

Harold gazed back toward Galidemus, his home for so long. Tall pinnacles rose into the sky, basking in the sunset. New oak front doors replaced the ones that had been damaged. The path that led to the stalls was overgrown with greening grass, dancing and swaying in the breeze. Orahton lay beyond, small brown flecks of houses in the distance.

Then his eyes wandered out to the pond. He saw the clear water, tapering off into a cascade of murky depth. He saw the ripples on the surface, jostling persistent water striders. Small clusters of foam and debris, collecting in the inlets, danced in the current.

He looked up into the trees, soaking in their enormity. Their leaves were fully grown now; the cottonwood's were green and glossy and the aspen's round and laughing.

Harold thought of these last few moments, how he would remember them for the rest of his life. Sitting here, waiting and waiting and waiting in the majesty of the world. And that's when an idea struck him. He had never tried calling for Swiftless before, though he doubted it would work. Still, he could try. It was better than doing nothing.

Harold stood up, rubbing his legs that had begun to fall asleep. The idea of hollering for his dragonfly in the peaceful evening made him feel silly, but he didn't care. Any minute, Mr. Porthand would come to fetch him, and all would be lost. Harold pursed his lips and took a deep breath.

The whistle came long and high, like a broken flute. He tried again, but no Swiftless appeared. He tried to make it higher, smoother, and lower. He tried to make it unique. But anyone could whistle. If Swiftless was out there, he would think it was anybody.

By the tenth whistle, Harold found himself on the edge of desperation. Tears filled his eyes. He swallowed, gulping the lump in his throat. He couldn't cry. That wouldn't help anything. He whistled again, but this time it faltered in the wind. He couldn't hold it in anymore—but he tried one last time. He couldn't make a single sound except a stifled sob.

He would never see Swiftless again. He would never feel the breeze, never brush the surface of the pond, never feel free again. He would never get to thank his dragonfly for saving his life. He fell to his knees on the trail. Tears were flowing down his cheeks.

The sun had set now and darkness was creeping in. The cold came with it, but Harold was numb to it. He looked up at the sky, peppered with stars. He could spot dark splotches moving against the stars, barely visible. *Birds*, Harold thought. Flying like he wished he could.

He curled into a ball, waiting for Mr. Porthand's voice to call him home. He would come any moment.

He had known all along it would come to this. Swiftless would disappear forever, and he would leave without him. He had known all along, but he was too afraid to admit it.

In the growing darkness, Harold heard a strange noise not far off. He couldn't see where it was coming from, but he could tell it was coming from the path. Mr. Porthand was on his way.

A shadow approached Harold in the night, but Harold buried his face between his knees. He couldn't bear to waste these last seconds— he wished Mr. Porthand had been late. The figure was so close, Harold could reach out and touch it. Then, it nudged his shoulder, and Harold raised his eyes.

Two eyes looked back at his, round and glimmering. A flutter of wings flickered. An antenna prodded his unruly, tufty hair.

"Swiftless?" Harold whispered, wondering if he was dreaming.

The dragonfly pounced onto Harold and the two were sent sprawling on the trail. Harold shouted in joy. Swiftless was back . . . Swiftless was alive!

After all these weeks, weeks of worry and pain, he was back! But how? Why had he been gone for so long? Harold didn't care. His dragonfly had come home. Swiftless had come home!

They chased each other and wrestled and ran in the darkness, laughing with pure joy. Relief flooded through Harold's bones; he never felt so relieved. Swiftless was home!

Long minutes passed before the two finally wore themselves out. Then they sat, staring at the bright stars dotting the sky. It was quiet now. The world was going to sleep. Harold stroked Swiftless's smooth, hard back and leaned into his dragonfly, exhausted.

"Swiftless, we're home now," he whispered. "We're going home."

Little did they know it was only the beginning of a new adventure.

THE END

For more information on the **next** book in the *Far Below Human Eyes* series, join Annabelle Healy's email list today at annabellehealy.com.

You can also stay up-to-date on

Instagram @annabelle.healy.writing

or on

Facebook @farbelowhumaneyes.

Happy reading!

ABOUT THE AUTHOR

Annabelle Healy is seventeen and loves to spend time in her fantasy world because high school AP classes and homecoming dances are too stressful. Her novels have received multiple awards, including a gold medal from the national Scholastic Art and Writing competitions, placing her beside award alumni such as Stephen King and Truman Capote.

Photo by Kailani Pico

She lives in Colorado with her parents and five younger siblings, and when she isn't writing, you might catch her playing goalie for her soccer team, painting watercolor, or attending youth group, and "dominating" the Ping-Pong table (or so she says). In general, she lives by the rule that you can never stay in one world for too long. God made big imaginations for a reason. You can find her on Instagram @annabelle.healy.writing or on her website at annabellehealy.com.